I0591147

A Plum Jaunt

Cenarth Fox

A Plum Jaunt

Copyright © 2023 Cenarth Fox

The real events, places and people in this novel are used fictitiously as a way of telling an invented tale. All other characters are fictitious and any resemblance to real persons, living or dead is purely coincidental.

All rights reserved. No part of this publication may be reproduced, transmitted or stored in a retrieval system in any form or by any means without permission in writing from the publisher.

Cenarth Fox has asserted his right to be identified as the author of this work in accordance with the Copyright Act 1968.

First published in 2023 by Fox Plays
Melbourne Australia

www.cenfoxbooks.com
www.foxplays.com

ISBN 978-0-949175-71-7

Cover design by Oliviaprodesign

This is Book 4 in the Plum series

A Plum Job
A Plum Jam
A Plum Jewell
A Plum Jaunt

Dedicated to

Dr Youra Livchitz, Robert Maistriau and Jean Franklemon
Three men from the Belgian Resistance
who, armed with a pistol and a homemade red lantern
stopped a train en route to Auschwitz-Birkenau
The train carried more than 1600 mainly Jewish prisoners
men, women and children
and thereby allowing dozens to escape

Chapter 1

The Cotswolds, Gloucestershire, 2002

Shakespeare nailed it when he compared beauty to a summer's day. Mind you he wasn't thinking of summer in Abu Dhabi or Alice Springs. No, he wrote about what he knew; an English summer, the type being enjoyed in June, 2002 in a village, deep in the Cotswolds.

Today's weather was pleasant with a zephyr caressing those in the garden of what you might call a chocolate-box cottage. The female gardener and homeowner was an octogenarian wearing an enormous sun-hat and still sprightly despite the odd arthritic twinge. Anything approaching a weed she tackled with vigour as her seven year-old great-granddaughter and the child's bestie chased one another around the beds of the glorious garden. The girls were on a sleepover at Grannie Plum's and having the grandest of grand old times.

The luscious lawn gave the girls a soft landing to cushion their tumbles. Angus, the woman's West Island White Terrier, tagged along loving the visitors and their joyous enthusiasm.

The blooms were more than precious to the keen gardener. 'Girls,' she called. 'Please be careful of the flowers.'

The little ones squealed, Angus yelped with excitement and despite these happy sounds the squeaky front gate was clearly heard.

I must find that can of oil, thought the elderly resident who turned to see a woman approaching. In stereotypical terms she was a student living on a diet of pot noodles and instant coffee. Too much junk food worked against her attractive features, her spectacles constantly needed pushing up while her mass of frizzy red hair was hogtied, unable to escape. She wore the loosest dress with a denim jacket which had never been buttoned. A bulging cloth bag hung over her shoulder with the bag matching the visitor's appearance.

'Good morning,' she said. 'I'm wondering if you can help me.'

'Good morning,' replied the gardener standing using a trowel as a mini-crutch before adjusting her Mexican-like headgear.

4

'I'm looking for anyone who may have heard of my great-grandfather, Peregrine Mortlake.' The gardener shook her head. 'I'm researching my family tree and found his details in the 1891 census. He and his family once lived in Arlington Row but the current residents only moved in last year. I've started door-knocking and you are my latest victim.' The visitor smiled.

'Girls,' called the gardener, 'enough running. Go and sit at the outdoor table and I'll bring the lemonade.'

More squeals of delight came from the youngsters.

'Peregrine's from my mother's side where there is so little detail.' The children went on a final lap. 'Where do they find all their energy?'

'Let me offer you some refreshment,' said the old woman who led Ms Frizzy Hair through the back Dutch door.

'How kind of you.' Inside, the stranger stopped and admired the kitchen. 'Oh what a gorgeous country kitchen, and what a view of your stunning garden.'

A jug of homemade lemonade fresh from the fridge with glasses and a plate with slices of a simple sponge were placed on a tray.

'Would you be so kind and take these goodies to the girls?'

'Of course; this is a real treat for me.'

'I'll be there in a jiffy,' said Grannie holding the door.

Outside in the shade, the visitor smiled at the girls who sat at a table displaying perfect manners as their elevenses arrived.

'Is Grannie Plum coming?' asked great-granddaughter Elspeth.

'I hope so.' Grannie appeared. 'And here she is.'

The visitor placed the tray on the table and all four settled as the family-tree investigator introduced herself.

'My name's Megan Hughes. I'm a post-graduate student at Cambridge writing a thesis for my PhD.'

The children understood nothing and Grannie introduced them. 'This is my great-granddaughter Elspeth and her friend, Henrietta.'

'*Best* friend,' chorused the besties.

'Hello girls and please call me Meg.' She turned to the hostess. 'And what should I call you?'

'She's Grannie Plum,' said Elspeth.

'She is indeed,' said the gardener pouring homemade lemonade.

'Well it's lovely to meet you all and especially you, Grannie Plum,' said Megan raising her glass.

Small talk took over and the young girls finished their cake and lemonade and asked permission to leave the table.

'Don't play in the stream and do keep Angus out of the water.'

'Yes, Grannie,' called the girls and they disappeared towards the back garden followed by a dog delighted to be in such company.

'A stream as well,' said Megan. 'You do have an ideal spot.'

Grannie smiled but wanted her visitor gone. 'Have you contacted the local History Societies?'

'I have but they take an age to reply and dealing with hard-of-hearing folk who still use quills and snail mail is not exactly ideal.'

'You need Esmeralda at Honeysuckle Cottage. She plays croquet on Wednesday mornings but should be home around now. Her knowledge of the village and the area is encyclopaedic.'

'She sounds wonderful.'

'I'll show you her place,' said Grannie heading to the front gate. Megan picked up her bag and followed the gardener who pointed.

'Thank you so much,' said Megan, 'and for the refreshments and showing me your delightful cottage and garden.'

'Good luck,' smiled the older woman and set off to check on the damage to her back garden and the possible re-distribution of H2O.

The girls sparkled watching Angus barking at the stream. Grannie decided a quiet time as in reading was overdue and sent the girls to the sunroom with its generous supply of suitable children's literature.

She collected the tray with a bee inspecting the cake crumbs. She returned the goodies, minus the bee, to the kitchen and came out carrying a small oil-can. She wanted to relax by resuming her gardening. Admiring the fruits of her labour brought satisfaction but she gained as much happiness when doing the physical work.

With the oil can, she approached the front gate and gave it a couple of swings. This pinpointed the squeaky spot. A drop or three, re-testing using swings, and honour was satisfied. The can was popped in the front of her apron as she wandered back to her previous gardening location.

When oiling the gate, had the gardener looked along her lane, she might have seen Megan crouched behind a tree holding one of the first Samsung mobile phones with a built-in camera, taking pictures of the chocolate-box cottage and its occupant wearing a giant sun-hat.

Chapter 2

Surrey, England, 1942

Louise Beatrice Wellesley, a.k.a. Plum, was thrilled to be alive and back in England having returned this time from war-torn Vichy France where a list of her daring adventures was as long as the stage-prop black-cane she once used in a Parisian nightclub. How many adventures you ask? Let me count the ways.

✓Living as a nun in a closed convent in Lyon with her religious qualifications being those of a lapsed Anglican
✓Captured and tortured by the Gestapo
✓Rescued by escaping RAF officers
✓Helping astonished Resistance fighters blow up a German train
✓Shooting a double-agent with an unbelievable gun
✓Fighting a wicked bishop in his magnificent cathedral helping the religious meet his Maker earlier than planned
✓Leading a group of Jewish refugees to safety by walking up and over the Pyrenees
✓Exposing a mole in the London SOE HQ
✓... and more, much more

There were enough ripping yarns in her latest French assignment to fill a novel. In London, her SOE boss, Colonel Maurice Buckmaster, naturally wanted to debrief his highly successful agent but Louise was less keen. Her family had become strangers of late—well her mother and brother Edmund—and a home visit to Farnham became Plum's top priority.

An initial truncated debrief took place before Louise caught the train and in an hour arrived at her local station in Surrey. Walking to the family home saw her mind spinning. Only big brother Henry knew her secret. She was never an actress performing the Bard on

7

tour Down Under but instead worked as a secret agent, spy and saboteur in war-ravaged France, first with the SIS and then the SOE.

Her heart thumped as she arrived to find her mother pushing brother Edmund in a wheelchair in the back garden. What a reunion. But if that was emotional, what happened next tipped her pulse into freefall. The man she fell in love with in Cambridge years ago knocked on the Wellesley front door. He was even more staggered to see her.

Louise walked Dr Tom Curzon through the garden and his visit and the luncheon proved a delight. Both mother and brother knew Louise had fallen madly in love with the medico who attended to the health of the Wellesley patriarch at Christmas 1938 when Charles suffered what became a fatal stroke. But the romance never grew wings. Why? Louise and her thespian travels obviously didn't help and the damn war got in the way of a budding love story.

The actress decided to keep her secret war-time life under wraps. There was still no sign of Hitler waving a white flag and her exploits in killing Nazis might be far too much information—at least for now.

After luncheon the couple went for a walk. The River Wey with its rich history, its swans, trees, bridges and badgers were of little interest to the actress and the medico. Both had so much to say and both were unsure when or where to start.

Louise had real concerns telling her mother about her life as a secret agent but wanted to reveal everything to "this man".

Tom had other priorities and reckoned kissing the actress was his most important assignment—ever. But when and how should he make his move? He knew she still cared for him. The way she slipped her arm into his, and the way she gazed at him screamed "get stuck in, my son" giving him a metaphorical kick up the backside.

Louise was the first to break ranks. 'Tom, I need to say something.'

His heart slammed on its brakes. *She's married! She has a child!*

He went to speak but she placed a finger to his lips which became his cue. He didn't care about her news. He squeezed her finger, kissed it; stared deep into her eyes then drew her to him. Their first kiss was gentle but lit a fuse. It fizzed to an explosion meaning their second kiss lacked any of the gentleness of the first and when they stopped, their eyes were shining. Ah, love!

He spoke seriously. 'I was right.' He kept staring at her while she appeared confused. He explained. 'I've long had a theory how kissing you would be addictive.'

She laughed then helped him reinforce his theory.

They continued walking and now the romantic gates had been thrown open, both were even more inclined to reveal their secrets. Yes, Louise was not alone in wanting to reveal all. Neither had any idea what the other wanted to say although both were certain it was, "I love you". As to secrets, well they could keep.

The river flowed at such a polite, apologetic pace they relaxed, sitting on the bank hoping the gentle water would calm their beating hearts.

'Tom,' said Louise, 'you know I fell in love with you over tea and cake after you came to a performance with The St Peter's Players.'

He smiled. 'Well I fell in love with you from my seat in the third row *before* the tea and cakes. My problem then, apart from being a cowardly lion, was telling you my feelings while you were grieving the death of your dear father.' She remembered and nodded. 'And your Spanish friend and her enormous fur coat and hat didn't help.'

Louise smiled, more inside, remembering her friend Matilda Gonzales-Jones. *Where is she now?*

He continued. 'And then a certain world war got in the way.'

She felt all warm inside and rejoiced in this serendipitous meeting. She was never so keen to tell this man everything about her life.

'Before I ask you on our first date,' he said sending a shiver up her spine, 'I need to tell you about my family history.' He paused and, in an instant, Louise switched from happiness to nervousness.

'My parents are English but I was born in the United States. My father worked for an international broking firm on Wall Street and when my mother was due to give birth, the First World War was in full flight and so I became a New Yorker, a Manhattan baby.'

Louise smiled not being sure what to say. A smidgeon of worry kept increasing as she suspected there was more to come. There was.

'You don't sound like an American and even if you did, it simply makes the man I love even more interesting.'

He kissed her. 'The Curzon family returned to England when I was a small boy and my whole life has been here ever since.'

'And your parents?' she asked.

'They're fine, a tad infirm and will be over-the-moon when I tell them their only son has met the girl of his dreams.'

Louise warmed up a little. *Is that his big secret? That's nothing.*

'I'm not sure how to explain this next bit.' Louise's warmth hit an iceberg. 'In the business of war there is such a thing as *The Official Secrets Act*. Have you heard of it?'

What is he telling me? She wanted to say she could recite the jolly document by heart but let him continue.

'I've signed it meaning I'm not allowed to discuss certain matters about the war or my part in it.' He paused, waiting for her reaction.

'I understand,' she said.

'Now the United States has entered the war, the US Army approached me to serve as a medical officer should the war take a particular turn.'

His announcement stunned her and she spoke without thinking. 'Do you mean when the Allies invade Europe?'

His face changed. He knew she was clever, a brilliant actress, but assumed she had little or no knowledge of the workings of war. The invasion was a matter of the utmost secrecy, well at least the date and destination.

'Yes and it's why I've been asked to sign *The Official Secrets Act*.

She saw he struggled so explained. 'The invasion is not a secret, Tom. We talk about it backstage and when the cast and crew are having a drink after a performance.'

'Of course,' said Tom and relaxed. 'But I think it's only fair I tell you I may not be based in these parts much longer and be able to take you for walks, to the cinema and dances if I'm at an army camp fixing bandages and helping men who may have terrible injuries from accidents.' He felt bad not only because he was telling her their romance had possibly struck a serious obstacle but because he was frightening her talking about the gory side of war.

It was then she knew she could never tell him her secret. Murder, rape, torture and massacres were once everyday events for her. If she told him her secrets, he might be seriously shocked. She imagined his reaction.

You've signed the Official Secrets Act? Twice?! Why?

They both saw how their romance might be interrupted a second time. They both knew couples who rushed to marriage because one or both could be killed in action next week. Many were.

There was one question Louise wished to ask. It had been troubling her since the night they met. Was this the right time to ask? She bit the bullet.

'Tom, forgive me for prying but when we first met all those years ago you told me about your wife and that she died.' He nodded. 'Do you mind me asking about her?'

'Of course not,' he said but she could see the topic hurt him to think about it. 'We'd only been married a few weeks and she tragically drowned.'

Louise shook her head. 'Oh I'm so sorry.'

'I blame myself. We had a dog, a feisty terrier. He went missing and we searched for ages without success. We went to bed but my wife was so worried she couldn't sleep. I was asleep when she got up in the wee small hours to search again. A storm hit and the police believed she slipped in the river and drowned. Her body was found a long way downstream.' He paused. 'Buster turned up the next day but my wife died trying to save the dog we loved.'

She squeezed his arm. 'She was a dog-lover which alone makes her a wonderful woman.'

He grimaced and nodded but said no more. They strolled back to the Wellesley home where Tom politely declined to stay for supper. 'I'd love to but my shift starts in half an hour.' He said goodbye to the housekeeper, to Victoria and Edmund. Louise walked with him to the front gate.

So much had happened in the last few hours. After what seemed an age they'd finally met face to face and expressed their love. Tom revealed his family history which meant he'd enlisted in the US Army. Louise said nothing about her hidden life.

She told him she would report to ENSA next week and gave him her Maida Vale address. They kissed and hugged afraid to let go. Louise fought hard not to cry. They squeezed hands before Tom kissed her hands, broke free and headed for the station. She waited until he was out of sight before going inside.

Mrs Crossley had long been a part of the family and now ate with them. She and Victoria were a similar age and like sisters. The topic of Dr Tom Curzon and his love for the Wellesley daughter did not flow. It barely got out of the starting gate. No-one wanted to ask if the pair were set to wed. Louise surprised everyone by revealing Tom's place of birth and his new appointment as a medical Major in the US Army. That got people chatting.

Victoria changed the subject by announcing Henry's news; a second grandchild was expected by Christmas. Louise sighed with relief and the new baby's name and gender were freely discussed.

They took coffee in the sitting-room when the phone rang and Mrs Crossley announced Henry Wellesley wanted to speak with his sister.

'How did he know you were here?' called his brother.

'I told him,' said the housekeeper and Louise picked up the phone.

'Big brother,' she exclaimed in a loud voice and the others went back to listening to the wireless.

'Are you okay?' he whispered from inside his study. 'Can you talk?'

She dropped her voice. 'I'm fine, everything's fine. I even met Dr Curzon who called to check on Eddie.'

Henry sounded interested. 'Did he now and what happened?'

'It was lovely to catch up.'

Henry became impatient. 'Yes but what happened?'

'He was born in America.'

'What's that got to do with him kissing you?'

She whispered. 'And we have one thing in common. We've both signed *The Official Secrets Act*.'

Henry paused. 'You're avoiding me, Plum.'

'No I'm not.'

'So if you won't talk about sex, tell me what's happened about you revealing your stunning heroics in France to the family.'

'I doubt it will ever happen, Henry. It would shock them and Mummy might never recover. It's as if I've betrayed her.'

'Nonsense, just break it gently.'

She changed the subject. 'And I hear congratulations are in order.'

'Thank you and let's hope it's a wee boy for the sake of the good old family name. So what's next for my hero sister?'

'ENSA I think.'

'ENSA? Listen Plum, you alone have the Austrian painter on the run. Hop in there my girl and finish him off.'

She laughed. 'I'll let you know if anything happens although you'll probably be told before me.'

'Ha, ha,' he scoffed. 'Better put the Mater on and never fear, your secret's safe with me, old girl.'

Louise swapped locations with her mother and resumed enjoying her hard-to-obtain coffee and homemade biscuits.

'How is the father of the century?' asked Edmund and they joked about his prowess. The younger brother knew there was something between his siblings and being intelligent and sensitive, never mentioned it. If told his siblings were both deeply involved in secret undercover work for their country, he would not be surprised in the least. Like his sister, he wasn't so sure about the mater.

Next morning Louise disappointed her family and Mrs C by packing her small suitcase and heading back to London. She was needed at SOE and wanted to sort her future as soon as possible.

'But what will you do?' asked Victoria.

'More touring with ENSA, Mummy,' she said and kissed them all and especially the family pooch, the now elderly Horatio who sported white fur as the foundation for his whiskers.

There was no-one to walk with her to the station allowing her to ponder her life. First she kept thinking about Tom Curzon before switching to her next SOE mission and then returning back to the medical man in her life. *When will I see him again? Will he be sent into action and never return? When will this bloody war be over?*

Chapter 3

Plum reported to Baker Street to undergo a seriously detailed debriefing. Maurice Buckmaster and his assistant Vera Atkins both admired her enormously and reckoned with more SOE agents like Louise Beatrice Wellesley, the Germans would seriously suffer.

After a good hour answering questions, having her experiences notated by clerical staff, Louise wanted a break. The finest cup of tea and cakes were on hand. Were there butter rations in Baker Street?

'So, young lady,' asked Colonel Buckmaster, 'what are your plans for tomorrow, next month and next year?'

Louise froze. She wasn't expecting that question or anything like it. *Why are they asking me and not issuing orders?*

'I was expecting you'd be describing my next assignment, sir.'

'Expecting, hoping or both?' he replied.

Now she was stuck. 'Have I blotted my copybook, sir?'

Apart from the agent, everyone in the room laughed.

'Hardly,' said Vera. 'You're about to be listed on our non-existent honour roll.'

Buckmaster moved to the young agent and put on a serious face. 'This is no easy decision, Miss Wellesley, but we have decided as of now you are too much of a risk to return to France.'

Louise's face showed shock and disappointment. 'What, never?'

'No, certainly not, but you are a wanted person. In Paris, the Resistance still thinks you betrayed them in the Hotel Meurice ambush. Before you fled the city, the French police were furious when Capitaine Bonhomme was killed.'

'But I had nothing ...' She stopped as her boss put a finger to his lips and whispered a soft shush sound.

'We know the double-agent Godfrey Silsbury killed the Capitaine allowing you to flee. But what we don't know is if Silsbury is still alive. If he is, you are his number one target, and the Gestapo most certainly have your picture in their office in Paris.' Louise felt her spirit being crushed. 'If you venture south, in Lyon the Gestapo is aware of your work with Father Flory and the local Resistance. Your exploits in wrecking a German train and killing two of their double agents again makes you a number one target. And don't even think about going to the Mediterranean and Marseille. What you did to the leading Gestapo officer, rescuing one of our own and then escaping from under their noses and climbing the Pyrenees was spectacular and magnificently brave. Tales of your exploits helping Jewish citizens are still being talked about in Vichy France.'

He stopped and stared at her. There was a pause before Vera broke the silence.

'You are too valuable to lose, Louise. Apart from wanting to keep you alive, we do not want to give the Germans an enormous psychological bonus by having them capture our brilliant agent.'

Louise saw their point but still felt sad.

'Thank you for your honesty,' she said. 'But if I am not to return to France then where do I go and what do I do?'

'Ah,' said Buckmaster returning to his desk. 'We think you deserve a well-earned rest.'

'A *very* well-earned rest,' added Vera.

That didn't excite Louise. In fact it made her further depressed.

'To keep doing your bit for King and country, why don't you go back to ENSA for a while? You certainly proved a hit last time.' He paused and dropped his voice. 'You know we received a note from the PM who demanded we fast-track your entry into the SOE.'

'We're sorry we missed the Windsor Castle panto,' said Vera.

Louise grinned as in a grimace and stood to leave.

'Now this won't be forever, young lady. You concentrate on entertaining the troops and we'll be in touch in the not too distant future.'

'Thank you,' was all she could muster as she shook hands with the leading lights of the SOE F Section and walked out into Baker Street.

'Bugger,' she whispered.

The head honchos at ENSA were thrilled when Louise first joined their organization. Being a brilliant actress, her star quality reflected on them. Then everything changed. She bunked off, disappeared after a performance. That was bad enough but when you add the fact the audience consisted of the Royal family, well, how unprofessional was that? The bosses demanded an explanation not knowing their star had been kidnapped along with a member of the Royal family by none less than the IRA. All publicity of the incident was shut down and the next thing ENSA discovered was the PM and the Royal family were two of Miss Wellesley's greatest fans. Say no more.

The ENSA response became, 'Please can you return and continue performing for our humble, little group of strolling players?'

Alas no. Louise was sad to leave and naturally did not disclose her next engagement playing a nun in war-torn France rooting out and killing Nazis.

The bigwigs at ENSA rued the day she left always hoping she would return and then, without warning, here she was, back in town and ready to strut her stuff.

Louise slipped inside the Theatre Royal and was spotted then mobbed. Performers and backstage crew who remembered her behaved like stage-door Johnnies and star-struck fans. Those who hadn't met her now wanted to.

When told of her arrival, the bosses flew down through the theatre and fought their way past the fans surrounding "their" star.

'Miss Wellesley, how wonderful to see you,' purred Leslie Henson.

'You look absolutely marvellous,' added Basil Dean. 'Please make our day ...'

'Our *year*,' interrupted Henson.

'And tell us you're available to re-join ENSA.'

Louise was impressed by their enthusiasm. She had nothing but fond memories of her time in *Cinderella* apart from the hair-raising clash with the IRA and a mischievous Princess of the family Windsor.

'Well if you'll have me, I'd love to play whatever role is available.'

She barely finished her reply as applause and cheering exploded on the stage, the cramped, overcrowded stage of the Theatre Royal.

Later she found herself in the producers' office where breathing and heartbeats were heading back towards normal; theirs not hers.

'We're gearing up to tour our latest pantomime, Miss Wellesley but alas the show is cast and well into rehearsals,' said Dean.

'But you would be a terrific asset to the company and the ideal understudy for our principal boy playing Jack,' added Henson.

Louise smiled. Normally performing on stage gave her an instant buzz, a thrill, and being a member of the chorus was fine but to be honest, she craved the rush of jumping out of a plane in the dead of a moonless night ready to tackle Germans in French France. Ah, maybe next month or next year—perhaps.

Being a talented actress, Louise got her real-life lines and sincerity spot on. 'I can't wait to start,' she said causing the smiles on the two men from ENSA to spread from ear to ear.

Rehearsals were well under way and the cast gave her the once over when she first arrived. Several females worried she was too good-looking to be stuck in the back row and a few of the gents thought their current gig just became a whole lot more interesting.

The tour was in the Midlands with the final weeks heading towards East Anglia. Norfolk and Suffolk were close to German-occupied France, the Netherlands and Belgium but by performing by day and away from major cities, the itinerary was deemed to be safe.

During a tea-break at her first rehearsal, Louise was approached by an elderly gent. 'Well knock me down with a feather, if it ain't Cinderella herself,' said Harry Bent.

Louise felt fantastic as she embraced her co-star in the previous pantomime, the one staged at Windsor Castle. She and Harry had squabbled as their characters fought on stage but offstage became the best of pals.

'How lovely to see you,' she said planting a solid smooch on the old boy's cheek. This reunion was noted by several company members.

Taking her aside, Harry turned anxious with a touch of curiosity. 'What happened to you after Windsor?' he asked genuinely concerned for the young woman he'd always tried to protect.

She worried about what to say. 'It wasn't anything like a few of the stories I heard. I didn't run off with the King's aide-de-camp or one of the palace guards.'

He appeared relieved but hung on her explanation.

'All rather boring, I'm afraid,' she continued. 'The cheeky little Princess Margaret wanted to run away with the circus so hid in the costume and props van which took off not knowing the Royal passenger was aboard.'

Harry was spellbound and Louise stopped on a sixpence.

'Oh damn, Harry, I was told to never breathe a word of this to anyone.'

'But I'm not anyone,' protested the fascinated old thespian.

Louise hesitated, knowing how a pause would heighten the tension. 'Okay, but if you breathe a word of this to anyone, I'll have to fill your pants with itching powder.'

He roared and she told him a made-up tale about how the van stopped at the Castle gate, how she climbed aboard and found the hide-and-seek Princess playing her game.

Harry seemed to believe Louise who had doubts. But finding her former colleague made this new gig one to look forward to—for now.

The touring panto went well. Troops on leave or new ones about to see action came along. Those with children made it a family affair. Watching another actress play the lead role gave Louise a few disappointing moments and not working as an SOE agent only made things worse.

After one performance, in a village, the usual thing happened. Excited audience members wanted to meet the stars of the stage.

In this production, Louise never developed a following but three young women, about Louise's age, saw her and called out.

'Excuse me, Miss,' said one.

'Hello,' replied Louise who was enjoying a cup of tea beside her caravan. 'Did you enjoy the show?'

She cringed inside as she was asked that question. Years ago her theatrical guru, Beauford "Nightie" Nightingale had given her a piece of advice about audience members.

'Never ask anyone if they enjoyed the show,' he said.

Louise squinted and so the wise thespian explained.

'If they enjoyed it, they'll want to tell you but if they didn't, you're putting pressure on them to tell the truth. Some people will express their true feelings but many don't enjoy delivering what could be considered bad news. They know you gave it your best but if you're told it was a load of codswallop, both critic and actor will be sad.'

'We loved it,' beamed all three women.

'I'm glad. Would you like to meet a few of the stars?'

'No thanks,' said one. 'We wanted to meet a girl who gets to wear a dress.' Louise was still in her pretty costume.

'It's because we live in these outfits,' said another.

All three were dressed in trousers; one had jodhpurs, and sweaters with holes, dirt or both.

'Don't tell me,' said Louise. 'You're Land Girls working for the Women's Land Army.' They were and smiled. 'You should be super proud. You're doing the vital work our boys would be doing if they weren't away fighting.'

'Actually we're Lumber Jills in the Women's Timber Corps,' said one.'

'Oh excuse my ignorance but I've never heard of you.'

'We're new. The Women's Land Army started back in the first War but we timber cutters have only been formed in the current conflict.'

This group of women was interrupted by Harry Bent wanting to check on his favourite chorus girl.

'I say, I say, I say, what's all this; a ladies' sewing circle?'

Louise introduced Harry to the fans. He loved audience members and especial pretty females.

'Would you care to see backstage where all the magic happens?'

Two of the Lumber Jills were keen and set off with Harry.

'I'm Alice,' said the remaining visitor.

'Louise,' replied the SOE agent in limbo and the two women hit it off. Louise asked about Alice's work and the Lumber Jill explained.

'So what were you doing before chopping down trees?'

'I was a teacher. I taught French and German in a girls' school.'

Louise was impressed but spoke without emotion. 'Donc tu parles Français und Deutsch?'

Instantly Alice's face changed showing a mix of surprise and delight. 'Are you serious?' Louise shrugged. 'You speak French *and* German?' There was still no response from Louise although a smile appeared. 'Were you a teacher too before you joined ENSA?'

'No, I've never taught. I learnt the languages at school and then went to Cambridge to study drama.' A silence settled as the two women felt a kind of bond between them. 'Do you fancy a walk?' Louise pointed. 'The river's rather pretty.'

They set off both wondering about the other.

'You're a strange mix, if I may say so,' said Alice. 'A Cambridge-educated woman, unusual in itself, multi-lingual and who now spends her days singing in the back-row of a touring pantomime.'

'You can talk,' replied Louise. 'You're a teacher of different languages now spending her days making telegraph poles and fence posts.' They laughed. 'Oh and bunking off work to go to the theatre.'

More laughter before they found a shady spot and watched the river drift by on its way to the North Sea.

They chatted about their families, their education and finally their love lives. Both were less than forthcoming on the subject of romance each wondering why the other held back.

'If you don't mind me saying, Louise,' I reckon there's more to your life than punting on the Cam and prancing about on stage.'

'Prancing!' retorted Louise expressing false indignation.

'I wouldn't be surprised if you were in Army Intelligence, decoding Nazi messages or interviewing double agents.'

Louise's heart beat jumped. *How the heck does she know that? What have I said that gives me away? Or is she guessing?*

'And I gather from your reaction I'm not too far from the truth.'

Apart from her surprise, Louise's mind snapped into gear. *This woman would make an ideal SOE agent.*

'I've never met a wood cutter but I'd be surprised if I met a hundred, they'd never be half as interesting as you, Alice ... I don't know your second name.'

'Promise not to laugh,' said the girl who was a whiz with a saw.

'It's not Alice Wonderland?'

'No, Woodhouse.' Louise did laugh. 'I asked you not to laugh and yes, I'm Woodhouse the wood cutter. So what's yours? Louise Thespian?'

'No, Wellesley.'

Alice reacted. 'Famous name, Wellesley. I once met Arthur Wellesley, His Grace the 5th Duke of Wellington; horrible, horrible man.' Alice froze. 'Oh god, you're not related to him I hope?'

Louise's heart rate, which had become busy before, now became even busier. 'I think the Duke's uncle is my grandfather's third cousin twice removed. Why, what makes the current Duke so horrible?'

The conversation turned serious. Each woman became cautious. They'd only just met. Both were intelligent, free-thinking and aware of the danger everyone faced during war with enemy agents everywhere. Alice decided Louise was a good egg, a person on the right side.

'I have a friend, well acquaintance more like, who joined Mosley and his Black Shirts.'

'Bad choice,' murmured Louise and left it there.

'He joined an organization called the Right Club—a bunch of wealthy, upper-class racists. My so-called friend tried to persuade me to join. Not a chance. Anyway he told me once the Duke of Wellington was a member and spoke at a meeting. His Grace reckoned he knew the facts of life. "This war," he said, "it's all the fault of the fucking Jews". Good job you're not his favourite great-niece.'

All Louise could do was nod and produce a pitiful smile. She changed the subject.

'So will you keep sawing logs for the rest of the war?'

Alice hesitated. 'Well I can't sing and dance like you Miss Wellesley so trees would appear to be my lot.'

'Where do you live, Alice? I mean if I'm ever performing out this way again, I could drop you an invite and a free ticket.'

'Seriously?' grinned the girl in trousers.

'You could bring that mysterious boyfriend of yours as well.'

They both laughed and Alice told Louise the address of the HQ of the Women's Timber Corps as they headed back to the caravans. Alice saw her pals and pushed off.

'Lovely to meet you, Louise and good luck with your tour.' She stopped dead and made a face of horror. 'Oh my God! I said "Good luck" to an actress.'

Louise laughed dismissing her new friend's concern. 'Tim-ber!' she called and they parted with smiles aplenty.

In her caravan, Louise couldn't stop thinking about Alice Woodhouse so hopped out of bed and wrote a letter.

Chapter 4

Concentration camps were well-named—at first anyway. They were to concentrate people, usually from a persecuted minority, in a small area. The Nazis became very keen on such camps.

One Nazi goal was to eliminate certain racial types—they believed no group of people could match the pure hypothetical Aryan race. The Third Reich, proclaimed to last 1,000 years, (it lasted 12) at first wanted to reclaim lands Hitler believed were originally and naturally German. And once the dominoes fell—Norway, France, and the Low Countries and then elsewhere including hopefully Russia, concentration camps were needed for another purpose—slave labour.

The Nazis planned on capturing vast numbers of people from Russia, enslave them in concentration camps and have them work until they died as slaves for Germany. Then there was the Jewish situation which grew into the beyond belief Final Solution.

This meant more and bigger concentration camps with Auschwitz in Poland a good example. It began life as a former army barracks and once the Nazis controlled different countries, expansion was necessary. By war's end there were dozens of camps and sub-camps within Auschwitz.

The Final Solution, the mass murder of millions of Jews, saw one section of the camp, Auschwitz-Birkenau, devoted to this horrendous task. The victims were both sexes and of any age.

This is where the railways were invaluable. The cattle wagons packed with humans pulled into Auschwitz-Birkenau where the poor wretches were ordered out—screaming the preferred method of conveying orders—and walked to the gas chambers. Being dead they were unable to place themselves in the ovens for cremation so other prisoners were assigned the task.

One Nazi aim was to incinerate 12,000 corpses a day so Auschwitz-Birkenau proved to be nothing if not efficient.

By the time it was running like clockwork, the Gestapo hunted Jews under every bed in other Nazi-controlled countries with Brussels in Belgium being a good example.

Louis Stern suffered from high blood-pressure. Being Jewish, ever since the Nazis invaded Belgium, Louis and his family were forced to move, to hide, to escape the enemy's clutches. Living in their home was out of the question. Despite the Queen of Belgium writing to Herr Hitler and obtaining his word Belgian Jews would be protected, everyone knew not for the first time he lied. Try asking Joe Stalin.

Louis and his wife Dina had four children. As a family they hid in the basement of a Gentile friend's home. Rumours and reports kept circulating of the Gestapo hunting harder for Jews. The increase in fanaticism seemed to be tied to Germany's success or rather failure elsewhere in the war.

The Russian disaster, *Operation Barbarossa*, saw a surge in anti-Semitic fervour. As the massive failure in Russia became known, much easier targets such as European Jews slipped into the Nazi crosshairs. The Nazis openly and proudly became mass murderers.

When the Germans first invaded the Low Countries in 1940, the Stern's oldest child, Jacob made the decision to leave his family.

'I'm going to join the Resistance,' he told his parents.

'No, no, no,' protested his mother. 'Jacob, they will hunt you then torture you then kill you,' begged his mother.

'They have to catch me first, Maman, and besides, they will hunt me anyway so why not give them a bit of their own medicine?'

'We are so proud of you, my boy,' said his father who took his son aside, gave him cash, kissed him and bade him farewell.

These were terrible times for millions of people but for the Stern family in Brussels they were heart-breaking.

Jacob was athletic with striking, attractive features. He studied at university in 1938 but now, as the Nazis dominated the Low Countries, he joined the fledgling Belgian Resistance.

The Belgian Resistance was smaller than in France but fragmented. Some wanted a communist country while others were royalists. The Belgian government decamped to London and set up in exile.

Outside Brussels, Jacob found a local Resistance cell and quickly discovered how dangerous life could be. Many of his colleagues found safe houses in the city but others, like Jacob, found safe houses on farms and flew by the seat of their pants.

The SOE in London sent agents to Brussels and those who survived did their best to help support and direct the Belgians. In Belgium, the Gestapo turned even more fanatical wanting Belgian Jews loaded onto trains and sent to Auschwitz-Birkenau.

The Sterns, like so many Belgian Jews, realised their fate was sealed. Hiding forever as a family could not work. Dina despaired and collapsed when her husband told her his latest decision.

'We must send the children away,' he said.

'Where?' she despaired, 'and how can we protect them if they are not with us?'

'I've heard Catholic schools, orphanages and nunneries are the best. The Germans do not hate Christians as they hate Jews. The boys will go to a school and Golda to a nunnery.'

'No, no, she will be terrified being in a strange culture and alone.'

'But she will be alive.'

Louis was right. Jewish children in Belgium who hid in Catholic institutions stood a much greater chance of avoiding being sent to Poland and a gas chamber. Parents were not so lucky.

The younger brothers were sent to a Catholic school, given new non-Jewish names and told to blend in with the other students. Kneeling, making the sign of the cross, going to confession and sticking out their tongue for "the body of Christ" were strange activities but the brothers followed orders. The communal showers became an issue when circumcision revealed a different culture but most importantly, they avoided a concentration camp.

Poor little Golda, all alone, the youngest sibling with a new name of Gretchen found herself deep inside a convent being dragged along by a nun dressed in a vast black habit. A friendly smile, a word of encouragement, even a little cuddle would surely have lifted the young girl's spirits but she received only reprimands and harsh tasks. But then she too was still alive.

Once the Gestapo ramped up the pressure on capturing Belgian Jews, Jacob got lucky. He was heading to what he thought was a safe house in Brussels when he turned a corner and nearly died. Gestapo goons came out of the house with one of his Resistance colleagues. The friend was a dead man walking.

It became the final straw for Jacob. He remembered the words of advice from his father.

'Go to England, my boy. Our government has set up in London. Change your name, find a job, find fellow Jews but find safety.'

He fled to the coast and found passage to England. Jacob became Jack Smith, lived with a family of immigrant Belgian Jews in London and worked at various jobs. As the war developed and news kept arriving of Nazi conquests in so much of Europe, Jack longed to return home and re-join the Belgian Resistance.

News of the murder of Jews in concentration camps drove him to despair. Radio messages to Belgians in London told horrific tales.

Jack preferred a job where he could move around. He believed the Gestapo had agents in England and being settled in the same place increased the chances of him being discovered. He wandered London and saw people going into a building, a theatre as it turned out.

In his French accented English he asked a group of women if there was work available in this building which was how Jacob Stern now Jack Smith found employment in London's Drury Lane Theatre.

The Stern parents couldn't sleep. Yes, their younger children were safer than with them but Gestapo patrols were more frequent and despite hiding in clever often horrible places, the Jewish couple survived—just. They constantly expected the worst.

Word raced around Jewish families. The transit camp at Mechelen was being prepared. It was the gathering place for Jews about to be transported by train to Auschwitz-Birkenau in Poland. There were no first-class or return tickets.

The train only left with a minimum of 1000 Jews hence the Nazis being extra keen to fill their quota. No wonder Monsieur and Madame Stern found it impossible to sleep. How would you survive knowing at any hour you were about to be arrested then gassed?

Chapter 5

Vera Atkins knocked on her boss's door and entered. 'Have a guess who sent us a letter?' she asked.

The fact his secretary brought the letter in person was enough to stimulate Buckmaster's curiosity.

'Go on, tell me.'

'Our agent the former Sister Claudine from Lyon,' she said handing him the missive describing Alice Woodhouse the wood cutter. 'I think we could find a new role for Miss Wellesley.'

'New role?' he asked still reading.

'She could help select SOE candidates and train them or both.'

Buckmaster nodded. 'Speaks French and German,' he said.

'Plum is too good to be wasted performing for ENSA. We need her back in harness and if it's too dangerous for her to tackle the Gestapo in France, let's get her training new recruits here in England.'

'She's certainly unique.' He pondered Vera's suggestion. 'Okay, let's have her in for a chat.'

'What about the lumberjack?'

'I think you mean lumberjill but yes, sound her out too.'

'Why not ask the actress to sound her out first? She already knows Louise and it'll give us a chance to see how Sister Claudine operates as a recruiting officer?'

'Where would I be without you, Miss Atkins?' asked her boss handing back Louise's letter. 'See to it as a matter of priority.'

Louise laboured on in the back row of the panto. She was a pro and always gave her best. The cast and crew were nice, fun even but the challenge for her on stage was at the lower end of boring. Still, Christmas loomed on the horizon and the panto was due to wind up before Santa came calling.

Changing out of her costume in her caravan, someone knocked on the door. She opened it and was surprised to see a dispatch rider wearing a helmet and holding an envelope in his large gloves.

'Miss Louise Wellesley?' he asked. She nodded struggling with surprise. 'Sign here, please,' said the rider handing her a clipboard and pen.

Transaction completed, Louise accepted the envelope, thanked the rider and read the letter written by someone she knew well.

Dear Miss Wellesley

Thank you for your letter regarding a possible new member of cast. Would it be possible to ask your friend to accompany you to the theatre on Friday January 2 at 10am?

I trust you are well and a Merry Christmas to you and yours.

Sincerely

Maurice Buckmaster

Maurice Buckmaster

Louise wasn't sure what to expect when she sent her letter to SOE HQ. She was thrilled to receive a reply and more so when it contained an invitation.

But hang on, she thought. *They want me to persuade Alice Woodhouse to attend an interview meaning I have to divulge my background, meaning they trust me to be a sort of recruitment officer.* She paused then whispered. 'Bloody hell!'

Her first task was to find Alice and convince her to travel to Baker Street for an interview. The panto was to end on December 23.

Her heart beat faster as she re-read the letter. Just when she thought the SOE had placed her in the too-hard basket, up bobbed a snippet of hope. It wasn't a call to don a parachute and prepare to jump out of a plane, but it was a start.

That evening she joined the usual band of cast and crew for a drink in the nearest pub. A few played darts, others cards, a couple who had started a relationship snuggled in a corner, and the rest smoked and chatted. Louise went for a stroll and found the local police station.

Her acting skills shone as she disturbed the sergeant in charge from eating sandwiches.

'Good evening officer,' Louise smiled and the copper sprang into gear brushing crumbs from his uniform.

'Good evening, Miss,' he purred faced with the glorious task of dealing with a young and gorgeous female.

'I need to contact my good friend who is a Lumber Jill working nearby but I only have her HQ address. Would you happen to have the telephone number of the local Women's Timber Corps? It's rather urgent and with Christmas around the corner, I do need to track her down.'

'Well I'm sure we can help, Miss.' He picked up the phone on his desk. 'Land Army business is it, Miss?'

Louise didn't hesitate. 'Oh it's much more important, Sergeant.'

She wanted to bite her tongue and kick herself thinking she'd told far too much. Mind you it was true but shouting your business from the rooftop was never recommended in any SOE manual.

The sergeant, lost in wonder at Louise's smile, spoke to a colleague who supplied the information. He handed her a slip with the Women's Timber Corps HQ telephone number.

'Oh Sergeant, you are an absolute brick. May I give you a Merry Christmas kiss?'

She didn't wait for his answer which would have been "Yes" a thousand times over. His watch-chain jangled and his whistle squeaked as the visitor left with a beaming smile. The officer touched his cheek which he planned not to wash or shave for a week.

Finding a public telephone was the easy part with the toughest being when a woman answered Louise's call at the timber cutting HQ.

Being unable to explain the real reason for her call and after unsuccessful explanations, Louise made her final pitch.

'May I ask, madam if you would be willing to tell Miss Woodhouse Louise Wellesley from the pantomime *Jack and the Beanstalk* would very much like to speak with her as a matter of urgency?'

The woman hesitated. 'How do I know this isn't a prank? You say you're an actress.'

'I *am* an actress.'

'Well we all know what they really are.'

Louise lost it. 'Well if that's your attitude, I'm afraid I'll need to refer the matter directly to the Prime Minister.' She stopped speaking and waited.

'No, wait, there's no need for that. I'll go and give Alice the message now.'

The sweet-sounding actress replied. 'How awfully kind of you.'

Walking back to the performing venue, Louise felt a buzz. Working for the SOE albeit in dear old Blighty beat the pants off performing. She gave her performance barely a thought and hurried to her digs as the cold December weather gave her the shivers; literally.

Half way up the stairs to her room she heard a voice she recognised.

'Do I see a famous actress?'

'Hello,' said Louise scampering down and leading the well-rugged-up Alice Woodhouse into the lounge.

The fire performed well and the two elderly hotel guests sharing the room were hard of hearing and dozing after their supper.

'Come and sit here,' said Louise and the two women stared into one another's eyes. Alice was fascinated and Louise struggled with what she would say.

'I knew you were not only an actress,' said Alice. 'So come on, spill the beans and please don't tell me you've fixed me up on a blind date.'

Louise smiled and explained the situation. Alice sat stunned.

'The SOE want us both to attend their HQ in London next Friday. Are you interested and available?'

'What a bloody silly question,' said Alice and the women grinned, clasped hands then hugged. 'Mind you, I have a hundred questions.'

'I can't say any more. If you're interested you may not be successful. Let's wait till next week and remember, nothing ventured, nothing gained.'

Alice gave a sort of snort. 'Well it can't be too difficult if they let the likes of you in.'

More laughter and Louise wanted her new friend to be successful.

'The panto season ends two days before Christmas and I'll be back in London on Thursday. Can we meet at the entrance to the Baker Street Underground at say 9am on the day? Their office is across the street.'

'Do I need to wear a red rose in my button-hole?' said Alice with a grin. 'I mean is that what you spies do?'

Louise's face gave Alice a sharp chest pain. 'If I have any advice for your application, Alice, it's don't joke about intelligence work and never, *never* refer to yourself as a spy.'

Alice frowned. 'Message received and understood.'

They parted on good terms and the out-of-work SOE agent started getting excited hoping her next visit to Baker Street might see a change in her employment.

Louise went home to Surrey for Christmas. Her mother and brother Edmund were there and along with Mrs Crossley and Horatio the family pooch, it was a quiet but friendly celebration.

Louise was able to discuss her life in detail given the fact it was all true and politically harmless. Her mother continued to age and her brother continued to try and improve. His chances of running again were nil but he was highly mobile in his wheelchair and using crutches, could move about the house with relative ease. His face now appeared much better, no longer being an eyesore.

'So what's next for my brilliant sister?' he asked with the other women all ears.

'More touring with ENSA,' she replied.

'Could you go back to proper professional theatre, darling?' asked Victoria.

'I'd love to Mummy but not many of the theatres are operating and probably won't until after this rotten war is over.'

'And when will that be, Plum? Have you thought about asking our big brother, the man who mixes with the high and mighty?'

'Edmund,' sighed Victoria. 'Your brother is playing his part.'

'Sorry mater, but all we know about Henry is he's producing children and never bringing them to visit his family home.'

That killed the conversation. Henry's wife had one goal in life which was to never have anything to do with her in-laws. *More fool her* thought Louise.

Mrs Crossley knew this family inside out and, sensing unrest and a possible argument, announced the arrival of a special Christmas cake she'd produced using a variety of the most bizarre ingredients ever placed in the same mixing-bowl. Rationing was alive and well.

The night before the SOE meeting, Louise slept fitfully in her flat in Maida Vale. She kept going over the possibilities which might occur in Baker Street in the morning. She caught the Tube and when she walked out into Baker Street, a grinning Alice Woodhouse was waiting.

They crossed the road and entered Number 64. After her French sorties in recent years, Louise was made welcome. Upstairs they waited until Vera appeared who was introduced to Alice. All three women entered the boss's office and after a low-key welcome—Louise knew why—Alice was interviewed. The leaders of F Section were impressed but stressed how many apply but not all were chosen.

Alice was given the address of the novelist Jepson and sent on her merry way. Louise remembered her trick of buying one of the man's novels before her interview. *Did that push me over the line?*

Louise went to leave with her friend, at least to wish her well but stopped when Buckmaster spoke.

'Once you've said goodbye to your friend, Miss Wellesley, please return so we may have a little chat.'

The two friends stood outside in the corridor.

'You're not an actress, Woodhouse, so I can safely wish you good luck. Here's my address so come and see me or drop me a line whatever happens.'

'Thanks for everything, Louise. Meeting you might turn out to be the best thing to ever happen to me.'

They hugged and Alice walked down the stairs. Louise took a deep breath, knocked and entered the boss's office.

'Congratulations, Miss Wellesley,' said Buckmaster. 'You may have found yourself a new SOE career.'

Louise was part delighted, part unsure. 'Thank you, sir but I admit to being confused about your offer.'

'It isn't an offer at this stage, merely a suggestion. How would you feel about becoming a scout, spotting would-be SOE agents?'

'You mean here in England?'

'I thought we explained our decision to not send you back to France where half the Third Reich wants your head on a spike.'

She nodded. 'Thank you, I'd be happy to help where I can.'

Being a woman, Vera knew Louise was disappointed. 'There could be more to your job. There might be a way you could help with training, especially women.'

There was little in the way of excitement from Louise. 'Again thank you so what should I do about these ideas?'

Buckmaster replied. 'Think about them, make a list of tasks you believe you could do and we'll call you back in say a fortnight.'

Buckmaster stood extending his hand. Louise shook it and turned to leave. He called when she was at the door. 'Oh, but don't give up your day job.'

It was a pathetic joke with the impact of a lead balloon. Louise gave a fraction of a smile and left. Going home seemed to take forever. A job that wasn't a job with the SOE and certainly not one with any excitement or danger, and the prospect of more touring with ENSA. At least it was many months before the next panto season.

Her misery was compounded as January rain settled in creating a typical London winter.

She reached the door of her flat and saw the small stick she placed there to expose any intruders had been moved. Her pulse exploded. Is big brother Henry inside?

Opening the door she paused expecting Henry to announce his presence. Nothing. On the floor having dropped through her letterbox she saw a telegram with the word *Urgent* on the top corner.

Chapter 6

Trembling, Louise picked up the telegram and read the brief note from her favourite, her only theatrical agent, Dickie Graves. He wished her a Happy New Year then made a simple request.

"Could you pop in and see me at your earliest convenience? If inconvenient, come all the same" he added with a nod to Sherlock Holmes.

What time is it? She wanted to leave now. He wouldn't ask unless he wanted her to consider a role. *Yes, but what is it?*

She started singing then ran a bath. No, she ran a bath and then started singing. She examined her wardrobe wondering what to wear. Life had gone from SOE nothingness to ENSA nothingness to possibly the most wonderful opportunity in her theatrical career.

Slow down, Louise. It may be a walk-on part back in Cambridge.

She bathed, dressed and set off back on the Bakerloo Line. She didn't want to arrive at lunchtime as if she was chasing a free lunch. She timed her arrival for after 2pm. When she entered his outer office, his secretary smiled and welcomed her.

'He's with someone at the moment but I'm sure he'll be delighted to see you. Please take a seat.'

Louise could hear muffled voices and wondered who was in Dickie's office. She reprimanded herself even thinking of her agent as Dickie. "Mr Graves" she whispered in her head.

Then the other person in the agent's office appeared and Louise gasped. *It can't be! It is! It's Mr John Gielgud.*

Graves was delighted to see his protégé and introduced her to the famous Shakespearean actor who treated her as an equal with Louise trying to stay calm and not say anything stupid.

Finally, alone in his office, Dickie Graves asked Louise all manner of questions about her family and work without ever being nosy.

'So Miss Wellesley, do I take it you are currently available?'

She struggled to keep her excitement under control.

'I am, sir, and would love to consider what you have in mind.'

'As you well know, many of the London theatres are no longer operating thanks to Herr Hitler and his bombs. In particular, the Old Vic has suffered major damage and is permanently closed.'

'Is it that bad? I didn't know.'

'One day we hope it will return to its former glory.'

Dickie Graves performed superbly, his introduction teasing Louise who desperately wanted details of any job offer. The agent continued.

'Because the Old Vic has been closed for years, a touring company was formed and has been presenting plays, mainly Shakespeare, in mining towns in England and Wales.'

Please, please Mr Graves, what's all this got to do with me?

'Sybil Thorndike and her husband are running the company and they have an opening for a young actress.'

Sybil Thorndike and the Old Vic! Louise clenched her hands to stop them shaking but caused her nails to make marks on her palms. Her heart needed to sit down.

'A young woman in the company has taken ill and they desperately need a replacement, and as they said, today would be ideal.'

'I can leave this afternoon,' said Louise without thinking.

Graves smiled. He loved her talent and personality but reckoned her enthusiasm was her best quality.

'Let me explain.' Louise tried to at least appear calm. 'There are bit parts and you'll also have to muck in with set-dressing, tidying up and packing. It's one of those old-fashioned rep touring companies where no-one and everyone is the boss. Does the idea appeal?'

'It sounds wonderful, Mr Graves, even on its own but after hiding away in the back row of an ENSA pantomime, it sounds like heaven.'

'I assume you've never lived through a Welsh winter?' She hadn't. 'For starters, I'd be borrowing your grannie's long winter woollies.'

They laughed. He made a telephone call which fascinated Louise.

'Is that the Savoy Theatre in Monmouth? May I speak with Miss Thorndike please? This is Dickie Graves calling from London.'

Louise thought she'd died and gone to theatrical heaven. She couldn't hear the famous actress but wanted to shout for joy when her agent finished the call.'

'Well there you have it, Miss Wellesley. The Old Vic touring company members are expecting you tomorrow. Now let's find the train timetable.'

Louise wanted to tell her mother who would be so proud her daughter would be acting with one of England's finest. Not knowing which plays or which parts Louise would perform became irrelevant.

Who cares? I'm back on the boards touring with theatre royalty.

She made a call to Farnham and gave a brief outline of the job. 'I'll write to you, Mummy once I'm settled and know the itinerary.'

Victoria bubbled with pride. 'Will you be coming to Surrey or going up to London?'

'I don't know. I'll send you the details. Now I must dash and pack.'

'Take your winter woollies, my darling. Wales is bitterly cold.'

'I won't and love to you, Mrs C and Eddie. Bye Mummy.'

Louise forced herself to hang up. She thought about calling the Vestys in Cambridge. Veronica would be thrilled to hear from her favourite pupil and would be beside herself to learn of the Old Vic touring company with Dame Sybil Thorndike.

Dame Sybil Thorndike!

Louise could hear Veronica screaming the name.

The train trip from London to Monmouth took an age. German bombs were no longer as frequent but track repairs and even basic maintenance meant delays and troop trains always had priority.

Louise held her suitcase in her gloved hand, tugged her scarf as tight as she could, pulled down her woollen hat and stepped onto the Monmouth Troy platform.

Wales patented cold weather where even your bones pulled your skin tighter. Louise placed her scarf over her face as she followed directions from the platform staff and fought the wind.

She found the theatre closed as if to repel boarders but a side door opened. She stepped inside where the temperature was lower.

Voices, she could hear voices and she knew the language instantly. They were speaking lines; dialogue written by the glover's son from Warwickshire. Forget the weather. Here be paradise.

She approached the sound of actors rehearsing. They didn't hold back. It was a performance fit for a packed house only the theatre was empty. The stage manager and a stagehand stood in the wings watching with not a skerrick of interest. Actually the SM was studying a form guide for the races at Ely in Cardiff next Wednesday.

Silently the new arrival crept into the wings. The stagehand saw her and stared. When the young woman pulled down the scarf covering her face, flat-footed Harry Thomas became seriously interested. He nudged his boss who gave up his racing guide.

'You the new lass then?' he asked.

''I am,' whispered Louise.

'Sit tight, love, they're on the last scene.'

Louise nodded and wanted to say, 'I know,' but didn't.

The run-through finished and Louise could hear a man speaking "ordinary" words and not those of the Bard.

'Well done everyone. My dear, we might have you enter further upstage for your final speech.'

'If you think so, Tyrone. Right now I'm gasping for a cup of Rosie.'

The actors headed offstage straight to the wings in which stood a nervous young woman with a suitcase.'

A man appeared and saw Louise. 'Hello. You must be the new ingénue. I'm Lewis and this is my wife Sybil.'

Louise shook hands with one of the best-known married couples in British theatre.

'Did Dickie say your name is Louise?' asked the wife.

'Yes, Dame Sybil, Louise Wellesley.'

'Ah, famous name there and don't be bothered with this Dame bit when we're all together. This is our director, Tyrone Guthrie.'

Louise shook hands with the towering theatrical genius finding the whole day to be a smidgeon more than overwhelming.

'Welcome Louise,' said the director. 'You are a godsend to our little party. We all know you're going to be wonderful because anyone recommended by Dickie Graves is a star in the making. Now you have a small walk-on tonight.' He called to his assistant. 'Michael, script for Louise, please.'

The director's assistant and general dogsbody appeared with a tattered script for the new arrival.

She was back being overwhelmed again. 'Thank you,' she said.

'Michael will fill you in on everything and when you're settled, come and join us in the Ritz for lunch.'

Mr Guthrie squeezed her arm, smiled and left with the others.

'Welcome to the madhouse,' said Michael. Handing her a schedule, he "filled her in". 'We leave for Carmarthen on Sunday where we're performing *Candida* and you're Prossy. Here's the script with your moves marked here. Our current digs are in a little hotel around the corner. I'll show you later. First you should find your costume for tonight and normally I would introduce you to our costumier except she happens to be you.'

Louise gasped and couldn't respond because Michael kept going.

'Apart from your small roles, you are my assistant in ensuring all props are placed in their designated spot and you alone must ensure everyone's costume is clean and hanging ready to go.' He stopped and drew breath. 'Now after all that, do you have any questions?'

He smiled which made Louise feel slightly better.

'It's a good job I like a challenge.'

'Good girl,' he said and gave her a tour of the dressing rooms. Then he walked her to the company hotel and waited downstairs while she went upstairs and unpacked. He walked with her to the "Ritz" which was one of the town's smallest and cheapest pubs. The cast were tucking into their lunch and all the males stood as everyone welcomed Louise to their table.

Her first meal and drinks were "on the company" so her feelings and happiness meter went from warm and friendly to wonderful.

Of course as someone new and unknown she was the centre of attention. Everyone wanted to know everything about Louise Wellesley, if she was related to the 5th Duke of Wellington and was she in love and if not, why not. Then, without waiting for her answers to finish, she was commanded to provide a detailed description of every role she had ever performed starting from Nativity Plays in her childhood. Describing her adventures with the St Peter's Players in Cambridge caused such merriment, other patrons even thought about asking the landlord to have those "bloody actors" turfed out.

When a short interval appeared in her "grilling", she sipped her drink and thought about her life in the last 24 hours. From the SOE she was offered next to nothing. From ENSA she reckoned it'd be another back row of the chorus job. The man she loved was whisked away to serve in the US Army and in general, she endured misery.

Then, from out of nowhere, she's working with three of the most distinguished figures in the world of theatre and being treated as an equal by a company of touring thespians in a tiny Welsh pub.

Now that's what one calls a change of fortune. She adored it.

She didn't at first realise Mr Casson and Dame Sybil were husband and wife because airs and graces were non-existent throughout the company. I mean, would you believe the famous actor and director, Lewis Casson was the company's bus driver!

Louise's time with the Old Vic touring company in the Welsh valleys was magical. She loved her roles, sorting costumes and props and the camaraderie of this group of strolling players. She reckoned she learnt more about stagecraft in those few weeks than ever before.

Their mode of travel was an old converted furniture van. Talk about a lack of luxury. Talk about lusty singalongs, bawdy jokes and unrestricted frivolity. It was bloody marvellous.

After performances, Mr or Mrs Casson would give her a small acting tip, nuggets of gold to an aspiring actress on how she better could move on stage or pause in a speech or give an emphasis to a word or words. They spoke at all times with love and Louise cherished every moment. You couldn't buy this education.

But as with all theatrical events, parting can indeed be such sweet sorrow. Louise despaired at the end of the tour.

'What's next for you young leading lady?' asked Michael as they packed up after their final performance.

'No idea, Michael but I've never been so sad, so devastated at the end of a season.'

He smiled and hugged her. 'I'm sure we'll see you again, Miss W.' She liked her new name. 'Something tells me you're due to tread some pretty big boards in the not too distant future.'

Her farewells to the famous actors and director and the others were equally as warm. Her gratitude and thanks were sincere. For the first time she reckoned her life as an SOE agent had found a challenge in terms of excitement and thrills.

I'd love to be a professional actress.

Chapter 7

Back in London, in Maida Vale, a letter arrived from Major Tom Curzon, MD, of the US Army 1st Infantry Division. Louise came alive. The fact his letter failed to begin with *Dear Louise* was a plus. The fact it opened with *My Darling Girl* was a heart-starter.

She thrilled to his news which included nothing about his location, future moves or anything remotely connected with matters of war.

Having his current army address meant she could reply describing her theatrical triumphs in the Welsh valleys with a few "unknowns".

She knew she must report to her kind and wonderful agent and so rang and made an appointment. En route the next morning she made a detour and entered 64 Baker Street asking if she might have a word with Colonel Buckmaster. The receptionist rang through and in a minute, Vera Atkins arrived to escort Louise upstairs.

'Have you thought about talent spotting and training work for the SOE?' asked Buckmaster.

Louise struggled to respond. 'I'd be lying if I said I'd been thinking about it much at all.'

Vera wasn't sure about Louise's thinking. 'You're still set on parachuting back into a French field at midnight.'

'Well yes and no,' replied Louise holding the attention of her listeners. 'The truth is I've been acting with a touring company in Wales and loving every minute of it.'

'Good for you,' said Buckmaster. 'Anyone we know?'

Louise hesitated.

'We're not all military robots, Miss Wellesley. Before the war I was a regular theatregoer and went to the cinema whenever I could.'

When she mentioned the names of her fellow performers—Lewis Casson, Sybil Thorndike and Tyrone Guthrie—there was a long pause. Buckmaster picked up a notepad and pen and handed them to Louise.

'May I please have your stage autograph, Miss Wellesley?'

She smiled, signed the page with a flourish and the mood relaxed, however, the visitor then decided to be, if not pushy, then certainly bold.

'May I ask if you have female SOE agents who have returned to France on several occasions?' Before they could reply she continued. *In for a penny, Louise.* 'And do you have female agents in France who have been there for months, even years?'

Buckmaster could see his agent was serious verging on angry. 'Miss Wellesley we are constantly searching for positions for you in occupied France which need your talents but in which your beautiful face is not plastered on the wall of every Gestapo office in the region. We regard the lives of all our agents to be precious beyond words. It's why our training is so thorough. Oh,' he stopped midstream. 'Your friend Alice Whitehouse ...'

'Woodhouse,' said Vera and Louise as one.

'Of course, Woodhouse the Lumber Jill has recently passed all our training tests and will soon become an active agent in France.'

Louise's anger and determination switched to joy.

'How wonderful. I only have her employment address. Is it possible ...?'

Vera interrupted. 'She told me yesterday she wrote to your London address and hopes you can catch up before she departs for France.'

'Brilliant,' said Louise and stood ready to depart.

Buckmaster added a thought. 'Please try and build her confidence for France.'

Louise got the message, shook hands with her superiors and left. There was a note under her door at Maida Vale. Alice left a phone number where she could be reached and the two women met and enjoyed, what was for them, a slap up meal.

Louise didn't have to give the new SOE girl any tips because Alice asked a hundred and one questions. They hugged and Louise wished her new friend the best of luck, good fortune and health. Would both of them see each other again? Would they survive the war?

Next morning Louise woke and stared at the ceiling. The wind had well and truly vanished from her sails. There was nothing from Mr Graves, nothing from the SOE and nothing from ENSA. Did this mean a trip to Farnham and a few days with the family?

She rang and Victoria sounded like a new woman. Her daughter was coming home, the daughter who as a professional actress, performed with several of Britain's finest and most respected theatricals. Why, Sybil Thorndike is a Dame.

Her mother and brother were pleased to see her as was Mrs C but Louise felt fear. Something troubled her.

'Where's Horatio?' she asked and knew the dog was the source of her fear. The faces of all three residents told the tale.

'We didn't want to write and tell you, darling,' said Victoria.

'He had a wonderful innings, old girl,' said Edmund.

'And I gave him his favourite lamb shank for his last supper,' added the housekeeper.

Louise lost it and cried like a baby. She loved Horatio; had done so since he arrived as a puppy. He was the one solid connection with the family home. Her father died. Her mother re-married and left. Her brothers went off to war. Only Mrs Crossley and the old black Labrador Horatio were permanent fixtures. He was a constant family member and it was the other one, the housekeeper, who hugged the weeping actress.

Of course the dinner conversation was dominated by tales of the tour in Wales. Victoria, who like Louise's father, didn't think a life upon the wicked stage was even remotely the life for her darling daughter had been converted. Years ago when a young Louise performed at the local church hall under Beauford Nightingale's expert direction, the scales were lifted from Victoria's eyes; from everyone's eyes. And now, all these years later when Miss Wellesley shared a dressing room with Dame Sybil Thorndike and acted under the direction of Mr Tyrone Guthrie, well, pardon me for boasting.

Alone with her brother, Louise was quizzed about Dr Tom Curzon. She knew Eddie was the only one who would understand and never interfere. She rested her head on his knee.

'We come from a generation, Plum, where a world war has turned millions of lives upside down. Our father died from wounds he copped in the first one, and you're kept apart from the man you love because of this current madness which has made me pretty much useless.'

She turned angry. 'Eddie, you're not useless, don't say such a ridiculous thing. With your brain you could do anything. And why can't you be a solicitor working from home?'

'Careful old girl, your optimism is showing.'

They sat in the dark as the fire in the hearth drifted to sleep.

'So when's your first London opening?' he asked.

She wished it was next week and her family and friends could come and then go for supper afterwards which she could afford as she had finally made it performing in a major West End production.

'I wish,' she replied. 'Instead I rather fancy I'll be singing for sixpence in an ENSA touring show and praying Dr Curzon is safe and well and coming home soon.'

He reached for her hand, held it for a while then lifted and kissed it. In the morning she packed to make a speedy exit.

'When I next come home, I will be most disappointed if there isn't a new dog living here—even two!'

Back in London she pondered her options. There was nothing from Dickie Graves, the boredom of talent spotting for the SOE or whatever ENSA had to offer. She picked the worst of a bad bunch and headed to the Theatre Royal.

She entered the stage door and met smiling faces. Many wondered if she would ever return. An actress with her looks and talent would never be happy in the back row of the chorus.

The producers were told their favourite leading lady was in the theatre and soon welcomed her to their office.

'So please, Miss Wellesley, do tell us what you've been doing?' asked Dean.

'We'd love to know,' added Benson.

When she explained she'd been touring with the Old Vic Company in Wales, the producers were more than impressed.

'But wasn't Dame Sybil a part of the group?' gasped Dean.

'And Lewis Casson and Tyrone Guthrie,' smiled Louise.

The two men exchanged glances. They knew she was good but obviously they were not alone. Mind you, Louise left out all the bits about being in charge of costumes and helping with props and having a few of the smallest roles in the vast catalogue of English plays.

'It's not the panto season, Miss Wellesley but we do have a new concert party about to start touring,' said Dean.

'You would be perfect,' bubbled Henson.

The producers stared at one another. Desperate minds think alike. There wasn't a leading lady role. In fact the one starring part or most-often-on-stage role was the emcee. The men communicated with their eyes and made a fatal theatrical mistake. They agreed to offer her a role they had already promised to another. Wrong!

Louise tingled; it's nice to be wanted, just ask any rejected actor or failed auditionee. Despite her excitement, she wanted details. Yes, getting a part is great but what is the role?

'It's a variety show, Miss Wellesley, with music, dance, sight acts and comedy.'

'We have excellent singers, musicians and comedians but to introduce them, to provide sparkling vignettes of brilliant wit and drama, may we introduce... drum roll ...'

The producers threw open their hands towards Louise and spoke as one, 'Miss Louise Wellesley.'

Now she understood or at least thought she did.

'So I'm to be the emcee.'

'Yes,' they nodded, grinning with enthusiasm.

'I don't understand these vignettes.' She didn't even understand the meaning of the word.

As the producers explained, her mind raced back to Paris in 1940. Sharing a dressing-room with Edith Piaf, Louise performed as an act between acts by telling the polite fairy tales and poems she recited as a child for her late Uncle Crispin, but in Paris in a suggestive even titillating way.

But I was dressed to display my legs and cleavage, she thought. *I couldn't dress like that for a concert party in broad daylight at a holiday resort in an English summer. There might even be families in the audience. There* <u>*will*</u> *be families in the audience.*

She slipped out of her dream to see the desperate producers hanging on her response.

'Please, Miss Wellesley,' begged Dean.

Holding a pen and a contract, Benson joined in. 'Please do sign.'

She did and, as a result, set off a chain reaction which would send her career in a new and deadly direction.

The two ENSA producers made a fundamental error—a schoolboy howler. Never offer a role to an actor and then give the part to someone else.

No matter what excuse you give for withdrawing the original offer, no matter how obsequious you become or how many gifts you bestow upon the sacked thespian as a form of compensation, you will have sown the wind and thus will most certainly reap the whirlwind.

The role of emcee had been offered to a senior and experienced West End actor, an old pro, Cranley Fogg. He accepted but when Louise Wellesley re-appeared at the Theatre Royal, and was handed the part with Cranley sacked, he found a fire of anger and hatred bubble up within his guts. Beware an actor slighted.

Of course the excuse for the change put up by ENSA was grandiose and pathetic.

'We have found a special role for you, sir, a testing role no-one but your good self could ever perform.' Baloney.

These lies were suffused within false sincerity and Cranley saw through them with ease.

He pretended to gracefully accept the move in which he was given a solo slot with a pedestrian monologue and his own bow in the finale. 'Fiddlesticks!'—actually when alone, he screamed something far more crude.

He fumed at effectively being sacked and more so when he fixed eyes on his replacement. He saw she was young, beautiful, young, talented and young.

My God, he hated the young. The youth were taking his roles. He couldn't retire. To do so would mean death.

And so this latest ENSA touring party included at least one unhappy cast member.

No, it was actually three because a husband and wife team, married for decades, and performing the same double act for longer, were having trouble on the domestic front. Hubby's middle-aged roving eye saw him chasing younger women, well, any woman, meaning his wife grew to loathe him and their now shaky future. Their dressing-room overflowed with silence or vitriol and sarcasm.

To further infuse this ENSA company with misery, the SM and one of the stagehands—a much younger person—who once were lovers were now no longer a couple with the stagehand having moved on.

Any mistake this stagehand made was regarded by the SM as a capital crime. The other stagehands kept well away and the tension throughout the company put everyone on edge.

Welcome back Louise.

At the first rehearsal, she picked up the mood of simmering anger and wished she'd not returned. When she discovered the business about Cranley being sacked enabling her to take the emcee role, she felt even worse. An attempt to break bread with the old actor went horribly wrong and before the tour had begun, Louise wanted to quit.

From her earliest days of treading the boards in amateur theatre, she discovered how an unhappy cast or rumblings within a backstage crew makes life a real pain in the backside.

To make matters worse, the joke about ENSA standing for *Every Night Something Awful* was true with Louise's latest show. The war, now in its fifth year, had seen the talent pool diminished both in number and expertise. There were fewer stars available. The young talentless woman Louise met in 1940 and who won the part of a fairy in Cardiff would have been a principal in this cast.

After the final rehearsal, Louise pondered her latest venture. Being tortured by Nazis was unthinkable but the alternative saw her on tour for weeks—*Please God not months*—with grumbling, frustrated and talent-starved thespians. She sighed.

Of course there were kind and professional performers in the company and Louise got on well with many of them but she avoided dressing rooms and drinks after shows like the plague.

The tour staged performances during the day meaning company members had their evenings free to wander around town, go to the cinema or a dance if one was operating or stay "home" in their digs and play cards.

The free evenings were Louise's escape from the unhappiest times of her performing life. She spent them alone longing for the tour to end.

Chapter 8

As the war progressed, Germany lost its dominance. Hitler fumed as the calamity in Russia unfolded. Underlings back in the Fatherland wanted to impress the dictator and saw a way. Round up "enemies of the state", mainly Jews, and send them to concentration camps. Auschwitz swapped *concentration camp* for *death camp.*

In Brussels, Louis and Dina Stern kept moving with their only source of happiness being the safety of their four children; one in England and the other three in Catholic institutions in Belgium. The parents were desperate.

Right now they lived—is *lived* the right word?—existed in the space between the ceiling and roof of an old engineering building on the outskirts of Belgium. It was still in operation; just.

A friend of the Sterns persuaded the building owner to let them stay there. There being a space in which lying down was the most comfortable position. Bedding consisted of old sacks with cardboard as a mattress. The dust and rats jumped every time a human moved. A bucket in one corner was available for you know what.

Their friend arrived late at night every few days. He was at risk of breaking the curfew and if found with supplies of food would be doubly arrested. If ever found by the aggressive Gestapo, the fate of those hiding was sealed. Many of Belgium's Jews disappeared. Some believed being arrested could be preferable to their current hell.

'I am dying, Louis,' croaked his wife, now speaking permanently in a husky whisper.

'You can't, my dear, at least not before the Sabbath. We are moving on Saturday and to a nice farmhouse in the country.' He lied.

She had no strength to reply. He had no strength to continue to encourage her. They fell asleep before both jerked awake due to crashing sounds. The factory was empty but the voices issuing German commands were not Belgian workers here for the morning shift. Here be Jew-hunting Nazis.

The Jewish couple stared at one another. They always slept close together and when clinging to life, it was easy to clasp hands.

'They are in the roof above the ceiling,' cried a Gestapo officer. 'Get that scum down here, dead or alive.'

The couple had been betrayed and by a fellow Belgian. What happens to collaborators when they die? Louis kissed his wife's forehead. He whispered. 'At least our children are safe.'

The ENSA concert party continued with all its unhappy company members. Louise hated the production, the travel and her role.

One night, again alone, she wanted a breath of fresh air (a) to think about her family, a certain doctor and her future if any with the SOE and (b) because the cigarette smoke in the parlour imitated a fog.

She strolled along a quiet street in the quiet and dark Suffolk market town where they were performing. In a square she came upon a young man sitting on a park bench and recognized him as a stagehand in the company.

'Good evening,' she said.

'Hello,' he replied standing as a lady "entered the room".

'May I join you?'

'Of course,' he said indicating the bench.

They sat. 'I'm afraid I don't know your name.'

'It's Jack, Jack Smith.'

Her mind became busy. *Will I offend him if I say something personal?* 'Jack Smith is an unusual name for a Frenchman.' He hesitated and she worried. 'Please, I didn't mean to offend.'

'I am not French, Miss,' he said. 'I am Belgian.'

'Ah, I'm losing my touch. I used to be able to pick an accent.'

He stood. 'Would Mademoiselle care to go for a walk?'

'I would,' she replied and off they set.

Gentleman Jack slipped behind her to take up the mud-splatter side of the footpath despite there being no mud or vehicles.

'Can I assume you speak French?' he asked.

'Oui,' she replied and continued in his native tongue. 'I should have noted your touch of Flemish.'

'I find it hard to believe you are English. Your French is perfect.'

'Thank you but certain French born people query my accent. "Where were you born?" they ask.'

He paused. 'And you reply by saying?'

She worried. *What am I saying? Who is this man? Jack Smith is obviously a false name. Why? Is he a German spy?* 'Ah, I usually laugh it off and blame my old French teacher.'

He gave a soft laugh. They continued walking and came within sight of the sea. It was more the sound of the sea as the darkness and lack of outdoor lighting made admiring anything in the distance impossible. He switched back to his accented English.

'I am not a lover of theatre, Mademoiselle, but I find your performances to be enchanting.'

'Thank you, you're very kind.'

She believed him and smiled. Their eyes met and lingered. He waited for her to speak again.

'So if you are not a theatre lover, may one ask why you are part of this production?'

'I need money and take pretty much any job I can find ever since I arrived in this country. I am a refugee from Belgium and need funds to help me return and fight Germans.'

'Do you mean Nazis?'

'No Germans; everyone who helped Hitler gain power. If the people of Germany had opposed him and his anti-Semitism, the world would not be in this mess.'

He was breathing hard. She glanced at him. His face changed. An unseen passion gave voice to his previously hidden fervent feelings. He tried to calm his actions.

'I do apologise, Mademoiselle. Please forgive my outburst but my family in Brussels is in danger of being arrested and taken to one of the many Nazi death camps.'

His breathing slowed and he refused to look at her. She paused.

'Is your family Jewish?'

He nodded.

She stepped closer, said nothing but grasped his arm and squeezed. He whispered, 'Merci'.

'Come,' said Louise, 'we should go back. Performers and their support acts must never neglect their beauty sleep.'

He struggled to produce a tiny smile but joined her in returning to their digs. Their previous small talk became tiny talk. All the way home and well into the night, he worried he may have said the wrong thing, and she worried about her present life entertaining troops while Jewish families desperately needed help across the water.

Louise and the ENSA party cracked on; another town, another show. The audience, war-weary troops were more than grateful for any distraction and when said distraction including good-looking females and especially ones in a glamourous costume, and comedians with a manly sense of humour, well bring it on.

Today's performance was outside in a genuine outdoor theatre. Never used in winter but today's sunshine made for a perfect setting.

Louise was backstage waiting for her next entrance.

A performer burst in. 'Where's me prop,' hissed a furious comic. He needed his suitcase containing its ventriloquist's doll. It should have been placed on the table in the Prompt Corner. The table was bare. 'Where is it?' he continued frothing as he searched in vain.

Louise appeared. 'Can I help, Syd?' She joined the search.

'It's that bloody Frenchie. I'll kill him if I miss me entrance.'

From the space beside the theatre, Jack Smith rushed in carrying the case. 'My apologies, sir, I was delayed.'

Syd opened his case to discover his prop sound asleep but wide awake. 'You'll be more than delayed Sunshine when the boys in London hear about this. I warned you last time.'

Louise made her entrance and padded out her intro allowing Syd more time to compose himself. She led the applause as the ventriloquist bounced on with the biggest plastic smile in Suffolk.

Jack stood there not so much afraid as desperate.

'Don't worry, Jack,' whispered the emcee. 'Syd's bark is worse than his bite. I'll smooth the old boy.'

The Belgian, gave a weak smile, said nothing and walked away. Louise didn't believe he was rude but left him alone as she was constantly involved, even downstage front in the finale singing *There'll Always Be an England* and finishing with audience and cast belting out *Rule Britannia*.

Show over, Louise went to find Syd. 'May I have a word, kind sir?' she asked in her usual polite way. Few men could resist Miss Wellesley. Being beautiful in a film star way with a smile to melt ice-cream, Syd stopped and admired her. How he wished he was 40 years younger.

'With pleasure, my darling, and thank you for the extra intro allowing me to get Archie up and ready.' She smiled. 'You're a real pro, Honey, and I can't believe one so young is so experienced. Who have you worked with?'

I can't say Edith Piaf or Django Reinhardt, and Dame Sybil would sound like I was boasting. 'Oh wonderful panto actors who, like you, have been in the business since Adam was a boy.'

He thought he was being buttered up, which he was, but only so she could settle the kerfuffle earlier in the wings.

'That young stagehand is a nice young man but his family in Belgium is being threatened with the death camps.'

'What?' flared Syd. 'Is he a bloody Yid?'

Louise copped a slap. Her attempt to help the stagehand hit a brick wall as another source of anti-Semitism reared its ugly head in peaceful Suffolk. She fluffed her reply and hated herself for doing so.

'No, no, he's one of us trying to give Hitler a black eye.'

She retreated to her digs with no interest in her supper. This was the lowest point of her latest foray back in the world of ENSA. The man she loved was going into active service and probably in France and she knew how deadly that country could be.

Jack, the young man she had befriended was waiting for news about his family being hunted by the Gestapo a hundred plus miles away across the North Sea. And here she was, smiling, singing and acting as part of a concert party without a care in the world.

This is crazy. How many people could play my role with ENSA? How many spies and saboteurs could play my SOE roles in Europe? I'm in the wrong country performing the wrong job.

She decided to contact SOE HQ in Baker Street.

The squeaky wheel gets the oil. I'll speak up and tell Colonel Buckmaster and his team I'm wasting my time at ENSA. Give me a job where I can give the Nazis a kick where it really hurts.

She wanted to tell Jack he was doing a good job. She saw how he was clearly upset this afternoon and with Syd now knowing his Jewish background, well, it didn't bear thinking about.

She found the production manager. 'Good evening Miss Rankin. I want to speak to the stagehand, Jack Smith. Do you know where he's billeted?'

'He's gone.'

'Gone! Gone where?'

'No idea. Gave me some baloney about a family disaster and took off. Didn't even wait for his pay.'

'Do you know where he went?'

'Station I expect. Back to London and the bombs.'

'Thanks,' said a now seriously worried Louise who headed towards the railway station. It was dark as she ran up the ramp and onto the platform. Two people waited for the last train and Jack was nowhere to be seen. She hurried back to the street and stopped when someone spoke.

'Bonjour Mademoiselle.'

She moved to him. 'Jack, what's happened? Is it true you've left the company?'

'Oui, Miss.'

'It's not a wise move leaving mid-season.'

She could talk. *Cinderella* and Windsor Castle ring any bells Miss Wellesley?

'I had to. I have received terrible news, Mademoiselle. My parents have been arrested by the Gestapo.'

'Oh no,' she groaned.

'My friends in the Resistance sent a message to my friends in London. I send them my locations on the tour and today they sent a telegram.'

'I'm so sorry but what will you do?'

He shrugged. 'What any son would do—try and rescue them.'

She gasped. 'But how? I mean how can you even return to Belgium?'

'I have made travel plans and now am waiting for my taxi.'

Louise thought this sounded ridiculous. She would never belittle his efforts but wondered if he had lost his mind.

'Here it is now,' he said and picked up his bag.

Louise gasped as a horse and cart plodded along the road and stopped. Jack went to climb up but froze.

'Oi,' said the driver. 'Money first, pal or we ain't movin'.'

Jack took cash from a pocket and handed it to the man. 'Half now and half when we're there,' he said and climbed into the back of the cart. Louise admired the stagehand's negotiating skills.

The driver secured his fee and went to start the horse.

'Good luck, Jack,' called Louise and nearly died when he replied.

'Come Louise, come and join me.'

He reached down and, without thinking; Louise grabbed his hand and found herself being hoisted aboard.

'Hey!' objected the driver. 'This ain't the deal we agreed.'

Louise climbed from the back and sat beside the man in charge. He could now see the woman up close. She smiled and the driver's mind flew straight to Fantasy Paradise. He flicked the reins and the horse set off. Yes, but to where?

This was arguably the slowest taxi in town, well, actually from out of town as the farmer lived a good two miles from the station. Jack's contacts in the Resistance in Brussels knew about Jews being arrested. Jack's former school friends in Belgium who moved to London knew about his arrival in the capital.

When told his parents would soon be on the way to the death camps, Jack jumped over more than the candlestick. The Resistance found him an escape route back home but it was only available tonight with no guarantee future opportunities would exist.

He stood up behind Louise and whispered in her ear, the one not close to the driver.

'I need to ask a big favour, Miss Wellesley.'

'Your English is very good, Monsieur.'

He grinned in the darkness. 'Please explain to Miss Rankin and the ENSA gentlemen how my family is in mortal danger and I have to do everything I can to save them.'

'I will do whatever you ask. But how ...'

She turned back and saw him smiling and raising a finger to his lips. He spoke to the driver.

'Please sir, how much longer have we to travel?'

'Not long an' jus' make sure you've got me cash.'

This was farming country, fields and more fields. Even in peace time there was no lighting. In the middle of a world war, the landscape was as black as a tin of Nugget shoe polish. If a farmer had a lamp inside his house, it was so weak no enemy bomber had any chance of spotting it. And why bomb a few sheep in the middle of nowhere?

The driver stopped. 'This is it.'

Jack stared into the gloom. 'I can't see anything,' he complained.

'Down the track,' pointed the driver. 'It's about two hundred yards beyond them trees.'

What is beyond "them" trees? thought Louise. *What are they talking about?*

'I'll go and look,' said Jack preparing to hop down.

The driver flared with anger. 'No you won't.' He grabbed Louise and threatened the stagehand. 'You pay what's owed or I'll give your lady friend here a bloody good seeing-to.'

His grip on Louise's hair was strong but rather than cause him Gestapo-like pain, she made a suggestion. 'Why don't you drive us down the lane, we'll be sure it's the right place, you'll have your money and you can drive me home.' She paused. 'Just me.'

What!?

Her last sentence was the clincher. It was the best offer Clarrie—*never* call me Clarence—had received this year; no, this century. Monks had better sex lives than this bloke in the sticks. He accepted the offer, released his bride-in-waiting and tugged the reins. Along the lane they went in the still and silent darkness. The copse of trees drew close. The passengers peered into the night. The driver peered at the chest of a certain former SOE agent and automatically licked his lips.

'There it is,' cried Jack as the clouds in front of the moon were moved by the lighting technician in the sky allowing a clear view of a flat piece of land.'

It can't be, thought Louise.

'Right, money,' snapped Clarrie and Jack did the right thing.

'I need to light the flares,' said the Belgian grabbing his bag, leaping from the cart and running towards the unusual field.

Louise went to stand but Clarrie grabbed her. 'Ah no me lovely. You stay right here.'

She was about to settle the matter there and then when a sound was heard in the crisp night air. A Westland Lysander aircraft purred towards them. It dropped lower and circled.

'Jesus, what's that?' exclaimed Clarrie.

A brazier caught alight and Jack's silhouette could be seen sprinting across the field. The fire and running human were mesmerizing. Even Clarrie forgot about his date and released his hold on the actress. He climbed down, Louise followed and they both moved towards the fire and sound of the plane.

A second brazier about a hundred yards from the first caught fire and the plane turned to begin its approach.

'He'll never land in the dark. He's gonna crash,' shouted Clarrie. The pilot couldn't hear him and did what he'd done a hundred times before.

The Lysander kangaroo-hopped along the field, settled then did a 180 degree turn and stood ready to take off. The pilot shouted something which Louise and Clarrie couldn't understand but Jack could and was already running towards the plane. He climbed aboard and the plane taxied.

As it drew level with the couple on the side of the landing strip, Jack stood up and shouted.

'Mademoiselle! Mademoiselle! Come with me! Hurry!'

The pilot lost it. One passenger, *one* was listed on his manifest. He was worried about fuel, the winds over the North Sea and any unnecessary weight.

She didn't need to think. This was the answer to her prayers. Depart a boring, unhappy concert party and dive back into the world of fighting Nazis. *Besides, they speak French in Belgium.*

Clarrie sensed her willingness to move. For him, that was never going to happen. He was on a winner tonight and intended to make every coital post a winner. He grabbed her.

'Oh no you don't, me darlin'.'

His grip was fierce but the contest was shockingly unfair; a highly-skilled SOE agent trained in unarmed combat up against an overweight, out-of-any-condition slob of a lazy farmhand. Where and how she hit him was never a part of the Marquess of Queensberry Rules. She struck and took off. Clarrie struggled even to collapse, unable to utter a sound. His eyes watered as his date for the night ran alongside the bobbing aircraft.

The Lysander gathered speed. Jack kept shouting, Louise ran like crazy, the pilot panicked not wanting to kill the woman but most definitely not wanting to hang around and besides, this was not the longest homemade runway in Britain. The copse of trees drew closer.

Louise and her rush of blood made for a hectic scene. Grasping a wing strut and Jack's hands she clambered up and onto the side of the fuselage beside the passenger seat. But it was taken. The engine roar made conversation a waste of time.

The plane lifted and Louise had no choice. She fell into the passenger seat with her lower abdomen flush against Jack's face. Her mother would have died. Matilda Gonzales-Jones would have shrieked with laughter.

As the Lysander soared, Louise managed to about turn and fall down onto Jack's crotch. He didn't know where to put his hands so settled for her waist. Interesting.

Alone in the darkness and suffering mental and physical anguish, Clarrie still couldn't speak leaving the horse downright annoyed.

'Is you coming or what?' it neighed and Clarrie took an age to climb aboard. Every move he made sent an arrow of agony through his body. It wasn't his night and the poor bugger was dead set stiff.

Louise once flew in another Lysander. In 1940 she made an escape from France with her big brother's best mate, Pongo Fingleton. They too shared the second seat although poor Pongo was badly injured and close to death meaning Louise became a contortionist to give the wounded Tommy a semblance of comfort.

This time her co-passenger was a young Jew, flying home to try and save his Belgian parents from their unwanted trip to Auschwitz.

Her mind raced. What will the ENSA producers say when they discover their beloved leading lady has absconded a second time?

'Miss Wellesley has gone AWOL!'

'Again?!"

Never mind the theatricals. What about Colonel Buckmaster?

Chapter 9

Somewhere above the North Sea, 1943

A Westland Lysander could take off and land pretty much anywhere and did so many times during WW2. In fields in the dead of night, they carried agents, ammo and articles (top secret). On the night Jack ran away from ENSA, a Lysander prepared to take off from an unknown "airport" in a Suffolk field about a hundred miles from Belgium as the crow flies. It flew low on a wing and a prayer.

There were two seats; one for the pilot, the other for the passenger and cramped is a fair description; although it's more accurate to say *very* cramped. Flying the Lysander was much easier than boarding it. Pilots and passengers of the slim variety were preferred.

This Lysander was heading to Belgium to collect an SOE agent and was diverted because of a request to help a Belgian Resistance fighter return home. Jacob Stern was that Resistance fighter and the plan worked a treat; so far. He and his new friend, the actress Louise Wellesley, a late entry, were aboard and on their way heading for Belgium across the North Sea.

The wind and the cold had little impact on the passengers who were interacting like never before being forced into an intimate union. Louise had no choice as to where she could place her bottom and Jack worried about where he should place his hands. He settled for her waist and they tried to relax but failed.

He leant forward and spoke into her ear. 'I don't know what came over me. It just happened.'

She turned her head to speak and their faces were close. 'I'm glad you did. I've never been to Belgium.'

'Will you get into trouble with Miss Watkins?'

Louise glanced at him, smiled and shook her head. She faced front. *Forget ENSA but the SOE might be tricky.*

He leant forward and kissed her neck. She felt a tingle and he held her tightly sliding his hands around her waist as the Lysander maintained her steady hum above the waves of the North Sea.

In Poland, Auschwitz started as a POW camp but grew over time. It became a major player in The Final Solution and by 1943 trainloads of human beings, most being Jewish, arrived regularly at Birkenau.

From the 1000+ passengers on each train, half a dozen young, at least reasonably healthy victims were separated, tattooed so as to identify them as workers in the camp, while the others were often murdered soon after arrival.

The chimneys above the ovens were tall so as to more easily dispose of the sweet stench of burning flesh as the gassed inmates were transferred to ovens in the "camp bakery" for cremation.

The locals knew what was happening and at other camps. The Allies knew too. So why was Auschwitz not bombed? And if such action was deemed barbaric, then why not bomb the railway lines?

24 hours earlier in the old engineering factory in Brussels, voices were heard; angry voices with German accents.

'They're in the ceiling.'

'Come down now,' screamed the German officer in charge.

Beneath the roof, the cramped, cold and terrified Sterns were as good as dead. In order to be murdered, they had to crawl to the small manhole then descend the vertical ladder bolted to the wall.

Dina went first facing the wall while Louis, with difficulty, stepped over her. If she fell, he would save her unless her weight and distress caused him to lose his grip and both would plunge to the concrete floor. That might be a kinder death than the one awaiting in Poland.

As they struggled, the Nazis shouted more obscenities. Talk about overkill.

If only the Sterns knew their firstborn had recently boarded a plane in a field in England and was heading for his homeland; it would have been a ray of hope within their abject misery. Hope was all they had left.

The Lysander settled into its routine. The engine hum gave comfort. All three knew if it spluttered and stopped, the North Sea would swallow the aircraft in seconds.

Sitting on Jack meant Louise was higher with a better view of their surrounds which consisted of blackness and a sea of stars.

Louise pondered her position. It wasn't so much she abandoned her professional role with ENSA with no reasonable excuse, again, or that she became a rogue SEO agent without any authorization; both unsatisfactory and one potentially fatal. No, she had thrown in her lot with people she barely knew. Who were these mates of her stagehand pal? Come to think of it, who was he?

And if all that wasn't bad enough, her preparation for the trip didn't exist. She didn't know where she was going or with whom? Her spare clothing ... what spare clothing? She had no toothbrush, no rations, no weapon, no foreign papers, and no clothes meaning not even a spare pair of knickers. Bloody hell! And doesn't Belgium have a King?

An hour into their flight, the pilot shouted back at the passengers.

'Coast ahead. Prepare to land. Hold tight.'

The couple had been holding tight since take-off. Jack's hands were numb refusing to release his hold on Louise. She moved and he discovered a new contour of her body. She turned back and they stared at one another. He wished the flight could continue. On land she would no longer be so physically close. She gave a weak smile.

It was pre-dawn as they crossed the Belgian coast. Louise tried to make out any landmarks. Breaking waves, possibly, but nothing else and her worry beads got a workout.

Am I in danger? These people, Jack's friends can't be German or on the side of the Nazis. But are they another group, Communists wanting to regain control of their country?

The Lysander banked to descend. Louise peered down. Yes, she was sure there were waves below. *We're not going to land in the sea!* She saw a flashing light with short flashes of a tiny beam.

They were pretty darn close to getting wet feet as they put down on a long stretch of sand. This airport depended on the tides.

The engine died, Jack patted Louise on the back and speaking French, four men appeared by the side of the aircraft. Three were from the Belgian Resistance, the other an SOE agent heading home.

'Bonjour messieurs,' said the first to the male pilot and Jack.

A second fellow blinked when he saw the woman. 'Who is this?'

All three Belgians stared at Louise and reached up to help her alight. *Who is this gorgeous creature?*

'This is my friend, Louise,' said Jack climbing down.

Jack and his friends thanked the pilot who helped the returning agent aboard and set to work preparing the plane for its getaway. Jack led Louise away from the aircraft and introduced his friends then asked the obvious question.

'So please Marc, what news of my parents?'

'They've been arrested and taken to the Mechelen transit camp. When there are enough Jews, we heard it must be at least a thousand, they'll be put in lorries and taken to the railway for the trip to the death camp at Auschwitz-Birkenau.'

Jack's face screamed despair. 'Can we attack the transit camp?'

'Too difficult, too dangerous,' said Davet, 'but we have a plan.'

'Wonderful, I knew you would,' enthused the former stagehand. There was a pause. He studied his friends who were reluctant to speak because of the stranger in their midst. Jack twigged.

'No, it's fine. Louise is my friend and one of us. She is English and hates the Nazis and her French is perfect.'

'Yes, but who is she, really?' asked Nev, 'and can we trust her?'

'Of course, now please, what is the plan?'

More hesitation and Louise took control speaking flawless French.

'Gentlemen, I understand your reluctance confiding in a person you've never met and a woman and English at that. I will walk along the beach while you discuss your plan. And do not worry; it is far too cold to go swimming.'

She left with the Resistance men watching her disappear wondering if angels often arrived by Lysander. The men spoke softly but excitedly. By the water's edge, the pilot joined Louise.

'You're a brave woman, Miss. Are you running away from someone or in love and running away *with* someone?'

Louise's worries about her spur-of-the-moment decision increased. *The resistance think I'm a double-agent and the pilot thinks I'm on a roundabout trip to Gretna Green with lover boy.*

She made light of the matter and wondered if she could bribe the pilot to make an immediate return journey. And as Clarence clearly carried a torch for the actress, might he still be there by the Suffolk International airport ready to light those braziers? Hardly.

'Mademoiselle,' called Jack as he approached. 'Everything is fine. My friends are happy to have you join our group. This way.'

She turned to the pilot. 'Please send a message to Baker Street. Plum's in Belgium and will report later.' He shrugged and nodded.

Jack led Louise back and introduced her to each man. She reckoned they were Jack's age or older. Their response appeared friendly but Louise never felt comfortable.

'Can you ride a horse, Louise?' asked Davet.

'A little,' she lied feigning a lack of confidence.

'Then you can ride with me,' he said smiling and taking her hand. His face suggested lust and Jack worried.

The group climbed through sand dunes and walked into a forest. They heard the horses before they saw them.

Jack went to Louise. 'We're going to a safe house where there is food. You can rest. We'll wait for other Resistance members and then, tomorrow night, follow our plan to kill Nazis and rescue my parents.'

'And others?' asked Louise.

'Of course. We try to rescue anyone captured by Nazis.'

Louise wanted to ask if there were any female members of the group but found herself being hoisted onto a troubled animal with Davet helping her using his hands in an ungentlemanly way.

She prepared to scowl and kick his face when a loud voice screamed in the pre-dawn light.

'Halt or we shoot.'

There was no doubting the German accent, a Gestapo officer as it turned out, when four men appeared pointing their weapons. Louise slipped down as the spooked horses ran away.

One Resistance member was about to snatch at his rifle when he froze knowing to continue meant certain death not only for him but everyone.

Each Resistance member had one thought. *We've been betrayed. How else would the Germans know we would be in this isolated place at this specific time?*

Actually the Gestapo didn't realize they'd stumbled on a Resistance cell. They were told this was a group of Jews and smugglers of Jews. The group's weapons were removed, they were bundled together and forced to sit. The Gestapo officer, Köhler, smirked as he surveyed his prize.

'I see you are not wearing your lovely yellow stars but do not worry, we have plenty although alas they are not bullet-proof.'

He grinned as his men laughed preparing to commit murder.

'Ah,' cried the officer spotting Louise behind Jack. 'We have a lovely Jewess.' He beckoned to her. 'Come Fraulein, bitte.'

She stood and every eye focused on the actress. She paused wanting to survey the scene seeking any way to escape.

The Gestapo officer grinned again with lasciviousness his calling card. 'Komm her,' he said beckoning.

She stepped away from the men in the cell and approached the Nazi. His men pointed their weapons at their prisoners ready to kill any who fancied saving their woman.

She stood facing the brute. He gestured waving a forefinger slowly in a circle. She pretended she didn't understand.

'Monsieur?' she asked.

He liked the game.

'Turn,' he said and continued with the finger waving. 'Slowly.'

Louise gave the impression of being scared knowing if she tried to resist, she was dead. The better her compliance, the longer she would live. Half way in her turn with her back to the Nazi he ordered a stop.

'Halt,' he snapped and Louise froze.

He moved closer standing behind her back. Maintaining his gloating and sexual yearning, he used the barrel of his pistol to push Louise's cardigan up her back.

'I have never seen a Jewess in the flesh, so to speak.' His words encouraged his three comrades to grin and laugh. Their business was to capture or kill Jews but all work and no play made Fritz a dull boy. The Resistance quartet knew this prolonged arrest would soon be over. An execution in this isolated place was a given.

Louise was not dressed for any long journey. After the show she changed into a shirt, cardigan, cotton trousers and plimsolls; not exactly Nazi-fighting clobber.

'Come along, Mademoiselle,' sneered the officer, 'do not be shy. Let us see your beautiful body, even if it is of the Jewish variety.'

Every male was infatuated. They stared at the actress as did audiences wherever she performed, including at the Folies Bergère. The pistol pushed the bottom of Louise's cardigan up her back. The officer leant in and whispered in her upstage ear. He stepped back and paused, then with his gun-free hand, slowly lifted the garment over her head and casually tossed it upstage, up forest. Jack wondered if ice ran in her veins.

The pistol was placed against the back of Louise's head. She flinched involuntarily. So, she is human after all. The Belgians were silently cursing with Jack weeping. They wanted their execution brought forward. Why this torture? Get it over with.

There was another whispered message from the Gestapo officer who again stepped back. Louise turned to face her torturer with thoughts racing back to Marseille when the Gestapo arrested her and applied horrific torture including a white hot poker on her right big toe, the pain being worse because it was not expected.

This Gestapo officer spoke with his pistol giving it a jerk as a signal to commence. Louise unbuttoned her shirt. She did so slowly to defy or deny her captor. It gave her time with the German enjoying his dominance even more. He too was in no hurry.

One by one each button was undone. Because she was now facing the evil man, audience members to Louise's left had a limited view of the stage. Belgian and German alike shifted slightly. German rifles remained locked in position pointing at the captives.

With the last button undone, Louise stood there. She had complied with his every request. He controlled the performance. She had no intention of continuing without direction. He sniffed then moved in close to her with his eyes gleaming, his whole body leering.

Using his pistol, he touched the right side of her unbuttoned shirt and moved it to his left, upstage. He could have ordered the shirt be removed but rather fancied peering behind the curtain, a private peek through the bathroom window.

As his pistol pushed the shirt and the weapon moved beyond Louise's body, the actress grabbed the firearm while at the same time she kicked her right shin up and into the officer's crotch. His pain became exquisite made worse by the surprise factor.

The pistol being grabbed by its barrel with one hand then needed two hands from the actress to have its handle locked into her right palm. The German guards were struggling to react to what was definitely not part of any striptease routine as performed in Berlin cabarets in the 1930s.

Their biggest problem being their cannons were facing inland and not out to sea as the enemy fleet arrived. As the guards swung their rifles towards the stage, the currently out of work SOE agent opened fire with speed and accuracy. The last of three guards to be hit was about to return fire when Jack grabbed his rifle and Nev smashed a fist into his genitals.

That distraction gave the actress the split second she needed to shoot the third guard dead.

The Belgians were on their feet and grabbing German rifles. The conductor of the orchestra, with watery eyes, no weapon and shock beyond belief, gaped at the semi-dressed "Jewess" whose ancestors may well have been related to his, as she pointed his pistol and shot him in the lower abdomen.

That was cruel. He was alive but in physical and mental hell. He dropped to his knees trying to speak. The Resistance men froze wondering how this wonder woman would react.

She paused, walked to within two feet of the wounded beast, raised the pistol and spoke in perfect German, 'Did you enjoy the show, sir?' paused, smiled then shot him between the eyes.

The forest fell silent. The forest floor turned red and those who were male and alive took forever to comprehend what they saw.

Jack's girlfriend, this English woman, beautiful and polite, could not be an actress. I mean she could be and actually *was* an actress, a brilliant one, but her unarmed combat skills which became armed combat skills were not to be found in a box of cereal.

Who is this girl?

Chapter 10

Three events happened simultaneously. (a) Vera Atkins walked into Colonel Buckmaster's office. (b) Four Belgian Resistance fighters froze with their mouths wide open, and (c) Louis and Dina Stern were shoved into a lorry in Brussels.

'You're not going to believe this,' said Vera. Buckmaster paused waiting for the next sentence. 'Our Sister Claudine, dressed in trousers, shirt, cardigan and plimsolls has landed in Belgium and has we think, joined the Belgian Resistance.'

Vera was correct. Her boss didn't believe it.

'What? How?' he asked wanting all the details.

'She was starring in an ENSA show in Suffolk, went looking for a stagehand who'd gone AWOL, and both were collected at the airstrip where we sent that Lysander.'

'But how did she know about it?'

'Apparently the Belgian stagehand wanted to re-join his Resistance pals in Brussels. She must have seen the chance to become an active SOE agent again and took it.'

'That bloody girl ...' He paused. 'That bloody brilliant girl.'

'It must have been crowded in the back seat of the Lysander.'

'What's the situation in Brussels?'

'God knows. The same Lysander brought back Agent Rickard who was shot in the thigh last week. We could send someone to his hospital bed in Essex.'

'Do it and make contact with whoever we have in Brussels telling them we want contact with you know who.'

Vera left with Buckmaster continuing to mutter. 'Bloody girl.'

In the forest near the Belgian coast, Louise shoved the Gestapo officer's pistol in her waistband and stared at the men she saved from certain death. She spoke in French.

'Gentlemen, I suppose an explanation is in order.'

'My God, Mademoiselle,' said a head-shaking Jack. 'Where the hell did you learn those tricks?'

'I'm SOE and have been an active agent in France.'

'Well I hereby claim you for Belgium,' replied Jack and his comrades wholeheartedly agreed.

'I'm happy to join any Resistance cell with an aim of smashing Hitler but I'm a follower. You must make the decisions, the first being what to do with these bodies.'

She told them they were in charge while subtly giving orders.

The men spoke over one another and immediately Louise worried. They could not agree. Two wanted to leave the corpses to rot, the others wanted them buried or at least hidden.

'They will hunt us like rats whatever we do,' said Nev, 'but the sooner we take off, the better our chances of staying alive.'

'I agree,' said Jack. 'Grab anything useful from the bodies and Louise and I will find the horses.'

Jack led her into the forest where they collected the equines.

'I will be honest with you, Louise. May I call you Louise?'

'Of course.'

'There are men in the Resistance who do not respect women. Ten minutes ago I would have worried for your safety. Now I worry for any of my comrades who treat you badly.'

'I'll be fine. Come on, let's find the others.'

'Beautiful, brave and brilliant,' he said as they headed back to the others. 'I am so lucky to have joined ENSA and found you.'

The Nazis had a simple plan in Belgium. Find as many Jews as possible, load them into lorries and drive to the transit camp at Mechelen. It was a former army barracks. Treat the Jews with contempt and if any die where they sit or lie, it's less work for the Gestapo tomorrow.

Most of Belgium's Jews lived in either Brussels or Antwerp and the Mechelen camp was ideal being half way between those two cities.

Louis and Dina had one suitcase between them. Moving from one hiding place to another forced them to travel light.

In the transit camp, Dina asked a question. 'Where are we going?'

Her husband chose not to say what he'd heard. *Why add to my wife's misery?* He also reckoned with their health being so poor, a speedy death might actually be a good thing. What a life.

Many Jews in Europe thought those thoughts now the Final Solution was in full swing.

'It may be we have to live in another country, my dear,' said Louis.

'But how can we see our children? They are here in those Catholic places. And what about Jacob? He is still in England. When will he come home to Belgium?'

'Soon, my dear, we must be patient.'

Louis was unaware his son was not a million miles away back home in Belgium. But Louis had other matters to worry about. His greatest fear was his wife losing hope and her mind. And worse, there was nothing he could do to help her with either.

He saw many Romani being forced underground. *At least we are not in the basement.* Louis heard those poor wretches were given no food or sanitation and many died.

Fuck this war!

Baker Street contacted their Belgian link telling them about Sister Claudine.

'Is she a nun?' asked the contact in Belgium.

The London officer worried. 'No, we'll give her a new code name and let you know. For now we'll call her Plum.'

'And what do I ask her?'

'Find out where she is, who she's with and, if possible, have her make contact with us as soon as possible.'

'Will do,' said the Belgian and the hunt for Plum began.

Sitting behind Jack, Louise rode with her new Resistance cell through the forest before reaching an old, dilapidated farmhouse far from civilization. Jack took Louise inside and introduced her to three more Resistance fighters, all male.

'We need clothes and footwear for Louise,' said Jack and the others shrugged.

One removed his jacket and tossed it to her. 'Here, Mademoiselle, please take care of it for me.'

The residents laughed until Jack explained how Louise had saved their lives and killed four Germans. Respect quickly replaced their rudeness.

When the original gang had taken care of the horses and returned, Nev took over. Louise wondered if he was the leader. He spoke.

'We are so lucky to have Louise join our cell. Christiane will be here tonight with supplies and news from Brussels. In the meantime, we need to check the weapons and items we took from the Nazis and prepare for our next attack.'

'Which is what?' asked Marc challenging Nev.

Observing, Louise thought she was back in France where dissent within Resistance cells seemed to be de rigeur.

What have I let myself in for?

The Sterns were two of hundreds of prisoners. Most were Jews and their eyes carried the same message—without hope and desperate. Why speak to other prisoners? Why listen to more tales of brutality?

Another lorry drove into the hollow square of the transit camp. The open space was surrounded by tall buildings creating an open-air prison. The vehicle stopped and guards moved to the rear and pulled down the tailboard. Canvas blinds were pulled back and orders shouted.

'Get down! Get out! Hurry!'

Louis, Dina and others watched with miserable eyes. What had these men, women and children done to be treated like this? Two middle-aged men, a son and a son-in-law stood on the edge of the lorry with an elderly woman between them. They were holding her, trying to lift her down. Each man took an arm and lifted the terrified woman. It was dangerous and difficult but it took time and held up the lorry becoming empty.

A Nazi stepped forward, grabbed the woman's coat and yanked. She fell as did the two men trying to help. There were many screams from the onlookers as well as the people in the lorry.

Louis wanted to go to the scene and offer to help but saw guards wading in and beating people demanding they move.

All this to transport us to a concentration camp. Why not kill us here? Oh, of course. They must have a simple way to dispose of the murdered bodies. I've heard about those very tall chimneys.

67

Vera told Buckmaster the news. 'Louise is with a group of Resistance fighters hiding out near Brussels. The agent asked for her code name. It can't be Sister Claudine so Plum was suggested for now.'

Buckmaster shrugged. 'As good as any,' he said. 'So now she's there, we need a project for the actress.'

'I think you mean projects, plural. Miss Wellesley was always good at juggling.'

He nodded and while he was angry she'd hitchhiked to an occupied country without permission, inside he warmed to the idea of this particular agent again fulfilling the PM's demand to, "set Europe ablaze".

The Sterns slept on the floor of a large, empty room, once part of the barracks for Belgian soldiers. The air was filled with groans and sobs. Those who snored were lucky; they were actually asleep.

An elderly Jew sat against the wall close to Louis. In the darkness their eyes met.

'There are 207 in here,' said the old man.

Louis stared at him. 'I beg your pardon?'

'They need at least a thousand.'

Louis started to follow. 'Do you mean for the train?'

'There's another two rooms like this with other Jews and I counted 129 Romani being taken downstairs to the cellars.'

'Poor bastards,' whispered Louis.

'I heard two guards. Our train won't go until they've found their quota. I reckon they're pretty close.'

Louis didn't know what to say but was glad of the conversation, any conversation. Neither man spoke but the old chap was definitely up for a natter.

'I know we're going to a camp called Auschwitz-Birkenau.'

'Do you mind telling me how you know these facts?'

The old chap tapped his nose with his finger. 'Gotta keep your wits about you. Once the old critical faculties are gone, you may as well be dead, my friend.'

Louis continued to think before he spoke. 'Faculties or not, I think we're as good as dead anyway.' For once his companion remained quiet. 'I hope I'm wrong of course.'

But the old chap, Chiram by name, replied with a vengeance.

'Of course, I would never question the wisdom of Jehovah but there are times, and now is one of them, when I believe he may have made the odd mistake.' Louis was hooked. 'If a father shows more affection to one of his children than the others,' ... Chiram wiggled his right hand suggesting uncertainty, a possible mistake. 'I reckon choosing favourites can lead to conflict.'

Louis nodded. He remembered times when he may have treated Jacob, his firstborn, more kindly than the younger brothers.

Did I upset my other children and were their complaints justified?

'You are my chosen people,' said Chiram. He wagged a finger at his student, Louis Stern. 'Was that a miscalculation on behalf of the great Jehovah? Did his favoured treatment of the Israelites upset other tribes and are we paying the price right here, right now?'

'You are a man of philosophy,' said Louis, 'but if you will forgive me, I must try and sleep before our long journey tomorrow. Shalom.'

'Shalom,' repeated Chiram then started counting Jews again to be sure his first count was accurate.

Chapter 11

Christiane arrived at the farmhouse around dawn. She could avoid German patrols, carry supplies heavier than many men could manage and always kept going.

She waited outside the farmhouse in the surrounding trees and gave her signal. Because the house was dark and quiet didn't mean there weren't Gestapo agents inside expecting her.

A man appeared in a doorway and barked like a dog.

Christiane picked up her rucksack and hurried towards the house. No lamps were lit although streaks of dawn made it possible to recognise the waking fighters.

'Good morning, gentlemen,' she said and placed her rucksack on the table. As she opened the bag and started removing the goodies, she stared at the grinning men. Then she stopped. One of the males was a female.

Louise stepped forward offering her hand. 'Hello. I'm Louise. Would you happen to have a bar of soap?'

The room erupted; the women greeted one another with both delighted to do so. Their company of two felt like twenty-two. And Christiane *did* have a cake of soap.

Nev took control. 'We can sort the supplies later but first the news. Christiane, what's happened?'

'The Germans have been given more bad news from their holiday in the Soviet Union.' The others buzzed. 'This has driven them crazy and they are even more cruel meaning the Jews are getting clobbered.'

Jack didn't hesitate. 'My family, have you any news?'

Christiane paused and the temperature dropped. 'They've been arrested, Jacob. I'm so sorry.'

Louise felt sick but wondered how in such a big city as Brussels, the cell would be able to pinpoint the condition of a single family. She didn't know Jack was the only Jew in the group and he had given Christiane specific instructions about his family by radio.

'Do you know where they are?' he asked fighting to remain calm.

'All the Jews have been taken to the transit camp in Mechelen, in the old barracks.'

'Then we must try and rescue them.'

There was a scary murmur from the others. All decisions were to be joint decisions. Targets must be agreed by all and preparation was key. No solo attempts were allowed on self-chosen ventures.

'You've been away, Jacob,' said Nev. 'There are rules within the cell. No heroics. It's bloody dangerous out there. You saw how close we came to being killed last night.'

Jacob fell quiet. But the new boy on the block wanted more.

'What happens to the prisoners after this transit camp?'

Christiane explained. 'They go by train to a concentration camp in Poland.' She paused. 'In reality it's an extermination camp.'

'That's where we can launch a raid. A train is much easier to attack than a building with guards all over the place.'

'No!' Nev laid down the law. 'You stay within the cell and only attack what we agree. No solo vigilante attacks.'

The silence grew louder. Nobody spoke until Louise broke the silence.

'I've had experience attacking trains and blowing up railway lines.'

One of the men who'd been in the farm all along had a go at her. 'What, with a bar of soap?'

Jack fumed. 'You shut your mouth. This woman single-handed killed four Nazis and saved all our lives.'

The joker took offence and went for Jack. 'You've been here two minutes and want to run the joint.' They tangled until Nev scared the shit out of everyone by firing his rifle into the ceiling.

He shouted. 'Enough! Our country's at war and all you lot can do is fight one another.'

Mutterings and half apologies followed. Louise decided to risk another outbreak of jealousies. She reckoned she was back in a French Resistance cell all over again.

'Where is the train going?' she asked.

'Poland,' said Christiane.

'It's a long way with plenty of possible places for an ambush.'

'Explain,' said Nev forcing Louise to justify her idea.

'We find the right place where we can hide close to the line. We choose a spot where the train slows—a bend, steep climb, both is better—then we stop the train.'

'Stop it? How?' questioned the bar of soap joker.

'At night we walk towards the locomotive with a red lantern. All drivers know the danger signal and stop the train. Guards will appear. We open fire then unlock the vans and the prisoners are on their own.'

'It's brilliant,' enthused Jack. He was alone.

Nev had comments. 'So abandoning our fellow Belgians to the countryside means they'll have no chance. All we're doing is delaying their death.'

Louise fired back. 'We choose a spot where their chances of survival are the best possible. Safe houses in the area will be one option. And before we go, we blow up a bridge or the track so future trains can't use the line for at least a few days if not longer.'

The way she spoke impressed people. The fact she'd done what she proposed before gave weight to her words.

Voices of dissent were raised. 'Should we be saving only one family. There are so many who need our help.'

'There will be at least a thousand on the train,' said Christiane. 'The Nazis stuff them in cattle cars like sardines. Only a few can sit down and they're lucky if there's a bucket in the corner. Imagine the stench. Stopping even one train allowing a few to escape is a bloody nose to the Gestapo and killing many of them has to be a good thing.'

'It's a great thing,' said a voice at the back.

'Well we can't stay here,' said Nev. 'Those dead Germans Louise killed will be found and then the hunt will be on. Let's move to a new safe house. I'll liaise with Jacob and Louise and form a plan. Once we're ready, I'll let you know. Agreed?' he called.

The response was muted but nobody complained. Christiane went to Louise.

'Come with me, Miss. You need more than a bar of soap.'

Chapter 12

Louise felt pressure. She'd scrambled aboard a small plane in England and unofficially re-joined the SOE. Within a few hours of landing in Nazi-controlled Belgium, she and a few Resistance fighters were captured by a Gestapo officer and his henchmen but thanks to Louise, all four Germans were killed; a great first impression.

Now firmly entrenched in a particular Resistance cell, she agreed to be part of a raid on a train carrying a thousand plus Jews to Poland's death camp at Auschwitz-Birkenau.

Time was against them. The train could leave any day. The line needed inspecting, and weapons, explosives and an all-important red lantern needed to be found.

One brilliant piece of good news involved fresh clothes and toiletries Christiane found for her fellow female Resistance fighter.

The trio, two females and Jack, set off outside Brussels to survey the line. Jack's emotions worried Louise. Of course he was emotional. His parents were due to be murdered. But the best fighters were those with ice in their veins and a hatred of Nazis in their cold heart.

Hiding in the forest beside the railway, Louise decided. 'This is a great place to stop the train.' The others agreed. She was SOE and a cold-blooded killer. They were amateurs wanting their country to be free.

'How many others will we need?' asked Christiane.

'Three,' replied Louise.

'Three?' said the others.

'We need one to carry the red lantern and stop the train. That's you Jack as a man will be more believable. Christiane and I with three others will deal with the guards then open the wagons. Then we get the hell out of here.'

Silence before Jack spoke. 'I need to find and help my parents.'

Louise switched to her reality gear. 'Jack, if the train isn't stopped, your parents will die in Poland, most likely as soon as they arrive. Stopping the train and giving the prisoners a chance to flee, is a far better outcome. Yes?' He paused then nodded. 'Giving your parents another chance at life is the best you can do.'

'When do we attack?'

'Once we know the train's departure time.'

'So come on,' he said. 'Let's collect the materials and the others.'

The Germans once used third-class carriages to transport Jews but the windows provided views, air and a possible escape route. The carriages were replaced with wooden cattle trucks. No windows and any openings were covered with barb wire; appalling conditions.

The Germans were renowned for their efficiency and sending a train with empty "seats" would never happen. The trucks were packed to the rafters with 1500 souls aboard all destined to be murdered. Louise and her five comrades waited in the forest.

It was a long journey from Belgium to Poland and this was no express train.

It was dark. The Resistance fighters shivered in the forest. 'Are we clear on the plan?' asked Louise. The others mumbled their agreement and Christiane said, 'Clear.'

They waited wondering if the guards on the train would kill them and any Jews who escaped. Resistance fighters were hated by the Nazis. Word spread like wildfire about the four Gestapo men shot in the forest and left to rot. Animals filled their boots and the state of the bodies sent revenge to the top of the German priorities. Reprisals were swift.

The Resistance cell heard the train. No whistle but the beat of the locomotive carried through the rural darkness. The chosen spot was good; a bend and an incline. The moon was out but so were clouds. It gave an eerie glow to the battle field.

'Good luck, Jack,' said Louise.

'Thanks,' he said and headed off to the chosen spot.

Louise had the handgun the Gestapo officer used to taunt her back in the other forest. Christiane had a pistol tucked inside her trousers and two free hands with a rifle slung across her shoulder. The other men had Sten guns thanks to a drop from Britain. All were taught how to open the sliding door of a cattle wagon.

The fighters peered into the night as the train came into view. It slowed because of the track curve and gradient. On the footplate the driver screamed to his fireman, 'Red signal!'

Brakes sprang into action and the sudden stop caused guards to spill forward. They yelled, the train stopped and guards climbed down with their weapons at the ready. Because of the bend in the line, no-one could see the whole length of the train.

In the cattle wagons, passengers suffered even more. They could hardly lose their balance being packed so tight.

Jack spoke briefly to the driver about a rockslide ahead then ran off into the forest. He had another plan. The officer in charge stormed forward yelling at the crew. They yelled back about the rockslide.

The Resistance fighters moved quietly towards the wagons. Christiane chose one where the guards were not close. She lifted the bolt used to lock the wagon, pulled back the flap and yanked the door. People inside helped. Did they ever! From inside many hands pulled the door across.

'Go!' yelled Christiane heading to the next wagon.

A guard spotted prisoners dropping onto the ground. 'Hey!' he screamed and ran towards the escapees. He stopped and raised his MP40 Maschinenpistole to spray death at dozens of fleeing Jews.

Louise fired a single shot and the guard never fired anything again.

His yell and her gunshot attracted attention from other guards. Several were on the wrong side of the train. It moved as the senior Gestapo officer pointed his Luger at the footplate crew. The guards on the wrong side of the train were too scared to dive underneath so had to wait an age as the long train inched forward. A few ran to the now approaching end of the train.

Jack counted on that and put his plan into action. In the darkness and confusion as the train moved, he went from wagon to wagon, pressed his face against the slats and called as loudly and yet as quietly as he could.

'Louis and Dina Stern, this is your son Jacob. Are you there?' No reply so immediately he went to the next wagon and spoke again.

Christiane unlocked another door, it slid open and more desperate Jews fell, climbed or jumped down. There were children and once free, their legs did the business. They had no idea where they were or in which direction they should run. They ran.

Guards were stung into action. 'Shoot them!' screamed the officer. They were unarmed civilians and worse, Jews. 'Shoot them!'

Louise and the other fighters lay flat on their belly, took aim and fired at the guards. Screams from wounded prisoners filled the night air. The locomotive picked up speed. It was obvious the train was being attacked and so healthy men in other wagons joined the escape working from the inside. They smashed the boards of the sliding door, reached out and unlocked their "cell". Another door slid open and out tumbled more people. Once they landed they fell as the train continued to gather speed.

'Get back on board,' raged the Gestapo officer watching, for him, the disaster unfolding. The train picked up speed. The guards scrambled to re-board the train. This stopped the flow of bullets allowing those Jews not wounded to flee.

Christiane gave up unlocking wagons. A guard seated above a wagon saw her and stood to fire. Louise fired and missed but the closeness of her shot distracted him thus keeping Christiane alive.

Jack continued with his message to the wagons. He heard nothing to suggest his parents were there and as the speed increased he could no longer speak. He dropped to his knees and wept.

The train disappeared and the other Resistance fighters faced the horrible problem of tending to wounded escapees and the grief of those who did break out of their cattle truck only to find their family member dead. People held deceased loved ones in their arms and wept. The scene matched those of battlefields when the fighting had stopped. The area was littered with corpses and people dying.

The train disappeared. Jack crossed the railway line and approached his comrades all the while scrutinizing the faces of people by the track hoping, desperate to find his parents. No luck.

He would think of this moment for ages. *Did they escape? Were they still on the train and heading to the gas chambers? Did they hear my voice calling their names? If so, would their spirits have soared to know their boy was alive and fighting to save his family?*

Several escapees wounded by the Nazis died beside the railway line. Later, members of a local Resistance cell arrived to remove the dead.

They left the Nazi guards where they lay pinning a large yellow star on the crotch of their uniform; the same yellow star many Jews were forced to wear.

When other Germans arrived the next day, the sight of their soldiers, dead and mocked with the Jewish insignia caused outrage in Nazi headquarters. The Germans who discovered the scene were ordered under pain of death to never mention the event. Such an order didn't apply to Resistance members who willingly spread the tale.

More reprisals followed. You'd think the Nazis would realize their additional brutal murders would never deter resistance. In fact their evil killings inspired even more attacks. But to not exact revenge would leave the Nazis looking weak and that for them was totally unacceptable.

This train attack was a savage psychological and propaganda blow to the Nazis and the Belgian Resistance success was largely due to a certain English actress.

When you think there were more than 1,600 prisoners on that train and 233 escaped with 118 making a clean break, it wasn't a raging success. But the morale boost it gave the locals was inspiring and contrasted with the so-called master race being humiliated.

Chapter 13

Louise, Christiane, Jack and the others met up with their cell. The mood was buoyant although a few of those not invited on the raid still harboured a grudge. Nev reported on what they believed to be the successful escapees and switched to a personal comment.

'I think we now know how lucky we are to have Louise join our cell.' Most of the others agreed.

'The train attack was all down to Louise and she saved my life at least twice,' said Christiane.

The general good feeling ended when a quietly jealous and seething wannabe leader, Udolf spoke. He led a small faction within the cell and took an immediate dislike to the Englishwoman.

'What happened to the plan to blow up the track?'

Instead of defending the missing part of her original proposal, Louise turned the issue into a challenge.

'Welcome to your next challenge. There's a bridge further along the line and if destroyed will stop the trains for a long time. I am willing to accompany a group of saboteurs.'

Udolf sneered. 'Is that accompany or lead?'

The atmosphere changed. People murmured. They were fighting amongst themselves—again. Jack took the lead.

'I am unique in this cell. I met Louise in England, we became friends and I brought her to Belgium. I've been with her on two Nazi attacks. She saved my life twice. Anyone criticizing her needs to take a good hard look in the mirror. She is SOE trained, experienced in guerrilla warfare and no-one, *no-one* I know is even half as brave as she is.' He paused. 'Does anyone have a question?'

The silence was loud. Jack continued.

'She taught me a few important lessons and one I'll repeat for those of you who doubt her commitment to driving the Nazis out of Belgium.' The silence dominated and even Louise was hooked.

'Our greatest enemy is not the Germans, although it's not possible to hate them any more than we do now. No, our greatest enemy is the collaborator. They are part of us, live among us, even fight alongside us but for whatever dark and evil reason, they collaborate, they work against us and help the enemy.'

People gazed without moving their heads, their eyes darting, trying to see the face of people they may have once suspected.

'Louise taught me that and she speaks from experience. Hunt Nazis but always, *always* be looking for collaborators.'

He turned away, his speech complete. Louise was mightily impressed. The humble stagehand stood tall, literally and metaphorically. The group broke up and she went to find him.

Nev interrupted her search. 'Louise, a word.' He led her aside. 'As you saw, we have a mix of people in our cell. I think, I hope despite their different political ideals, we are all as one in fighting Nazis.'

She admired him and more so when he told her the news.

'We've made contact with the SOE in London.' Louise's heart jumped. 'We told them of your arrival and your first encounter with the enemy.'

'And?' she asked.

'They already knew you were here thanks to your pilot. Would you like to speak to London?'

She blurted her answer. 'Yes; when?'

'Soon; I'll come and find you.'

He wandered off and Louise resumed her search for Jack. It was like old times. The stagehand was alone in the dark and saw her approach.

'You *are* allowed to mix with people,' she said joining him on the grass. He barely smiled. 'Thank you for your kind words, Jack. I was touched.' He nodded. 'I'm so sorry you couldn't find your parents.' He remained silent. 'Take pride in your valiant effort.'

He checked his watch. 'That train should be well through Germany by now. Next stop Poland.'

Then it happened. His emotions overflowed. Escaping back to Belgium, discovering his parents were arrested and certainly being taken to Auschwitz-Birkenau, joining the attack on the train, calling their names and then failing to rescue them pushed him to despair. He lost control, silently weeping, his body shaking.

Louise put an arm around him. She stroked his head not speaking and allowing him to let it all out.

After a minute his misery softened. He felt embarrassed. Louise produced a handkerchief and gently wiped his eyes. He took a deep breath and turned to face her.

Their eyes locked and then their lips locked. Their friendship was always there from their first meeting. Having flown together in a cramped Lysander helped stir romantic feelings. When you throw in two separate life and death situations, it's easy to understand how passion became the hottest of hot topics.

The kissing was energetic and Louise wondered where this was going. She had a pretty good idea when Jack began to undo her shirt buttons. Still kissing, although with less fervour, she gently removed his hand, kissed his nose and whispered.

'I must go, Jack. London is calling and this will be my first chance to explain how and why I ran away with a Belgian stagehand.'

He accepted her opinion and helped her to stand.

'Can I escort you to the schoolmaster's office, Mademoiselle?'

She laughed easily being in his company. 'Merci Monsieur but I do not want you to hear all my lies.'

She kissed him lightly on his lips then walked back to the safe farmhouse noting how her heart continued to race.

The Resistance radio operator was skilled twice over. She knew her Morse and kept moving locations. The Germans were experienced at finding signals and anyone sending or receiving and staying in the same place inevitably gave up their job thanks to a bullet or three.

Nev led Louise into the forest. She was glad he knew the way. After about half an hour he grabbed her arm and pulled her behind a tree. He peered out then whispered.

'It's okay, she's over there.'

The radio operator had her aerial over a branch about 15 feet above the ground. She met Louise.

'I understand you have been making a name for yourself.'

She was Flemish but her French parfaite. She made contact with Baker Street and received a reply.

'Colonel Buckmaster hopes you are well.'

Louise winced and offered her apologies. She followed the toing and froing of the Morse.

The operator turned to Louise. 'Do you have any questions?'

'Only my orders,' she said. Her smile grew bigger once she grasped the reply.

'Carry on and try to stay alive, Sherlock.'

She followed their thinking. Baker Street had given her a new code name. The Gestapo knew about *Plum* and *Sister Claudine*. Having worked with Sir Arthur Conan Doyle's youngest daughter in Louise's previous London triumph, *Sherlock* seemed an appropriate moniker.

Nev announced to the cell. 'Louise is now officially approved as an SOE agent here in Belgium and will be a member of our team.' Most of the group greeted the news with delight. Jack found his heart beating faster.

'Because Louise has experience working with the Resistance in France, I would like her to give us her thoughts on how we should continue in Belgium.'

Louise accepted the invitation but with reservations.

'Thank you, Nev. I am no expert. In France I was arrested by the Gestapo and only by luck and a few brave British airmen did I escape. I think we all know the Allies will invade Europe. When it happens the Resistance will play an even bigger role and I am happy to fight beside you to smash these bloody Nazis.'

Because Louise had already proved her worth since landing in Belgium and her words now were inspirational, applause erupted.

'Does anyone have any questions?' asked Nev.

'How can we blow up railway lines without the proper equipment?'

Another voice called. 'How can we do real damage to the Germans without reprisals?'

People murmured forcing Nev to intervene. 'All right, please, one at a time.' They settled. He invited Louise to speak.

'Again, I'm no expert but I would choose your objectives, list the material you need then request drops from London. The SOE provides highly-trained agents and the right materials but they can better help Resistance groups when we are well organized and clear on our targets.'

Most of them noted her use of the word "we".

Nev invited Louise to the next meeting of the cell's executive. She suggested Jack join because of his time spent in England. The group made two lists. One involved targets for which they didn't need material from the SOE and the other where explosives and weapons were required.

One group were the sugar and bolt team. At night they would pour sugar into fuel tanks and remove bolts which secured rails on the train network. This sort of nuisance usually didn't provoke reprisals but made the Germans take longer and reassign manpower instead of fighting or searching for Jews.

Greater damage was caused by setting explosives on railway bridges and in tunnels. Another attack like the one carrying Jewish prisoners was abandoned knowing the Germans would have doubled the guards.

Louise and Jack walked back to the safe farmhouse. He never felt more in love with her. She liked him but reckoned her love for Tom Curzon and a new SOE assignment in, to her, an unknown country were more than enough to handle without another romance.

She could see his disappointment when she gently turned down his advances. 'Sleep well,' she whispered, kissed him lightly and headed into the quarters reserved for the females.

It was 3am or thereabouts and everyone woke when a cell member ran into the farmhouse shouting, 'Plane crash! Plane crash!'

The Resistance fighter gave the details. It was three or four kilometres away elsewhere in the forest. Downed planes, usually British or American, were sadly common in Belgium. They were mainly aircraft coming home from a raid over Germany.

Louise joined the others and headed off into the night. Locals knew the way and she followed. They made steady progress until someone shouted in a controlled voice.

'Down!'

Everyone took cover.

'What's happened?' whispered Louise to the person beside her.

'We're close to the crash site but we don't know if the Germans are here already.'

A fighter crept forward and returned to say it was all clear. The group moved and when closer could see parts of the plane were still burning.

'Over here,' called someone. Louise headed to where two men in flying suits lay on the ground. Both were groaning.

Someone speaking French asked them if they were British. They helped no-one. Louise moved forward. She studied their insignia and spoke English.

'Hello,' she said, 'are you Americans?'

Both men nodded relieved beyond measure. They had survived the crash and were not being prodded by rifles owned by Germans.

'Where does it hurt?' she asked the first officer. He touched his hip and winced. 'Stretcher here,' she called and spoke to the other man. 'And you, sir, where is the pain?'

'Everywhere and will you marry me?'

She called again. 'Whisky here and he can walk.'

Nev approached and led her aside. 'There are four bodies in the fuselage or what's left of it. Can you take charge of the survivors and we'll meet back at the farm. Don't hang around. The crash and the fire will have the Germans here sooner rather than later.

Back at the farmhouse, Louise used her first-aid training and with a nurse in the cell did what they could for the aircrew. One could walk and with bandages and a crutch, the other could at least hop.

'I'm Louise,' she said.

'Rich,' said the cheeky one.

'I'm Roy,' said the chap with obvious injuries.

'Pleased to meet you, gentlemen. Try and relax and we'll have you sorted in no time.' Studying her made both feel a lot better.

Nev and Davet took Louise aside. 'We have a rescue trail helping downed airmen.'

'I know the O'Leary Line. Pat is a Belgian doctor isn't he?'

'Yes but their contacts start in Northern France. We use the Comet Line which starts here in Belgium. How do you feel about travelling with these men and see they arrive safely in France?'

Louise wondered why she was chosen. 'If you think it will help but I've never worked in Belgium or Northern France before.'

'You will have two other Resistance members with you and your French and English is the best. Once the airmen are safe in France you can return and help us kill even more Nazis.'

He watched her and she thought, *Why not?*

'Okay and please send a message to London to say *Sherlock's gone south*. Can you do that?'

He nodded. The airmen rested the next day and at night, Louise and her two passengers were ready to depart. Nev took her aside.

'You are armed of course?'

'Of course, she said.

Leaving with her was Leroux, a red-haired fighter with an appropriate fiery temper. The surprise was a good-looking Belgian, Jacob Stern. Louise wondered if Jack had volunteered.

As Leroux was the only experienced Resistance fighter who knew the Comet Way methods and contacts, Louise worried about the group's success if Mr Redhead copped a bullet or for whatever reason departed the team. They'd be on their own.

He explained their route and their first safe house. To Louise's surprise it was in Brussels. The Americans said nothing. They had no choice. Their first mode of transport was a farmer's open cart pulled by a sturdy equine. The airmen were helped aboard and Louise thought about a recent trip she took with Jack in a similar conveyance and remembered the result of that little adventure.

Living in the forest gave her a sense of security but once they reached the outskirts of Brussels, her worrying began.

They stopped in a dark street. 'Hop down,' said Leroux.

Louise translated. 'Kindly dismount, gentlemen.' They did.

Leroux led the way always in the shadows. Jack was assigned Roy, the less nimble of the aviators. Outside a house the leader stopped and the followers stopped. He opened a gate and beckoned. They walked along a path beside the house. He tapped a pattern on a door. It opened and all five visitors entered.

The food and drink were wonderful and the welcome even warmer. After about half an hour, Leroux stood and said it was time to leave. Louise was confused. What he meant was Leroux, Jack and she were leaving and the two Americans were not.

Then she twigged. It was the same principle when she fled from Lyon. You are taken to a safe house. Then the people there take you to the next refuge along the line. You only know details of the next safe house—nothing else. There is no list for the Germans to find.

Once told, both Americans became uneasy. 'I'd feel safer if the lady who speaks such good English could come with us,' said Rich.'

'Me too,' added his pal. 'We heard she's in the SOE?'

The couple in the safe house were impressed.

'But she's never lived in Belgium before,' butted in Jack. 'Her language and SOE skills together with my local knowledge will make the next move so much safer.'

Louise worried about Jack's motives. Leroux didn't give a damn. 'Are you sure about this? I mean it's a long way to Tipperary and the chances of you being stopped are about odds on.'

Louise wasn't sure but the faces of the airmen convinced her. 'I think we'll risk it,' she said and then spoke in English making the Yanks feel so much better.

'Okay,' said Leroux, shook hands with the airmen and left. The four visitors studied the couple who smiled. The husband spoke.

'Do you have the necessary papers?' he asked.

Louise felt sick and wanted to run after Leroux.

'What did he say?' asked Rich.

'Papers, have we got the necessary papers if we're stopped by the Germans?

The Americans shook their heads. 'We've got nothin',' said Roy.

Louise couldn't believe the situation. She explained the situation to the people in the house. They spoke quietly amongst themselves and the discussion became heated. The husband overruled his wife.

'We go,' he said, 'and the people in the next house will help you with papers. But pray we do not get stopped before then.'

And so the husband and wife, the US airmen, Louise and her besotted stagehand set off they knew not where.

Chapter 14

Colonel Buckmaster studied the message from Belgium. 'Sherlock's gone south,' he read. 'What the hell does that mean?'

'Miss Wellesley is bored with Belgium and longs for the bright lights of Gay Paree,' replied Vera.

'I've given up trying to control or second guess that young lady. She has the luck of the Irish and can't even spell the word *fear*.'

'Should we notify our SOE agents in France?'

'And say what? The one agent the Gestapo would love to capture, torture and slowly kill is heading your way. I suggest we tell nobody, have her locked in the safest house in France and bury the key.'

Vera produced a grim smile. Many SOE agents in F Section, including females, were in a special category of bravery. Their ability to hurt the Germans and avoid arrest was truly remarkable. Louise Wellesley had earned her membership badge within that group.

The next stop for the airmen and their buddies and leaders was deeper into Brussels. This was because the normal next safe house had nothing in the way of scientific or technical equipment. A special safe house was required.

Through the suburbs of the capital they went always in the shadows. Main roads were out of the question. The husband led and used hand signals. If danger threatened, his hand signal spoke volumes.

A truck turned into their road with restricted headlights probing the sides of the road. The husband and wife leapt over the front fence of the nearest house and lay flat in the garden. Louise and Jack pushed their American partners. The truck slowed as the travellers chewed grass. It kept going with nobody moving. When the homeowner opened the front door and came out holding a torch, the party of six grew wings.

This cat and mouse routine continued until they reached their goal. A secret code being tapped saw the back door open and everyone pile inside. Only then was a dim light switched on. A short, elderly man with thick glasses, a beard and hair which could fill three pillows, and wearing clothes he lived in permanently, grinned at his visitors. It seemed he did his own dentistry with a bottle of whisky and a pair of pliers.

'This is Drugi,' said the husband. 'He will make you papers and we will bid you a safe journey.'

'They're leaving,' said Louise and the Americans were full of gratitude as the married couple left.

'Who are you and where are you going?' asked Drugi.

Louise spoke for them all. She pointed. 'These are American airmen going to Spain.' She pointed at Jack. 'He is a Belgian helping the Americans cross into France.' She pointed at herself. 'I am English, SOE, also helping the Americans cross into France.'

Drugi frowned. 'You are SOE and have no false papers?'

'Ah, I left England in a hurry. Sorry.'

The old man shrugged, made them a hot drink which was neither tea or coffee and then got busy. He photographed everyone, printed the photos, trimmed the edges with a razor blade and glued them on fake travel documents. He stared at the Americans.

'Your name?' he asked in heavily accented English.

'Richard Jones, Chicago Illinois.'

Drugi struggled in disbelief. Louise helped.

'Gentlemen these are fake documents. You need a fake name from a country not at war with Germany; France or Switzerland.' She spoke to Drugi. 'Make them Swiss businessmen.'

The whole procedure took over an hour. Louise and Jack became French and if stopped could easily converse in the local lingo. The Americans, if dressed in suits might pass for being Swiss but their cover would be blown the moment they opened their mouth.

Sleeping arrangements proved interesting as the two guest bedrooms provided two singles in one and a double in the other. The Yanks were on their singles in a flash while Louise and Jack entered their room with hesitation. The main issue was the size of the bed. Landlords would call it a double; the rest of the world would mock.

'I'll sleep on the floor,' he said and glanced at the rug on the carpet free boards.

'Don't be silly,' said Louise regretting her every word. 'I'm sure you are a gentleman, Jack so please keep to your side of the bed.'

'Would you like to use the bathroom, first?'

She smiled, grabbed her tiny bag of toiletries and left.

She returned and they stepped around one another as if each had a contagious disease. He left with his bag of toiletries; a toothbrush. He would have liked to shave but having no razor killed the idea.

When he returned and closed the door, the darkness meant all he could see was a lump. He walked to the other side and carefully lifted the sheet and blanket. Exposing Louise in her expensive negligée would be exciting but impolite. Her sexy night attire consisted of exactly the clothes she'd been wearing since, God knows when.

He slid into bed and a loud twang sounded. The bed was as old as Drugi. 'Pardon,' said Jack and froze. Louise giggled and after a moment Jack laughed. The unresolved sexual tension faded a little.

They settled. 'Goodnight,' whispered Louise and turned her back towards her sleeping partner.

'Goodnight,' he said with feeling. 'Sleep well.'

Both took an age to fall asleep. Both thought about their brief moment of passion after the Resistance meeting. Louise was the first to sleep and Jack found the sound of her breathing to be both relaxing and arousing. He eventually slept.

Hours later, he woke because someone was touching him. A hand lay across his chest beneath the blankets. His body stiffened and his pulse started jogging.

His thoughts multiplied. *Does she know about her hand? Is she asleep? Did she place it there deliberately? What the hell do I do?*

He decided, gently lifted the blanket and took hold of her hand. As he placed it back on her side of the bed, she woke. It took her a moment to discover where she was. Their eyes met and she smiled.

'Good morning,' he said lowering the blanket.

'Good morning. What time is it?'

'Why? Are you going somewhere?'

She smiled again and he was never more in love. They lay there side by side staring at the ceiling. The only window in the bedroom was covered with an old and never-cleaned blind.

'I've been thinking,' she said. He hoped it was about them. 'We should split up.' His hopes shattered. 'On their own, those Americans will be caught in five minutes. We take one each and if stopped at least we can make a fist of talking our way out of any trouble.'

'You're right,' he said. 'I'll take Roy. If he needs help, I'm stronger than you.'

She was about to say, "Who says?" then realized their current situation. To kill any temptation to give in to her sexual desires, she hopped out of bed. 'I need the loo.'

After the flush stopped, she heard a sound. Curious she followed it and entered the kitchen, dining and sitting-room combined where Drugi was hard at work.

'Ah, Mademoiselle, you slept well I hope?'

'Thank you, Monsieur, I did.'

'And your boyfriend? Did he keep you warm?'

Louise wondered if God did her a disservice creating her with so much natural beauty. Remarks by males with overtones of sex were on a loop.

'How are your documents coming along?' she asked.

'Nearly finished and your tailor and escorts will be here soon.'

Soon meant right now as the window or door tap message was heard and three people were admitted. It was still pre-dawn but the two men and a woman were as fresh as a daisy. They greeted Drugi and he introduced them to Louise as the visitors began to undress.

Louise was asked to unzip the woman's outer garment. She soon twigged; these people were delivering clothes for the escapees. Carrying such garments would have the Germans arresting them on sight. Wearing them increased their body shape but it worked.

The voices brought Jack, Rich and Roy from their bedchambers. Introductions followed, more mugs of the hot stodge were poured and, thank God, rolls with ham were pulled from pockets of the newly arrived clobber carriers. Louise asked Drugi for a prop.

Eating and dressing ensued until the serious stuff began. One of the two male visitors explained the documents expertly created by Drugi and handed out four train tickets. All his sentences were translated by Louise for the airmen.

With instructions over, Louise explained their plan about going as two pairs rather than one quartet. No-one argued. It made sense and Louise spoke with such calm confidence, it was natural to follow the leader.

The main difference this time was daylight. None of this creeping along darkened streets and hiding at the sight or sound of anything German. Now they were citizens of France or Belgium going about their daily business and, for them, scary didn't even come close.

With clear directions to the station, they thanked Drugi and his comrades and set off. Louise and Rich went first with Jack and Roy to follow five minutes later. The second group were to try and keep the others in sight.

Good luck.

At the station, Belgian railway staff checked tickets and German soldiers checked papers. Louise had instructed the airmen to say nothing. She and Jack were the talkers.

The officials didn't need to speak. Passengers knew the routine. The travellers had chosen to be step-siblings. Louise held out her new ID which had aged by adding a few food stains from the kitchen of chef Drugi.

Rich held out his ID. Before the soldier could question the American, Louise spoke. 'We have a family funeral in Wallonia, officer. We will return on the 6.23 train.'

The ID was thrust at Rich who broke the inviolable rule—do not speak. 'Merci,' he muttered in his Illinois accent.

Louise's heart stopped beating as she half pushed her "step-brother" forward. The German soldier either didn't hear or didn't understand and the "siblings" walked to the train.

'Sorry,' he whispered. 'I don't know what came over me.'

'Are all Americans dumb ass morons like you?' He gasped at her rudeness and language. She was even more shocked at her reaction. 'I apologize. I don't know what ...'

'No, you're correct. It was damn stupid and it won't happen again.'

They found their seats and looked back along the platform watching for their friends. The pressure kept mounting. If they were caught, being apart meant Louise and her sibling should be okay.

Jack and Roy came along the platform and all four passengers glanced at one another without making it obvious. So far so good.

Once the train started, a ticket-collector checked their tickets but said nothing.

The journey took about an hour. Louise saw a sign and whispered to her fellow traveller. 'We're next.'

Rich glanced at her and then across the aisle to his mate and Jack. The train stopped at Wallonia. They'd been told at the farmhouse and again at Drugi's they were to exit around the middle of the group. Keep others in front and behind. They did so and on the platform were hoping like hell a person was there to meet them.

It was busy when from out of the crowd a middle-aged woman grabbed Louise and excitedly pounced on her.

'Michelle, hello,' said the woman and kissed her "relative" with the name Michelle on Louise's ID card.

Stepping out of the line of traffic, the woman whispered her name and asked about the others. They saw what was happening and, still apart, all five made their way to the exit gate. Their tickets were taken, including the platform ticket for the woman and the contact led the two groups to a local park. In a quiet corner they chatted in quiet voices.

Smiling at the airmen, she spoke in English. 'I am your sister,' she said in English and the Americans were delighted to have a local they could understand. 'We will leave soon as we are going to our mother's birthday party.'

Rich understood. 'Happy birthday, Mom.'

'So now it is time to say goodbye to your friends from Brussels.'

The airmen stood, kissed Louise, shook hands with Jack then wandered off arm in arm with their "sister". At the park entrance they turned and waved. Would they make it across the borders; French, Spanish and more?

Louise and Jack wandered around the park. 'Jack, I've decided not to return to Brussels.'

He stopped. 'But it was agreed. You are part of our Resistance.'

'I know but I have unfinished business in Paris.'

He felt sick. Apart from her breaking their agreement, his heart was seriously attracted to this young woman. He floundered.

'I can come with you.'

'No, it's too dangerous.'

'But I will be there to protect you.'

He knew she was a trained SOE agent and he a semi-skilled stagehand. He needed her to protect him and appeared sad and pathetic.

She yielded. 'Okay but after Paris, you're on your own.'

He hugged her with strength then grasped her shoulders and kissed her with passion. She didn't join in but didn't resist.

She set off. 'The Paris train leaves in ten minutes.' He ran to catch up realizing this was something she'd been planning for some time.

They exchanged their tickets to Brussels for ones to Paris, paid the extra and waited on the platform. Louise carried a small bag, Jack nothing. Their lack of luggage was more suspicious than any bulging suitcase.

And crossing borders was more difficult. Their ID within Belgium was fine but now both needed to show a passport. Drugi had done an excellent job and both travellers were fluent French speakers. Their train arrived.

'I think we should pretend to be lovers,' she said. 'If stopped, it will be more believable than siblings.'

He couldn't stop smiling.

Chapter 15

They crossed the French border with papers accepted and when questioned, both spoke fluently with confidence. To the authorities, this couple were who they claimed to be.

As the train headed south towards the French capital, Jack spoke quietly. 'May one ask what you meant by "unfinished business in Paris"?'

She stared at him and as he was already staring at her, their eyes locked. 'It's something I must do alone. I know a safe house where you can stay.'

He nodded feeling disappointed. He loved her, yes, but also wanted to help her even save her as she once saved him.

In Paris, they stepped from the train and Louise felt her skin begin to crawl. Only three years ago she lived and worked in this city as a sleeper for the SIS. The SOE had yet to be formed. Louise slipped on the spectacles given to her by Drugi.

There were people milling around and the war of 1939 was nothing like the war today. Louise lived here when the Germans first marched down the Champs Elysées. Jack saw fear in her eyes.

'Come on,' said Louise. 'I want this over today.'

They travelled through Paris not speaking. Louise's silence was obvious to her companion. He worried not knowing the reason.

She stopped outside an apartment building, gave it the once over then climbed the steps and knocked on the door.

'Who is this at my door in the middle of the day?' called a woman.

The door opened and the two women screamed. Madame Baudin was the landlady who changed the life of Mademoiselle Juliette Beauchamp. She gave Louise, then Juliette, accommodation and a job reference. Then she gave her an outfit for another job in a Parisian club and finally sent the Gestapo on a wild goose chase when they burst in hunting for the young Englishwoman.

'Come in, come in,' ordered the former showgirl still wearing a pound of make-up and smoking continuously. Inside Madame Baudin turned to examine Jack.

'And who is this young man? Have you brought me a lover at last?'

'Madame, this is my boyfriend, Jack. We are passing through and need a bed for the night please. Naturally we have money.'

The landlady scoffed. 'Who am I to stand in the way of true love? For you, ma chérie, there will never be a charge.'

Louise kissed her and indicated Jack. 'If you could allow my friend to hide upstairs, I will return in an hour or two.'

Jack didn't know what to say as Louise kissed him and left. Madame Baudin studied the stagehand.

'You are a lucky man. She is a wonderful, wonderful woman.'

Louise knew where she was going and found her memory of certain parts of Paris to be as if she had never left. Despite the fact the war in 1943 was far different than in 1940, there were still German soldiers on the streets, in cafes and she knew Gestapo officers could blend in anywhere.

She reached the street with the building where once she was held captive by the Resistance. Her conscience and heart worked overtime. Did she want forgiveness or to repay what she believed was her debt? She didn't know.

She turned into a lane and climbed stairs. She removed her spectacles, knocked on a door and lost control of her heartbeat. Footsteps sounded, the door opened and Louise knew she was in the right place. A man's face rang a bell. More to the point, he knew her.

His eyes blazed. He grabbed Louise, dragged her inside, closed and locked the door and shoved her and as she sprawled on the floor knocking over chairs, the disturbance brought Resistance members into the room. None of them had ever seen Louise before.

'It's her,' spat Émeric. 'This is the bitch who betrayed us at the hotel Meurice where all our comrades were slaughtered by the Gestapo.'

The atmosphere oozed hostility. Émeric spat on Louise lying on the floor and prepared to kick her. Another member, a woman, grabbed him.

'Stop! What are you doing?'

'She's responsible for half our cell being wiped out.'

'Then why is she here? If what you say is true, why would she return? Does she have a death wish?'

'I agree,' said another member. 'Let her speak.'

Émeric backed off muttering. A couple helped Louise to stand while the others stared at her waiting for an explanation.

'My real name is Louise Wellesley. I'm English and came to Paris in 1939 as a sleeper, an agent for the Special Intelligence Service based in London. When war broke out, I was trained to start work here and wait for instructions from London. I worked with Edith Piaf and she introduced me to an Englishman, Godfrey Silsbury.'

There was a sharp intake of breath.

'Go on,' said someone.

'It's a long story but I knew a high-ranking Nazi was staying in the Meurice Hotel. I told this Resistance cell and helped them plan a kidnapping. Silsbury pretended to be a loyal Englishman while all the time was a double agent. He betrayed me and this cell and was the reason your comrades were killed.'

She paused and her words had a ring of truth about them.

'Where have you been the last few years?' asked someone.

'I'm an active SOE agent. In Lyon I attacked a Nazi train, killed Gestapo and Wehrmacht officers, uncovered and killed German spies and helped French and German Jews walk across the Pyrenees to freedom.' She paused. 'Did you hear about the bishop in Lyon falling from on high in his cathedral?' Heads nodded. 'I helped him fall.'

Her words kept hitting home.

'Who is the head of the SOE?' called someone.

'If you mean the F Section then it's Colonel Maurice Buckmaster.'

'Anyone can discover his name. Your fine words may be true but why are you here now?' snapped Émeric. 'Is this a double bluff, another trick to have us all killed?'

The silence dominated as all eyes fixed on Louise. 'I want to apologize for what happened before and to ask for a chance to seek revenge for your lost comrades.'

Wow. No-one was expecting that answer.

'I know,' said a man. 'Have her kill Silsbury.'

The others murmured their approval and Louise gasped.

'He is still alive and here in Paris?'

'Do you accept the challenge?' Émeric pushed hard.

Louise struggled. 'Well yes but I would need to know where he is and what you know about him in order to plan his assassination.'

'And you would have to work alone,' fired back Émeric. 'The last time we trusted you, all our comrades were killed.'

Louise decided to fight back. 'If I was ever a traitor or am still today, why would I bother returning here now? I know this is your safe place. Why did I not send the Gestapo here already?'

Silence settled. Even Émeric ran out of questions.

'Tell me all you know and give me 24 hours,' she said.

They did and she left with nerves buzzing. Her task was overflowing with risks and danger; find and kill Godfrey Silsbury.

She knocked on Madame Baudin's door and was welcomed again with joie de vive. 'Come in, my little darling.' She studied the SOE agent. 'But yes I was correct, you are even more beautiful today and what have you been doing these last few years?'

'You would not believe me, Madame.'

'Go on, I love a good story and especially one with sex. And I think your present lover is gorgeous.'

'Please Madame, I apologize for my rudeness but I have a very important invitation to accept tonight. When I've finished, I promise to return and tell you everything. Now a favour if I may.'

'Of course; a sexy dress or even one of my old costumes?'

Louise smiled. 'Thank you, no. All I need is a small card, an envelope and a pen.'

The older woman reacted with surprise but went to a desk covered with knick-knacks. She found the items and placed them on her desk. 'Here, sit,' she said offering Louise a chair.

There was little writing and the inquisitive former entertainer tried to see. Louise was quick, placed the card with the message in the envelope, addressed and sealed it and stood and kissed her wonderful former landlady.

'Please might I borrow a hat, Madame?' she asked. And the woman took exquisite pleasure in selecting a range of headwear for Louise. Madame Baudin was re-living her youth. Dress to impress was her motto through life and the young Englishwoman allowed her to live vicariously.

With a chic and classy hat, Louise kissed her former landlady and headed out. 'Please tell my friend I will be back soon.'

The Resistance cell knew Godfrey Silsbury had been seen in Paris but knew nothing of his address. A few members wondered why they'd been unsuccessful in finding and executing this double-agent and hated collaborator. He was obviously well protected.

Louise walked briskly through Paris heading to possibly the most dangerous destination in the city—Gestapo headquarters. She thought of her family, Tom Curzon, the SOE leaders in Baker Street and even Jack Smith risking his life to follow his girl.

Why am I doing this? The chances of success are slim. How is my Deutsch?

The hat gave her a touch of class. Her dress was fine and her slim body eye-catching but the hat set her apart. She wanted to exploit her natural beauty. She wanted it to distract from her mission.

Outside the building, she added her spectacles, took a deep breath then walked into the foyer. Her acting ability shone. A uniformed soldier stepped forward to challenge her although being a woman and beautiful and he thought unarmed, his challenge was not aggressive. Louise spoke softly in German.

'I have a message for Herr Godfrey Silsbury,' she said and held up the envelope.

'Over there,' said the soldier using his head to indicate. His hands were fully occupied with his weapon.

A woman was typing but stopped when Louise approached. A certain hat caught the receptionist's eye. Louise's beauty caught everyone's eye.

'This is an important message for Herr Godfrey Silsbury. Please see it is forwarded to him without delay.'

She finished her routine, placed the envelope on the desk, turned on her heel and strode out of the foyer with several pairs of eyes hooked on her every move. Time to return to Madame Baudin.

She knocked gently on the door of "their" room and Jack was on his feet in a flash.

'Sit,' said Louise removing her hat and pouring herself a glass of water. 'I have a mission tonight, Jack. Once it's finished, we will make plans to return to Belgium and re-join our friends in the Resistance.'

'But where have you been?' he asked worried sick. He was alone in Paris with no idea where his comrade was or what she was doing.

'Some business from when I was last in Paris.'

He wanted to ask so many questions but felt it might upset her if he did. Besides, she exuded confidence or at least he thought she did. Possible false bravado didn't come into his thinking.

They sat in the room which was dominated by a bed. It too was a double although of the smaller variety. He thought of them being alone here tonight.

'We'll pay Madame Baudin for food and then you must wait here until I return.'

They ate then Louise slipped out to the lavatory. She returned to find him holding her pistol.

'What are you doing?' she hissed.

'What are *you* doing?' he replied.

She strode to him and took the weapon. 'If you want to travel with me, you must do as I say. You know I work for the SOE. You have little training in fighting Nazis. Do as I say or you are on your own.'

His face shouted fear and sadness. He didn't want to be on his own in a foreign city and country and he most definitely didn't want to be separated from the woman he loved—madly.

'I need sleep,' she said and slipped into bed. 'Wake me at 11.'

She turned her back to him. He sat on the chair in the dark and worried. His parents were certainly dead although his younger siblings he hoped were alive. The hours ticked by. He checked his watch then gently touched Louise's shoulder.

She was instantly awake and out of bed. Splashing water on her face at the basin, she dried her face and hands, tied her hair with a ribbon, checked the contents of her bag then stood close to Jack staring at his eyes.

'When I return, we will make plans for our future. Okay?'

'What if you don't return?'

They stared at one another. 'Have I ever let you down?'

She stood on tip toe and kissed his lips in a firm but brief movement. Then she was gone. He despaired. After a minute he couldn't stand the tension and went downstairs. Outside the landlady's door, he tapped softly and whispered.

'Madame, are you there?

The door opened. She appeared wearing one of her striking dressing-gowns and spoke. 'She has gone to the Eiffel Tower.'

'What?'

'Come in.'

He moved in a flash and she closed the door. 'I saw her writing a note and part of it mentioned the Eiffel Tower.'

'Why, what did she plan to do?' She shrugged. 'I am worried, Madame. I think she is in terrible danger.'

'Then go and make sure she stays alive.'

'Thank you,' he said and kissed her on both cheeks. He stopped at the door when she spoke.

'Here, you must take this.' She held out a small pistol.

Louise had no idea Silsbury was in Paris, if he received her note or, if he did, if he would do as asked. It was a cryptic message but she knew the man and how he hated her. She was the one who blew his cover and the reason England wanted him dead and why the Germans must still tolerate him. If caught by the British he would be tried for treason and hung. Yes, he hated Louise Wellesley, his little plum!

It was well after curfew and she remembered the night she escaped from Silsbury's murderous attempt on her life as she raced through the streets of Paris. From side street to side street, from shadow to shadow she ran through the City of Light now dark.

The vast Eiffel Tower stood tall, the perfect setting for a deadly game of cat and mouse. But who was the mouse?

She stared through the gloom. The giant feet of the Tower beckoned. *Is he here? If so, where?*

She squatted behind bushes, keeping still and watching carefully she withdrew her pistol, the one she "borrowed" from the Gestapo officer near a Belgian beach two or was it three days ago? Time flies when you're having constant death encounters every hour.

She listed midnight as the time of their appointment. Her note mentioned, "something to your advantage" and was signed by "a long and trusted friend".

If Silsbury knew it was Plum who wrote the note he would be there with bells on. If he wasn't sure, he would come anyway in case it was her. But he was no mug. No-one could be a collaborator and survive in a German-occupied city for years without taking precautions.

Not knowing if he was around, she bent low and scurried to the closest of the tower's massive feet. She crouched and pressed herself inside its vast metal structure. The silence crowded in on her. Could she be seen? Would it matter if Silsbury was nowhere near? She wondered. *Did he even receive the note?*

'Good evening, my dear.'

She froze. Yes, he bloody well did get her note. She heard him loud and clear. She strained peering into the darkness in the direction of the voice; *his* voice and saw no-one.

Feeling vulnerable, she crept around the frame so as to have it between her and the target. *Do I speak?* He spoke.

'It was a lovely surprise to hear from you. I felt sure you were long dead but this way I can be sure you will soon be no longer with us. I'm awfully sorry, old girl.' He never could stop lying.

She wanted to speak but held back. The few night sounds of Paris went unnoticed.

'So how do you wish to play this, my dear? Drop of a hanky, ten paces then turn and fire? Being a gentleman of course I would abide by the rules. But then you being a fucking bitch, makes me more inclined to stay hidden.'

'Like a rat, you mean?' she said without thinking.

He loved it. The first sign of provocation and she took the bait.

'Oh you are there. Well come on, m'darlin'. You asked for the rendezvous. Put your cards on the table. Show yourself.'

She cursed herself having no plan. Colonel Buckmaster would be ropeable at her lack of preparation. She decided to creep around the tower support then spring out and fire in his direction hoping her new position and firing would force him to reveal himself.

About to move, she froze when a round metal object pressed against the back of her head. It was unmistakeably a gun barrel. 'Move and you're dead,' said a male voice she knew.

The silent support team member whistled and pushed Louise towards her enemy. Silsbury called.

'Drop your weapon, Plum old girl.' She hesitated. The gun behind her pressed harder and Silsbury snapped. 'Drop it.'

It made a sound clattering on the ground.

'I see you pick your collaborators from the top of the pile.'

'Ah,' replied Silsbury walking forward, his weapon trained on the SOE agent. 'The best traitors are the ones hiding in plain sight.' He called. 'Am I right, Émeric?'

The Resistance leader laughed. 'Abso-bloody-lutely, old bean.'

Louise was never big on prayer but right now wished Father Flory from Lyon was in the vicinity.

Émeric moved out of the line of fire as Silsbury drew closer.

'I know it sounds crass, Louise, but apart from shagging you, putting a bullet between your beautiful breasts is the next best thing. Now please do stand still you bitch so I don't have to waste a bullet.'

Her mind exploded with a million thoughts as his grinning face came into focus albeit partly hidden by the gun he pointed at her. She closed her eyes not wanting to see the gun fire. Bang!

Where's the pain?

She opened her eyes to see Silsbury on the ground. There was no time to examine him as Émeric fired once then twice. Louise flung herself towards her own weapon, rolled once then again as the traitorous Resistance fighter turned his weapon on her. He fired and missed, twice, and then she fired and didn't miss.

What the hell? Three bodies lay beneath the Eiffel Tower.

Louise saw her two enemies were dead. She ran to the third body and saw the stagehand from Suffolk coughing blood. She knelt and cradled his head.

'Oh Jack, what have you done?'

'I thought,' he coughed, 'if I couldn't marry you, at least I could save your life.'

He coughed and his death was heart breaking as Louise's tears mingled with his blood. She placed his head gently on the ground, kissed his forehead, picked up the strange little pistol beside him and fled.

This was not the first time she raced through Paris at night having shot and been shot at. Twice she survived and reckoned third time *un*lucky would be very much on the cards. Get out of town, girl!

Chapter 16

Louise made it back to her favourite landlady. Madame Baudin outdid herself with fussing as Louise told all. There was blood on the clothes of her favourite showgirl, a dead boyfriend and dead Nazis. But one was a Frenchman, a traitor! Putain!

Time changed direction. It was a blast from the past. The landlady ran a bath and in the wee small hours—she was always awake then having spent her life in night clubs which only became busy around midnight—Louise scrubbed and was scrubbed until she glowed, was revived, refreshed and ready to go.

'You hide here, ma chérie. The Germans are losing and soon Paris and the whole of France will be free. You can make a triumphant return to the stage and have sugar daddies falling over themselves to kiss not just your hand but the rest of your divine body.'

The woman's magnificent heart proved a boon but Louise knew in Paris she was a dead woman walking.

Where to go? Back to Brussels? And to what? Jacob Stern was dead. Head to Vichy country but to where? Face the Gestapo in Lyon and a hike over those massive mountains? Please God, no.

Then if not those places, where and how? Right now, all she wanted to do was sleep.

In the morning, Madame Baudin's breakfast arrived from Heaven.

As Louise feasted on eggs—hard to find unless you had contacts—she quizzed her hostess. 'Please Madame, what is the quickest and safest way to England?'

'You are asking me? What would an old Folies Bergère dancer know about wartime escapes?'

Louise nodded knowing it was a silly question for a Parisian who had never lived more than a kilometre from the Seine.

'But I did have a lady staying here who entertained sailors who worked on those fast boats at Cherbourg.' Louise stopped eating. 'Apparently they can fly along at 80 kilometres an hour and cross the

English Channel in no time. But I doubt they would give you a ride even if you were to perform your best nightclub dance for them. Besides they are Nazis.' She laughed.

Louise laughed too but her brain worked overtime. 'Do you know this woman, Madame?'

She shook her head. 'Not for ages but she met her sailor friend in a club on the Rue Pigalle. He called it Pig Alley and the club has a cheeky sculpture in the front window.'

In a clean dress, clean underwear and a different hat, she set off to explore the city she once came to love. Could she, should she return to the Resistance safe house? Would they believe one of their top fighters was a collaborator?

She needed to contact Baker Street but could she find a radio and an operator she could trust? She found the club in Pig Alley closed.

What about the police? Did today's officers think she was responsible for the death of their colleague Capitaine Bonhomme?

News of the two collaborators and an unknown man shot at the Eiffel Tower would be all over Paris and in particular in Gestapo offices. Madame Baudin's suggestion about hiding at her place and riding out the war was the best or simply Louise's only option.

As she walked "normally" along a busy street her SOE training kicked in and she observed a car following her. It slowed and a man in a black leather coat hopped out and crossed to her side of the road. Gestapo agents had no idea of the word *subtle*.

Louise fitted the description of the woman who entered Gestapo HQ to deliver an envelope for Mr Silsbury. She was a main target.

He kept his distance but Louise needed a distraction. She approached a church and without breaking stride or moving her head, she walked across the lawn and entered the Basilica dedicated to Saint Clotilde.

A handful of people were inside. Most were praying. Two lit candles. Having once been a pretend nun, Louise knew the routine and did the usual. She sat in a pew beside a huge pillar. A worshipper came out of a confessional followed shortly after by a priest.

Louise was up and at him. 'Forgive me Father, for I have sinned.'

He studied her, had never seen her before but shrugged and re-entered the confessional. He did the usual and asked how long it had been since she confessed.

Louise remained calm but reckoned she needed to take risks. If the Gestapo were serious, they'd be doubly suspicious if they followed her into the church and she was not there.

'Father, I'm an English secret agent, the Gestapo are following me and unless you can hide me right now, they will arrest me and I will be dead in an hour.'

He stared through the grill, stunned by her words. She persisted.

'Do you know Father Flory from St Nicholas Church in Lyon? He will vouch for me. But please Father, help me now.'

Her brilliant acting skills worked helped by the fact she told the truth. He stood and whispered, 'Follow me,' then left the confessional and swept along the side of the church towards the altar. She hurried after him.

He opened a door and waited till she entered. He closed the door and headed along a corridor. In another small room, he opened a cane basket, extracted a nun's habit and ordered her to dress.

'Put this on, stay here, don't make a sound and I will come and fetch you when the Gestapo have gone.'

'Thank you, Father. You are a saint.' He grunted and left. She heard the door being locked. *Is that for my safety or capture?*

In the darkness she handled the garment and had no trouble putting on her old uniform. Memories of Sister Claudine flooded back. Escaping the Gestapo gave her spirits a fabulous feeling but the question remained.

How do I get home? Or rather, how do I get out of this room?

Silence helped her. No barking Gestapo voices. Then footsteps which were definitely not jack boots. Someone tapped on the door. 'It's Sister Bridget, Mademoiselle. I'll open the door.'

She did and in the light, two nuns, one real and one pretend, stared at one another. 'I think you need a hand with your wimple, Sister. Allow me to assist.' Louise's costume became shipshape.

'I can't thank you enough, Sister.'

'Don't be silly, Sister. We brides of Christ must always stick together.' Their eyes locked and Bridget gave a short wink.

'Where should I go?' asked Louise with heart racing.

Father Patrick suggested the best hiding place to be in plain sight. We'll go into the church and pray and when Father gives us the all clear, I'll take you to our nunnery.'

'Thank you,' breathed Louise.

They entered the church. People knelt in prayer.

'This way,' whispered the real nun. Louise kept in step but in keeping her head lowered, her eyes swept the church. Damn. The same leather-coated, Gestapo man was kneeling about ten rows from the front and on the end of a pew near the side aisle.

'Kneel,' whispered Sister Bridget and Louise copied her. This part was easy. Her religious "training" meant she knew what to do. She was a tad rusty and found she needed to surreptitiously lift her habit and move it forward a little. No problem.

How long will this go on?

Not long as she sensed someone approach. No way would she turn and look. The voice told all. He spoke French with a German accent.

'Do not move Sister, or whoever you are. We do not want an act of violence in the House of God and certainly not in front of the altar.'

She glanced up and saw the Gestapo officer facing front holding his standard issue Luger pistol hard against his belly but pointing at Louise from 18 inches away. He couldn't miss.

Sister Bridget froze with fear.

He continued. 'You should have changed your shoes, Sister.'

Louise cursed her stupidity for (a) wearing smart fashionable shoes and (b) hitching up her habit exposing her pumps.

'The two of us are going to walk to the side then head past the altar and out of the rear of the church. Try anything and you will be shot here in this building. Trust me; nothing would give me greater pleasure. Now move.'

Louise decided death away from the place and people who gave her sanctuary was the right thing to do. She moved well, her deportment and gait perfect for a humble nun. Bridget watched from her kneeling position. Once they were past the altar she stood and followed without being seen by the Nazi. She wore nun's shoes.

Louise could feel the handgun in her back. They were close to a door leading out of the church when it opened and Father Patrick appeared. He was shocked but knew exactly what was happening.

'Sister?' he queried, 'I asked you to tidy the vestry.'

'Stand aside, priest,' snapped the Nazi producing his Luger for the benefit of the man of God.

The tension grew wings and Father Patrick wanted desperately to save the visiting "nun".

'Move, Father or I'll shoot her and then you,' were the last words Gunther Gestapo ever spoke. Sister Bridget was Irish and grew up in a good Catholic family with six brothers. She was in the middle and needed to be strong with so much testosterone floating around.

She crept after the couple having collected a statue of the Blessed Virgin. It wasn't big but heavy and when the Holy Mother's head smashed into Gunther's skull, well, lights out permanently was the end result.

Bridget was in disbelief crossing herself repeatedly. She was not worried about breaking the Sixth Commandment as much as having used the statue of the Mother of God to commit the act.

Louise wanted to kiss Bridget but knew there was a more pressing issue at hand.

'Help me move the body, Madame,' said the priest dragging the Nazi into a cupboard. 'Clean the floor, Sister,' he ordered and the clean-up began.

'What about the body, Father?' asked the practical SOE agent.

'Leave it to me. He'll be in the sewers by nightfall. Now you need to flee as far from here as you can and don't bother returning the habit.'

Louise now wanted to kiss the priest. 'I can't thank you enough, Father.'

'Good luck,' he said. 'And I spoke to your friend Father Flory and he asked me to have you get in touch.'

Louise bubbled. 'How wonderful but I don't have his telephone number in Lyon.'

'No, he's here in Paris at Saint-Gervais-Saint-Protais on the 4th arrondissement. Just don't lure any Gestapo officers with you this time. Au revoir, Sister.'

She left the church via a back entrance, surveyed the narrow street and seeing no-one, set off. 'Think Nun,' whispered Louise and adjusted her gait.

Finding the correct street was easy but the church could be anywhere. She couldn't see any religious structure. *Which way? How silly would it be for a nun to ask the way to a church?*

From behind her came a voice. 'Good day, Sister. Are you going to Father Flory's Special Mass?'

'I am indeed,' she replied and became religious for a moment in order to believe in miracles. 'I'm Sister Claudine.'

She walked with the married couple, parishioners of Father Flory, and was able to say how well she knew him from another parish far away in the south of the country.

They reached the church with many people gathered outside in the sunshine. She was introduced to other parishioners and then joined them in entering the church.

The Mass was to celebrate Father Flory's 40th anniversary as a priest. A monsignor led the service and his "sermon" was to tell tales about the priest formerly of Lyon.

Louise watched from a distance but realized she was in trouble when the Sacrament of Holy Communion began. Both clerics served the body and blood of Jesus Christ and Louise was in the wrong queue. She could hardly push her way into the Monsignor's list.

She knelt and the priest spoke in his normal voice. 'The body of Christ,' he said, studying her face and added and 'God bless you Sister.'

The Mass ended and members of the congregation made their way to the church hall next door. Despite the exorbitant prices in war-torn Paris, the ladies of the parish were able to cobble together a reasonable spread. Father Flory was mobbed and Louise stood back nodding to parishioners all of whom had no idea who she was. Her minimal make-up saw a few tongues start wagging.

The priest kept moving around chatting to people but stopped when he was close to Louise. With a surprised face, he stared at her and spoke in a clear voice.

'I don't believe it. Is it really you, Sister Claudine?' He moved towards her with people stopping their conversations and staring.

He stopped in front of her. 'It is.' He clasped her hands. 'My favourite nun all the way from Italy.' He kissed her hands. 'It is so wonderful you have remembered your old friend Father Flory. How are you, Sister?'

'I am all the better for seeing you again, Father. You look well.'

Their voices dropped but people kept staring, trying to hear.

'What have you been up to, Sister? Still performing for your audiences?' He whispered. 'I heard you were in top form last night.'

She whispered back. 'And only an hour ago as well.'

He hadn't heard about the statue and the Gestapo agent, and was genuinely shocked. 'Another curtain call today!'

She nodded and didn't know how this chat would end.

'I will hear all your news later, Sister. You must stay for supper.'

He drifted away and she was surrounded by inquisitive parishioners who wanted to know everything about the priest's favourite nun.

Father Flory was mingling and Louise didn't know how to break free or where to go. An elderly lady dressed in black approached.

'Excuse me, Sister. I am Madame Aubert the housekeeper and Father Flory said I am to show you to your room.'

'Thank you, Madame,' said Louise wanting to kiss her fairy godmother. They reached the kitchen and Louise was served the weakest cup of tea in the history of the Republic. She loved it and the women chatted freely discussing a certain priest.

About an hour later he appeared uttering apologies. 'My dear Sister Claudine,' he said then to Louise's surprise and the housekeeper's shock, he embraced the pretend nun and kissed her passionately on both cheeks and then the lips.

Bloody hell, Father, that's not in the script!

'What a sight for sore eyes, you are, Sister. How can I ever forget your time at St Nicholas in Lyon? Why, even Bishop Vaine thought you were marvellous until he suffered his unfortunate accident.'

Father Flory's choice of words fascinated Louise. Was he speaking in code in front of his housekeeper? She couldn't possibly be a collaborator. He turned to the old woman. Please Madame, will you tell Brother Vincent I wish to see him.'

'Now, Father?'

'Yes please, immediately.'

The housekeeper left and Father Flory pulled out two chairs and they sat facing one another.

'We have no time for a reunion, Plum.' She thrilled at his use of her name. 'You are in trouble and half the Nazis in Paris are searching for you. You need to leave Paris today. Do you understand?

Her thoughts raced. *Who is this man? A patriot? Yes. Does he want France to be free? Of course. But now he sounds like a Resistance fighter.*

'I will do as you say, Father.'

'I have contacts with the Free French Resistance and while there is next to nothing left of the French Navy, there are men who bring arms and people into France. They pick up and drop people around the Needles on the Isle of Wight? Do you know this place?'

'I do.'

'Then you must leave tonight. There are perfect conditions—the tide, no moon and rough weather. The vessel will arrive around midnight. You will be taken to the coast to a place where the Germans are, how do you say, not heavy on the ground, where you will be rowed out to sea and to your rendezvous. But it must be tonight.'

Louise thought ocean rowing in bad weather sounded ominous.

'You must wear better clothes. We can find them.'

'I can't find the words to thank you, Father. Without you I would have been killed in Lyon and now here in Paris.'

'I tell you, Mademoiselle, you have not been forgotten back in Lyon. True French people remember what you did but sadly the Nazis also remember you. They have your photograph in all their offices and now you have killed a top Gestapo collaborator under the Eiffel Tower, the price on your head will have doubled.'

'You know there was a collaborator with the Resistance cell.'

'Those bastards are everywhere. The Gestapo survive thanks to traitors. But people like you, Mademoiselle are why France will one day be free again. I hope when the Government of France is restored, you will be honoured for all you have done.' A young man entered. 'Ah Brother Vincent, this is Sister Claudine better known as Plum.'

'Hello, Mademoiselle? I have heard many good things about you.'

'Brother Vincent,' smiled Louise wondering what good things.

Flory explained. 'He will take you now to a safe place where you will be prepared for your journey back to England.'

Louise was in a tizz. Her day was overwhelming. She was stalked by the Gestapo, became a nun again, watched a real nun using a statue of the Virgin Mary kill a Gestapo officer, discovered Father Flory had moved to Paris and finally, she was offered an immediate passage out of France and back to a certain green and pleasant land. Yes, you could call her day remarkable. And there was more to come.

She embraced the priest she came to love; her admiration for the man was already sky-high.

'Father, may I ask one favour please?'

'It depends,' he said with a bluntness surprising her.

'Could you please tell my dear friend and landlady, Madame Baudin I have been called away but will write to her as soon as I can?'

'No promises,' said Flory but leave her address with Brother Vincent. Now go!'

She kissed the priest and followed the seminarian out into the still bustling city of Paris.

Vera Atkins entered Buckmaster's office. 'I'll tell you what happened and you have to guess who was involved.'

Buckmaster threw down his pencil. 'Try me.'

'Senior Gestapo officer and Resistance collaborator both shot and killed beneath the Eiffel Tower at midnight.'

'But how does she do it?'

'You haven't told me who we're talking about yet.'

'Juliette Beauchamp, Sister Claudine, Louise Wellesley,' he replied his voice getting louder as he shouted, 'Plum!'

'The last report came from Father Flory saying the agent in question is heading to the coast for a rendezvous with what's left of the French Navy with her destination the Isle of Wight.'

Buckmaster shook his head. 'Well if we do actually bring her back to Baker Street, I'll slap a charge on her for being *too* bloody successful.'

Vera laughed. 'Apparently another Gestapo officer was killed in a Paris church and Plum had nothing to do with it.'

'I don't believe it.'

'The Nazi had his skull smashed by a real nun using a statue of the Virgin Mary.'

More head shaking from Buckmaster. 'Who do we know on the Isle of Wight?

Chapter 17

Father Flory sent his housekeeper, Madame Aubert, to tell Madame Baudin her favourite tenant had left Paris unexpectedly but would be in touch once she was free to do so.

The housekeeper had trouble rousing the landlady but when she managed to gain entry, the old dancer's door was open. A gentle knock produced no reply so the visitor stepped inside.

The message about Plum was not delivered. Madame Baudin received a visit from desperate Gestapo officers and when the loyal, loving and likeable lady refused to reveal anything, even under cruel-beyond-belief torture, she was shot between the eyes.

Such news would drive a knife into Louise's heart but right now, she was changing into appropriate clothing in a safe house on the outskirts of Paris. The residents in the safe house were proud to be French and keen to help anyone helping France win back its freedom.

It was getting dark when Louise was told to leave. Her escort, a slip of a girl would lead Louise to the station from where her train would head towards the coast.

'Papers Mademoiselle?' asked the mother of the girl.

'Oui,' replied Louise showing her forgeries. The passport would not be needed on a French beach.

'Here is a little British money for when you arrive in your own country. Louise kept feeling better. She did worry about crossing the Channel by sea and the thought of U-boats and the superfast E-boats gave her heart a start. But the thought she might be back in Blighty tomorrow kept shivers being active all over her body.

'Merci, Madame.'

'Do you have your firearm?'

'Two,' said Louise taking Madame Baudin's tiny pistol from a bag and tapping her trousers to indicate her stolen Gestapo pistol strapped to her thigh.

'There will be a friend at the station to meet you.'

'How will I know them?'

Back came the same answer. 'They will know you. Now go with my daughter and I will pray for your safe return to England.'

The women hugged and then Louise and her guide slipped out into the night. Again the darkened streets were their friend. Being young and nimble, the two females were able to duck and dive whenever something suspicious or dangerous appeared.

'There,' said the young girl pointing. 'It's the train soon to depart for the coast. Travelling at night and alone is risky. If you walk away from the station and then back along the tracks, you might be able to board the train without being seen.'

'You are brilliant, Mademoiselle. Thank you and please be careful going home.'

They kissed and the girl vanished. Louise studied the layout and pondered her best move. A sea passage was useless if she couldn't reach the coast about three hours away.

She opted for the "sneak on board" idea and walked away from the station. On a road, she reached an overpass, climbed the small wooden fence and slid down the embankment to the railway track. Back to the station she went walking on the sleepers.

The subdued lights on the station made it hard to see. She crouched and observed. The rear of the train was about fifty yards away. She decided to walk alongside the carriages but not on the platform side. If a carriage door or window seemed a possibility, she would climb up and sneak inside.

She kept low and was about to reach the end of the train when she heard voices. Flattening herself on the ballast caused pain. *Did they see me?* No, the voices belonged to railway staff loading the guard's van. Louise rose and crept towards the platform.

'Come and help me,' said one worker and both men headed towards a goods shed. In a flash, Louise was on the platform and darted inside the open door of the van. She could hardly see but moved to a corner. Moving boxes of what she didn't know, she crouched out of sight as the workers returned and loaded more material.

Then a whistle sounded close and the inside went dark as the door slammed shut.

Great. No inspection of papers but can I escape? She was about to stand when she heard a belch. *Shit! I'm in with the guard.*

The locomotive whistle sounded and the train set off.

There were a number of stations before the station by the sea. Stretching would be nice and Louise remembered a flight from Gibraltar where she squeezed in with cargo and turned numbness into a disease.

The train stopped at a station. The guard hopped out and she heard muffled voices. Then he returned and the train set off again. The same routine happened at the next two stations.

The fourth station was reached and Louise sensed danger. The door opened and a voice from the platform could be heard loud and clear.

'Did you bring my parcel?' asked the person on the platform.

'Yeah, it's right here,' said the guard and approached Louise's corner of the van. She panicked and reached for her gun.

The parcel to be removed covered Louise's upper body. The guard took hold and lifted. It was dark but the muted light from the platform was enough for him to see the top half of a woman.

'Come on,' said the voice on the platform.

At the last second, before being revealed, Louise dropped the idea of the gun and clasped her hands together in a sort of begging pose.

The chosen container moved. 'Shit!' whispered the guard shocked at his living cargo.

'Please,' begged the hitchhiker and the guard swung around and handed the box to the man on the platform.

'Sign here,' said the guard finding his documents. The parcel collector left, the guard sent the train on its way and closed the van door. He lit his lantern, faced Louise and spoke.

'Come out, Mademoiselle, now.'

Playing the role of the helpless female, broke, desperate to escape her bully of a boyfriend, Louise rose in pain, her circulation crying out for a chance to start moving.

'Please, Monsieur, I am desperate. I have no money and must reach my family on the coast tonight.'

'I should report you to the stationmaster at the next station.'

The actress put on the sob routine. It worked as the guard was thinking how he could benefit from the situation. Of course he did.

'No, no, no, Monsieur. Please, I am begging you. I am not a criminal. I have suffered terrible misfortunes and only my family can save me.'

The guard sniffed and Louise knew she'd fooled him.

'The next station we reach the coast.' Louise was rapt. 'It will be half an hour so we have a little time to get to know one another better.' He paused. 'I'm sure you understand my meaning, Mademoiselle.' He smiled. With his lamp revealing the appearance of his passenger, the guard's mind easily entered the realm of fantasy.

'You are most kind, Monsieur. I am truly grateful for your understanding.'

'How grateful?'

She played the innocence card. 'I'm am so sorry, Monsieur but as I told you, I have only a few francs.'

He decided to put his cards on the table and began to undress. Louise reacted with faux horror.

'I don't want your money darling, only your company. Now get your gear off.' She undid her belt, slowly, and removed her trousers keeping herself in the shadows where possible and her legs close together.

'Good girl,' he said disrobing. The movement of the van meant disrobing saw him lose his balance. His cap, jacket, boots and trousers were removed quickly and tossed aside. In his socks, shirt and underwear he was ready for action.

Louise stood there, her legs on show. The guard now understood the expression, "all his Christmases had come at once". He moved towards her. The lamp behind him meant he blocked much of its light. He grabbed her shoulders ready to pull her towards him. The train wobbled. She slipped out of his grasp and about turned. Front or back, he was happy to start at any location.

He touched the outside of her thigh. He purred. She stirred. He stroked her thigh, hit the strap on the outside of her leg and reckoned he'd found the top of a stocking. He turned her round and their eyes locked. He moved his hand inside her thigh and hit a solid object. Curious but excited he fondled the item.

His face radiated fear when he realized the cold object was unmistakably a pistol. Before he could move, her right hand, holding

114

the late Madame Baudin's tiny firearm, shot up and its pointy end was pressed hard against the horny guard's left cheek.

'Move and you die.'

It wasn't only the words but the sound of her voice and her body language. The innocent, naïve young woman became a deadly assassin. Keeping the gun hard against his cheek, she walked the now trembling man backwards. He was bathed in the glow of his lamp.

'Drop on your knees.'

He did but started pleading. 'Please Mademoiselle; I have a wife and three children.'

'On your belly, lie down.' He didn't argue but the firearm was no longer against his face. 'Face down.'

He complied. She put a foot on his neck and pressed. It hurt. Him, not her. She'd spotted the ties hanging on the wall to be used to lock down certain items. She reached across and grabbed two.

'Hands behind your back.' He hesitated but not when she resumed the foot on the neck position. She expertly tied his hands then moved and did the same with his ankles. Casanova went limp all over.

He could hardly see but strained to watch as she re-dressed pulling up her trousers hiding her Gestapo gun. Then he nearly died as she stepped over him and kept dressing. Louise put on the guard's trousers, jacket and cap. They were all too big but not ridiculously so. She buttoned the jacket and certainly could pass for her fellow passenger on a moon-free French railway station in the dusk with the light behind her.

The train slowed. She pulled a handkerchief from one of the guard's uniform's pockets, knelt and crammed it into his mouth. He made the odd unintelligible sound but stopped when she grabbed a handful of his hair, lifted his head and returned it to the floor of the van with considerable force. He took a vow of silence.

Slow, slower, stop and the train pulled in at Louise's station. Now came the tricky bit. She paused, waiting for someone to arrive or at least call out. Nothing. With her bag around her neck under her new uniform, she opened the van door, checked to see all carriage doors were closed, blew the guard's whistle, waved his flag, tossed both back in the van, closed the van door and dropped off the platform.

It was low and as the train steamed away into the night with a full complement of staff, she crouched on the tracks beside the low platform.

There were a few people in the area but so far away you couldn't see their faces or intentions. She reckoned her luck had held and did what she did in Paris and walked away from the platform.

Once out of sight, she climbed the slight embankment, heard the sea and headed in that direction.

On a road heading back to the station, a voice made her stop.

'Monsieur! Monsieur!' It was a man's voice and he clearly wanted to attract Louise's attention. She realized. *He thinks I'm a railway employee*. Keeping her head low and her cap lower, she grumbled.

'Monsieur?'

'I have lost a passenger, a young woman was supposed to be on the last train. Did you see ...'

Louise whipped off her cap and shook her hair free. The man gasped. 'I have borrowed this uniform, Monsieur.'

He hugged her and helped her into the trees beside the road. She understood and removed the jacket and trousers.

'We must hide these, Mademoiselle and never leave any sign we have been in this area.' He grabbed the uniform. 'Hurry, we must be at the rendezvous in twenty minutes.'

They headed off the road and through sand dunes which reminded Louise of her arrival in Belgium only ... goodness, she couldn't remember how many days it was since she crossed the North Sea. Now she was about to cross the English Channel.

The sound of the surf was unmistakeable and the wind pushed her backwards. *And I'm going into the ocean in what? A rowing-boat?*

Her contact knew where he was going. He turned his head to check on his charge. He spoke but his words were swallowed up in the wind.

She had no choice. The sand became friendly and filled her shoes. On and on she went until she saw people; her contact talking to two men. Once close they greeted her, adjusted her bag and strapped it to her body.

No time for questions, comments or complaints. The contact stepped into the surf and held the small craft as the other two each took an arm of the SOE agent and lifted her up and on board. It was a rubber dinghy, the type used by commandos on one of their raids. She landed in the dinghy and was given one instruction.

'Do not let go,' said one sailor pointing to a rope running around the inside of the vessel. She grabbed the nearest piece of rope.

Her contact yelled 'Good luck,' before pushing as hard as he could.

The other two men paddled like crazy and the dinghy hit a wave and pointed towards the black sky before slapping back down again. Louise fell back clinging to the rope.

She could see her two crew members and the white cap of a wave when it collided with their dinghy; oh and blackness.

Where are we going? How will we find this bigger ship?

Having been tortured by Nazis and faced death at different locations including a desolate mountain range, a magnificent cathedral and the Eiffel Tower, drowning struck her as being even a worse way to die. A boiling ocean in the dark had to take the biscuit for one's finale, her last curtain call.

The crew used every skerrick of their muscles and the one behind her screamed to the other. 'This is it.' Louise hadn't a clue. *This is what?*

The men changed their paddling to a holding pattern. She glanced around then back to shore and saw a tiny light blink. The mystery deepened as the dinghy bobbed like the proverbial cork in the sea.

'There,' screamed the sailor at the front. Louise stared into the night. *What? I can't see anything!* Then she froze. This shape, dark, big and getting bigger appeared about 50 yards away.

Her fishing trawler, her UK version of an E-boat was a submarine!

It was a swap; one French Resistance fighter returning home and one SOE Agent doing the same only in the other direction. There was no time for introductions. Submariners held the dinghy as steady as possible while the human cargo swapped places.

'Bonjour, Miss Wellesley,' said the captain as he ordered his crew to dive. A crew member escorted her to a tiny room—mind you every room on the sub was tiny—and Louise began her first journey as a submariner.

Chapter 18

Hitler once planned to invade the Isle of Wight. He invaded the Channel Islands but only bombed the Isle of Wight which was as close as two and a bit miles from Hampshire.

As Louise's sub hummed along below the surface of the English Channel, the skipper knocked on the frame of her room.

'Are you comfortable, Mademoiselle?'

'Thank you, sir, I am.'

'Have you been in a submarine before?'

'My first time.'

'We will surface soon and you will be put ashore on the Isle of Wight.'

'And do you know what I will do afterwards?'

He shrugged. 'You are English. I am French. I deliver you to England; the rest is up to you.'

'I understand.'

'I will send for you in a few minutes.'

'Thank you, Captain, I am most grateful.'

He smiled and was true to his word when a few minutes later a sailor appeared.

'It is time, Mademoiselle.'

She followed the young man to the control room and experienced the pressure of the male crew members staring, checking out her body. The submariners formed a single-sex crew and anything remotely female proved attractive, and in this case, mightily so.

She watched the captain operate the periscope. He brought it down and gave the order. 'Prepare to surface.' There were noises Louise had never heard. Her heart beat faster. The captain sent the periscope back up and moved it around then closed the handles and sent it back down.

'Open the hatch. Lookout aloft.' A sailor scrambled up a ladder and Louise enjoyed a breeze as fresh British air sweep into the control room. Other men scrambled aloft.

The captain held out his hand. 'Your turn, Mademoiselle and the best of British luck.'

She shook his hand, thanked him and stepping out of the vessel, found several sailors waiting to hold her even if she was stable. The sea was less choppy than on the French side and the dinghy at this end was sitting in a friendly, a better way for a passenger transfer.

A wide selection of hands offered their support as she used a rope to step down and into the bobbing rubber vessel.

One of the two sailors each holding a paddle, greeted her in a voice she reckoned hailed from the Tottenham Court Road.

'All right, Miss?' he asked and pointed to the rope. 'Hang on there.'

She was an old hand at this caper by now and waved to the French submariners whose faces and sighs displayed their disappointment.

'Why here, gentlemen?' she asked the British sailors.

'There are mines bobbing about closer to the mainland and U-boats and E-boats ply the Solent, Miss. Here there's a better chance of landing you on Blighty in one piece.'

'Thanks,' she said and meant it.

As they approached the island, specks of lights could be seen. Hitler's bombs landed here in huge numbers in the early years of the war. The Isle was on the way to Southampton and Portsmouth but now the Luftwaffe, with fewer planes and pilots had other fish to fry.

The dinghy hit the sand and both paddlers were out offering a hand to Louise. She stepped ashore and loved the crunch of a British beach. She was about to ask where she should go when a chap approached.

'Miss Wellesley? Good morning, I'm Captain Harrison from the Hampshire Home Guard.'

'How do you do, sir.'

'We got a call from a Colonel Buckmaster up in London asking us to collect you and take you up to Ventnor. If you come this way, Miss, I've persuaded our friends from across the ditch to put on a car for you.'

She waved goodbye to her two paddlers and walked up the beach and into a jeep. It was an American vehicle with an American driver.

'Howdy Ma'am,' said the driver and with Louise riding high in the back, the Home Guard Captain in the front but on the right, they set off as the dawn crept above the horizon.

As they bumped and bounced along, Louise decided to ask. 'Am I right in assuming you're an American, sir?'

'Correct, Ma'am. Private Danny Fitzpatrick, all the way from Dayton, Ohio.'

'I have a friend serving with the US 1st Infantry Division.'

'Fine outfit, Ma'am.'

'He's a doctor.'

'Well God bless him, we sure need the medics.'

She wanted to ask what if anything he knew about the Division but asking anything specific about troop placements and the like would earn her a rebuke and rightly so.

They drove through the gates of a large house in Ventnor. The island featured many and Queen Victoria spent summers nearby.

At last Louise discovered females in uniform and greatly appreciated being greeted by smiling English faces. One ATF girl took Louise in hand and showed her the mess and the female facilities.

'I'm a bit lost,' said Louise. 'I want to cross to the mainland. What do you suggest?'

'Are you army?' asked the woman. 'Or shouldn't I ask?'

'Nothing special but a word with your boss might help.'

'Why don't you freshen up and then come and find me.'

'Thanks, you're a dear,' said Louise and stared in a mirror. Ouch!

Ten minutes later she entered the officer-in-charge's office. 'Please have a seat Miss Wellesley. I understand you're rather keen to hop across to the mainland.'

'Is it possible, sir?'

'More than possible and with a request from SOE HQ in Baker Street, I should think we'll have you sailing on the next ship.'

'Ship sir?'

Yes we have several freighters plying between Southampton and Portsmouth and here and touch wood, since the war started they've not been bombed or bumped into any Nazi mines. Do you have a destination preference?'

'No sir but the sooner the better would be perfect.'

He signed a piece of paper and handed it to her. 'This'll put you aboard and landed at Southampton by lunchtime.

She hesitated.

'Something wrong, Miss Wellesley?'

'There is, sir. I think I should hand you these weapons.' She retrieved both handguns placing the tiny pistol on his desk and while the officer examined it, she discreetly produced her Gestapo souvenir and placed it too on the desk.'

'My, I gather there's tale behind these two little beauties.'

She smiled and opted to say nothing other than her sincere thanks. Outside, tiredness kicked in.

When did I last sleep? Once back on the bigger island, I need to ring Baker Street and Mummy. Phew!

The ship, *The Hound*, and her sister ships must have had the sailing gods smiling down on them as in nearly four years sailing supplies back and forth, never once had Jerry even damaged this small fleet of workhorse vessels. At the quayside she showed her slip of paper to a purser by the gangplank.

'Up you go, Miss.'

'Thank you. Will I be seasick?'

'You won't have time, Miss.'

He was right. She stood by the railing watching the Hampshire coastline draw ever closer. With the ship secured, passengers were free to disembark. Her heart took flight. Her mad dash to Belgium then into France with action and deaths galore was over. A crazy unplanned adventure and now it was time for family and rest.

At the bottom of the gangplank she froze. *Oh no!*

'Your papers, Miss,' asked the official.

She produced her fake ID and fake passport, superbly crafted by Drugi of Brussels and knew she was in trouble.

The official studied the documents and then her. 'Where have you come from, madam; it was Miss before—and how did you travel?'

She returned his stare and put on her best acting outfit. 'Three or four nights ago I hitched a ride on a Lysander from a field in Suffolk to a beach in Belgium. I picked up these false papers in Brussels and snuck into Paris. Last night, from an unmanned French beach, I travelled by dinghy to a French sub which dropped me off the coast of the Isle of Wight and from there I hopped aboard this magnificent ocean liner which brought me to this quay and to you, my good sir.'

He swallowed, stamped her documents and waved her through.

She grinned inside and out and set off into Southampton.

Right, Louise, train station and a ticket with the fastest train up to London. Then out to Maida Vale and a bath and change of clothes; a sleep followed by a phone call to Mummy and a visit to Baker Street. That's the plan, girl, now get cracking.

She asked for directions to the station and set off. Walking through the city she overtook a young woman and a soldier arguing. Passing them she could hear their conversation.

'But why *your* Division? Why the 1st? It's always the 1st.'

'Now Honey, it's only for a month. I'll be back real soon.'

The man in uniform was clearly an American. Louise slowed.

'I'm going to complain to your General,' continued the English sweetheart.

'Aw, come on, baby. You wanna get me arrested?'

Louise stopped. The couple saw her staring and returned the stare. 'Forgive me, sir, miss,' she said. 'I have a friend serving in the US 1st Infantry Division. Are they stationed here in Southampton?'

'Not for long,' said the woman.

'What's your friend's name, lady? I might know him.'

'Dr Tom Curzon. He's English but serving with the US Army.'

'Can't say I've heard of him but the medics are based at Frogmill House which is a ways out of town.'

Louise's body reacted. She couldn't control her rapid heartbeat.

'Do you know if there's a bus?'

'There ain't,' said the woman having walked the three miles before to see her lover. 'You need a cab, lady.' She tugged at her American true love's jacket and they headed across the road.

Louise opened her purse. She had enough money for a train ticket but a cab fare would see her stuck in Southampton. And what if the good doctor was not in his office or even at this camp? She kept walking towards the station. Her body kept misbehaving. She desperately wanted to see the man she fell in love with in Cambridge years ago before this crazy world war had even started.

Turning the corner, she saw the station. In front of it was a taxi rank with one vehicle sitting, waiting. The driver was leaning on his cab reading a paper and smoking.

The cab appeared strange, unique. A large bag-like fixture sat on the roof with a metal bowl on its back. The vehicle had been adapted to run on coal thanks to the heavy or total restriction on petrol for civilian use.

Louise followed her heart.

'Excuse me, sir; I want to go to the US Army camp at Frogmill House.'

The driver sprang out of the blocks. A fare was a heart starter in itself but when the passenger was a cracker of a girl, his chauffeur skills magically appeared.

'Certainly, Miss,' he said opening the door for her.

Setting off, he kept checking his rear view mirror. 'I haven't seen you around these parts before, Miss. Is you local?'

'No, I'm from London.'

'My sister married a bloke an' they live in the East End. Bloody dangerous is that part of the world. You know it, Miss?'

'I do.' She didn't want to chat only because she kept rehearsing what she would say if a certain medical officer happened to be on site.

To his credit, the cabbie got the picture and started whistling. Louise stared out of the window seeing nothing as her head and busy heart were swamped with what might happen in the next ten minutes.

The cab pulled up at the front of the camp. 'That'll be two bob, Miss.' She fumbled in her purse. Her nerves came out to play. She paid, stepped out and the cab departed. Another problem appeared.

A uniformed soldier stepped out of a sentry box and gave the impression he knew every word in the handbook, *How to Refuse Entry*.

'Ma'am?' he said in a voice Louise knew was negativity writ large.

'Hello officer. My name is Louise Wellesley and I am hoping to have a word with Dr Thomas Curzon who is a medical officer serving with the US 1st Infantry Division.'

She reckoned her speech was straightforward, covered every part of her mission and should require no further information.

The sentry spoke to his colleague. They asked to see inside her bag. A tiny pistol or folding knife might, at a pinch, be hidden. There was nothing suspicious and the woman's clothing on her slim body showed no bumps or hidden dangers.

'Private Jones will escort you into the camp, Ma'am.'

His comment was the cue for a major internal body movement, rapid hormonal activity causing full-blown excitement. Louise smiled and followed the young American soldier into the camp. As they passed men working on vehicles, all of them stopped and stared at what they perceived as a vision of loveliness which for most was a polite way of describing raw animal lust. Comments were made. Then a certain whistle soared into the air. Tent flaps fifty yards away swung open and men appeared. The ogling multiplied.

The soldier and the woman reached a magnificent old house. It was the massive home on a country estate taken over by the Americans as they prepared for an invasion of mainland Europe.

Louise enjoyed a sense of relief having escaped the enthusiastic and obviously sex-starved soldiers. In the foyer of the country house, the escorting private explained his cargo.

'Lady to see Doc Curzon, sir.'

The private saluted the sergeant and left.

'What name shall I say, ma'am?'

She hesitated then said one word. 'Plum.'

'Plum? Just Plum?'

She nodded finding her emotions were getting the better of her.

The sergeant spoke to an underling. 'You heard the lady.'

The private walked to the impressive staircase leading to the floors above and headed upstairs. Louise stood there trying to remember her breathing exercises from drama lessons. The sergeant studied her but said nothing.

A serious serving of tension wafted around the house. Then the silence was shattered.

'What!' screamed a voice. The yell was heard upstairs and downstairs and in my lady's chamber.

Louise trembled. Loud footsteps were heard and the medical officer born in New York to English parents appeared at the top of the stairs. He wore a white coat with a stethoscope hanging around his neck.

He saw the message was true and took off. Louise began to cry. Anyone in the vicinity elsewhere in the house appeared. Tom hit the floor running and Louise moved towards him. They collided and did what true love demanded they do. Forget the bloody onlookers. They hugged and kissed and kept on doing the same.

Tears mingled from both and Louise could think of nothing but the man she loved.

Spontaneous applause broke out from the stalls and the dress circle and the applause grew forcing the couple to realize where they were and what they were doing. Still holding one another they glanced around and saw beaming faces and clapping hands.

Tom grabbed one of Louise's hands and headed for the front door. He led her around the house to a part of the glorious garden. They entered an area with flower beds and a large hedge. Once beside the hedge, Tom stopped and stared at his girl.

'I can't believe it's you. This is the best day of my life.'

She cried again and he wiped her tears then stopped to kiss her again only properly this time. They came up for air.

'I overheard a soldier in Southampton talking with his girl about the US 1st Infantry Division. I asked if he knew you. He didn't but told me about this camp and here I am.'

'But if you were performing in Southampton, why didn't you write and tell me. I could've come and seen your show.'

She hesitated and he reckoned she was hiding something. He had wanted to ask about her missing times when they met back at her family home and walked along the river where they both said, 'I love you'. But forget any such questions now. Love conquers all.

He led her deeper into the sprawling garden then stopped.

'I bought you a present ages ago and have been dying to see you. I carry it with me wherever I go.'

He reached into a pocket and produced a little box, the sort used to carry a small even precious object. Louise's heart had tossed in the towel by now as she stared and wondered.

Tom opened the box revealing a simple but stunning diamond engagement ring. She gasped and he dropped onto one knee.

She blinked hard to stop a tear blurring her vision.

'My darling girl,' he said, 'please will you do me the honour of becoming my wife?'

Silly question. All she could do was nod. He stood and they kissed. She broke away to confirm her response in writing or rather the verbal equivalent of same.

'Yes, Thomas Curzon, I would love to be your wife.'

Their immediate kiss was interrupted by a man who spoke. 'Oh blimey, I didn't know you was there.'

Ernest Tharker had been head gardener on this estate for nigh on forty years. He became the first person to congratulate the doctor and the actress on their engagement. Well done, Ernie.

The ring was a perfect fit and as the couple wandered back to the country house—they took the long route—Tom got serious; not that he hadn't been already.

'Louise, things are hotting up. The Allies are getting serious about the invasion everyone is talking about. If it happens, I'll be going over with the other medics and I fear we'll be kept pretty busy.'

She blurted her response. 'Tom, I don't want you to go.'

That was pretty rich coming from a woman who put herself in danger dozens of times when fighting in France and now, more recently in Belgium.

He tried to reassure her. 'They don't put the doctors working in field hospitals on the front line.'

She knew he had to go. 'When is the invasion?'

The Official Secrets Act was thrown away because she wanted to know everything about his future and that her man would be safe.

'I'm leaving on a training exercise, it's a dress rehearsal for the main show, and I don't know when I'll be back. So how about we get married now.'

She gasped. 'Now? What, you mean now?'

He laughed. 'Now usually means now. Or have you an acting role which will make you even more famous?'

'No, nothing. I'm free to become your wife.'

'Are you sure you don't want a big church wedding with flower girls and half a dozen bridesmaids?'

'Only you,' she said and they kissed.

'What about your family?'

'Aren't you listening?' she said with a reprimand like voice.

'Right, I'll check with the padre. We'll probably need to give 24 hours' notice. Where are you staying?'

Louise panicked. Telling him the truth would open a massive can of worms. *Nowhere. I've arrived via French sub after killing half a dozen Gestapo officers in Belgium and France.*

He didn't wait for her answer. 'I'll need to obtain special leave. But my darling, I'm sorry it'll be one of the shortest honeymoons in history. Do you mind?'

What a silly question.

Tom asked Louise to wait in the foyer of the country house while he went to see his commanding officer. It was not an unusual request. Many men in uniform wanted to marry pronto. They could be dealing with Nazis next week and exchanging bullets and bombs.

Louise sat feeling a dose of reality seep inside her body. *Should I tell my mother? Should I have my family present? Should I tell my husband-to-be my true role in this war?*

Minutes ticked by and she worried. *What's keeping him? Has his request been denied?* She need not have worried as everyone Tom went to see gave him their permission or blessing or both.

He emerged smiling. 'It's all set, my darling. You and I will be married tomorrow at ten here in the smaller sitting-room. The Reverend's given us the go-ahead and I lost count of the number of people who volunteered to be a witness.'

Louise struggled to say, 'Tomorrow morning?'

'There's a summer house we can have for our 48 hour honeymoon. Is there anything I can do to help you prepare?'

She shook her head. Overwhelmed did not come even close.

'I'll arrange a lift back to town for you and I'll see you back here in the morning for your big day.'

Does he mean our big day?

He squeezed her hands. 'I know an actress would never miss her entrance.' He kissed her again then walked her outside to the transport depot established off the driveway.

He spoke to the sergeant in charge. She stood there studying her hand. She flexed her fingers and examined the ring she recently acquired. It sparkled and so did she. This morning, only a few hours ago, she arrived by sub and dinghy landing on the Isle of Wight. Now here in Hampshire she was about to get married in the morning.

Chapter 19

'Why haven't we heard from Louise?' asked Victoria. She and Edmund were having lunch with Mrs Crossley.

'Silly question, Mother; please accept your daughter's a busy star and impresarios demand she grace their stages.'

Edmund was still a wounded soldier although his face was much better with its gruesome features repaired or re-arranged thanks to the wizard plastic surgery of the Kiwi Dr Archibald McIntoe.

Mrs Crossley offered her tuppence worth. 'I'm surprised Dr Curzon hasn't been in touch. When he was last here, I was sure Miss Louise and he had finally decided to wed.'

Edmund laughed aloud and his mother despaired. She became sad wanting her daughter's happiness. 'Whatever their feelings for each other, this rotten war will keep them apart.' She turned to her son. 'Tell me when it will happen, Edmund.'

'Do you mean the war ending or Plum getting hitched?'

Mrs Wellesley did a Queen Victoria with her expression equating to the words, 'We are not amused.'

The trio of humans finished their ration-restricted luncheon in silence being totally oblivious to the impending marriage of the sister and daughter in question.

'Where can I drop you, ma'am?' asked the driver as he and Louise arrived in Southampton.

'The centre of town please; I have a spot of shopping to do.'

He pulled over and she hopped out carrying her small bag with her miniscule number of possessions.

Standing on the footpath, she assessed her options. Find a bed for the night here in Southampton and get married in my current outfit looking like the wreck of the Hesperus. Hightail it back to London, buy something fetching for both my wedding and honeymoon and ... and what?

She headed to the station and waited till the ticket window was free of passengers. The chap behind the counter was far too old for military service. She wondered if he had a granddaughter her age.

'Yes Miss?'

She emptied her purse's coins on the counter. 'Please sir, how far to London will this get me?' she asked with the sweetest of smiles.

He counted the coins and Louise held her breath.

'It's exactly the right money, Miss,' he said handing her a treasured piece of card with a free wink. She thought about the possibility of travelling with a randy guard as she did the other night. Hang on, that was *last* night!

She gave the elderly railway gent a dazzling smile and went out to the platform. Trains travelling during the day were less likely to be attacked by German planes and the trip up to London was uneventful.

With no money, the next journey to Maida Vale meant a decent walk, at least 4 miles. She could drop in to SOE HQ in Baker Street and beg a few shillings. But it would mean a huge delay having to explain her recent unofficial expedition to Belgium and beyond.

She wished Madame Baudin lived in London as she would fall over herself to provide her favourite showgirl with exquisite outfits in which to marry and dress or undress for her honeymoon.

Vale Madame Baudin.

So walking it was. She thought about breaking railway by-laws or praying for a friend to spot her in the street and lend her a bob. And her shoes were not the best for fell climbing but onward she pressed.

Her method of entering her flat remained the key buried in a specific spot at a nearby park. The last time she placed it there she followed advice from her SOE training days.

She buried her key even deeper then covered it with soil before burying a useless key even higher. Making sure she wasn't being watched, she reached the spot beside the tree near the cricket pavilion and removed the grass, then wrapped her new ring with a handkerchief and attacked the soil with the heel of her shoe. The false key was still there. She breathed easier and continued until the right item was found.

She replaced the soil and reckoned—hoped—this might be the last time she performed such a task.

Climbing the stairs to her flat, her whole body cried out for relief.

Inside, she ran a bath and put on the kettle. She entered her bedroom and collapsed on the bed. She fell asleep and only a whistling kettle woke her in time to prevent a bath overflowing.

A cup of tea in the bath with questionable cheese equalled paradise. She wanted to stay soaking forever. Then her mind became busy, frantic more like.

What will I wear? What outfit, shoes, hat, underwear, jewellery, makeup, gloves? Will I need a going away outfit? Who will give me away? What will I wear on my honeymoon? Her answer made her smile. Matilda Gonzales-Jones would know. 'On your honeymoon, darling, you wear nothing,' she would cackle.

Where is Matilda today?

She thought of her father. He would be so proud. And he met Tom. Briefly, yes, but they met albeit in hospital.

It was time for action. She dried, dressed and recovered cash she kept in a clever hiding place. Outside, with key buried in her purse, she set off for the Tube. Shopping became her sole goal.

There were early trains from Waterloo and the bride was bright and early. She wore a coat over her wedding dress, a scarf over her hair and had various outfits and accessories in her suitcase. Her wedding shoes were in a separate box.

She bought a single and a friendly gentleman offered to put her case on the rack in their compartment.

'Going far?' he asked hoping his innocent remark would prepare the ground for something, anything to his advantage later.

'Southampton,' she said not keen to chat having one particular event on her mind.

The fellow traveller wasn't giving up easily. 'A beautiful girl like you means it must be for an important occasion.'

She paused as her dramatic training allowed, smiled and spoke two words. 'My wedding,' she said and stared out the window.

'Oh,' said Henry losing his hooray. 'Lucky chap.'

He departed at Winchester and at Southampton Louise had to fetch her own case. This she did and landed on the platform with all her bibs and bobs. Her previous experiences at planning for an event had more to do with blowing up bridges and railway lines but the principles were the same. For a wedding at 10am, she needed to be at

130

the venue by 9.30am. The taxi would take 10 to 15 minutes. She was early but left the platform and glanced along the road to the taxi rank. The same vehicle with its alternative fuel supply sat waiting for a fare.

If she hailed the cab now she would arrive at "the church" well before time. *Aren't brides supposed to be late?* If she held back and someone else took the cab, she might be left high and dry.

Thinking she could book the cab for half an hour later, she set off. Wonderful, it started to rain. Struggling with suitcase, shoe and hat boxes, she fought to raise her umbrella. The rain got heavier. The taxi fired up and moved.

'No!' cried Louise in frustration. 'It's my wedding day!' she called to no-one as the taxi pulled in beside her and the cabbie hopped out.

'I thought it was you, Miss,' he said taking her case. 'Back to the Yankee base it it?'

'Thank you, so much,' she said climbing in the back with the cabbie holding the door. *This man will get a serious tip.*

He stored her luggage, climbed in and waited for instructions. 'All set, Miss?'

'Not exactly,' she replied and the cabbie did nothing. 'I'm sorry to be a nuisance. I'm getting married this morning but not till ten o'clock.'

'Oh congratulations, Miss, I hope you'll be very happy.'

'Thank you but if we leave now I'll be an hour early making life a little awkward. Can I book you for later?'

'You could, Miss but where will you go until then and in all this rain?' She could only think of a tea-room or back to the station. 'I tell you what. I'll drop you at my place and my wife can give you a hand with your hair. It's become a little wet under your scarf.'

'Thank you, you're most kind.'

'She's a retired hairdresser so you'll walk down the aisle and turn a few heads. I'm Fred Weatherly, by the way.'

He pulled out into the road as the blushing bride enjoyed relief and fear thinking of a headline; *SOE Agent disappears on way to her wedding.*

She didn't have time to worry as the cabbie lived two streets from the station. He hopped out and held her umbrella. 'I'll bring your luggage, Miss, this way.'

He banged on his own front door and a woman appeared.

'What's the matter ... oh, who's this?'

'This is my wife, Ethel and this young lady is getting married at 10 and needs shelter before I take her to the church.'

Ethel had the same generous nature of her husband. 'Come away in, Miss and have a seat in the front room. Where's Fred?'

'I think he's gone to fetch my case. I'm Louise.'

'Well give me your coat and scarf, lass.' The bride handed them over and Ethel reacted with a tinge of shock.

'Goodness, who did your hair?'

'I'm afraid I did.'

'Well we can't have you getting married with messy hair. Sit there and I'll fetch my basket.'

She disappeared as the cabbie returned. 'Here's your case, Miss. Where's Ethel?'

She entered. 'I needed my basket to fix Louise's hair.'

'This is too much,' said Louise.

'Nonsense,' said Fred. 'A girl's wedding day is her special day.'

'Sit nice 'n tall, Louise,' said Ethel spreading a cloth around the bride's neck and shoulders. 'When is she leaving?' Ethel asked her husband.

'You've got half an hour.'

Off went Ethel, combing and brushing, tying ribbons and trimming here and there.

'So will you live in America, Louise?' asked the interested cabbie.

Ethel twigged. 'Oh, you're marrying an American.'

Louise explained and the couple's curiosity ended with smiles.

It made a change for the SOE Agent and actress to be playing herself. Ethel handed her a small mirror and Louise gasped at the result; it was a coiffure to amaze and despite Louise insisting, Ethel refused to take any money.

'It gave me a lot of pleasure, young lady. Now Fred, you drive carefully.'

He did and Louise paid the fare keeping her pledge to add a generous tip.

The rain had eased when they reached the sentry point of the wedding venue. Orders had been given. They knew the female arriving was the bride about to marry the popular doctor known as Doc Tom, and Louise was driven in a staff car along the drive to the grand entrance of the country house. Soldiers carried her goods. The same female member of staff greeted Louise in the foyer and led her to a room they'd set aside for the bride.

'I like your hair, girl. It's real pretty.'

'Thank you, said Louise wanting to ask about the groom.

'The doc has scrubbed up real nice too. I'll leave you to freshen up.'

Louise had a better chance to study her hair and her complete outfit in the full mirror sensibly provided. She changed her shoes. Thinking she was about to cry gave her the willies.

You're supposed to be happy, girl.

The only disappointment, despite her overall happiness was thinking of the people she would dearly love to be present. She ran through a list of absent family and friends when someone tapped softly on the door.

'Come in,' said Louise immediately frightened it might be the man she was about to wed.

A middle-aged woman entered and spoke in an American accent. 'Good morning, my dear. Oh, don't you look lovely.'

'Thank you.'

'I'm Prunella, wife of the Reverend Clarkson who's going to marry you. I'll be your attendant and one of the witnesses. Now, would you like me to say a little prayer before we go in?'

Will it be a Protestant prayer? 'Thank you,' said Louise and closed her eyes. *But I'm a former Catholic nun.*

Prunella held Louise's hands, spoke her prayer and loved the experience when she discovered Louise still had her eyes closed.

'Here we go,' said Mrs Clarkson and led Louise to the door.

Talk about a pounding heart. Prunella opened the door then stepped aside smiling at the nervous but determined bride. This was her cue.

The smaller sitting-room was bigger than Louise's flat in London. The expensive furniture had been positioned to make a passageway leading to a small table with a white cloth behind which stood the minister in charge of proceedings.

There were two men in uniform, one a colonel, standing to Louise's right. She knew the other one. He was smiling and his smile filled her with happiness, excitement and a wonderful feeling of joy.

There was no organist, piper or music of any kind. The thickness of the carpet meant her footsteps were silent. Prunella stood to Louise's left and whispered. 'Off we go.'

All her stage performing meant Louise's posture and movement were excellent. She held the attention of the minister, groom and the other witnesses spellbound. Looking stunning was a given but the way she carried herself seemed a damn shame there were so few in the audience. Actually there was no-one.

Louise stopped beside Tom and he spoke to her. 'Good morning, Miss Wellesley.'

He surprised her and for once, the actress fluffed her line. It didn't matter as the minister began his speech. Normally, when on stage, Louise could say the cue lines in her head. Here she needed a prompt. *Will Mrs Clarkson whisper my lines?*

Tom spoke confidently always gazing at his bride. She thought he was a natural and would make a brilliant actor. His confidence and relaxed demeanour gave her strength.

Tom produced two gold rings and as they exchanged same she realized her hands were shaking. She came back to Earth when the reverend gentleman said, 'You may kiss the bride.'

Constantly smiling, Tom didn't need to lift the veil as it was more a dressing, a trim on her perfect hat, so he held her arms in a soft grip and gently kissed his new wife.

Congratulations flowed from the rest of the wedding party. The colonel was up for a kiss. No music, no congregation but, for Louise, a wonderful feeling of relief and contentment.

The colonel led the way to a side door and Tom took Louise's hand. As they stepped into the dining-room, a huge cheer erupted and confetti rained down on the newlyweds. What a thrilling surprise. Every officer and female on the base clapped and smiled and gazed in awe at the happy, beautiful and surprised Mrs Curzon.

It was a wedding breakfast to remember. Where the food and drink came from was listed under the *Don't Ask* category.

Louise met more people in the next hour than she could ever hope to remember. The colonel made a brief speech but Tom made up for the brevity and his speech brought many to tears.

He spoke about her brothers calling her Plum and, knowing the guests were fans of baseball, wisely chose not to explain the origin.

But there was a war on and while this wedding was a diversion giving everyone a fabulous time, people soon disappeared. Louise thought she was kissed by more Americans than she'd fired bullets.

Tom followed the Clarksons to the door, closed it and turned to face Louise. She was sitting on a plush settee and trying again not to cry. He strode over, offered his hand, helped her to stand then kissed her gently. They stood in the middle of the dining-room, noses touching and saying nothing. Finally Tom broke the ice.

'So, Mrs Curzon, how do you like married life?'

She laughed and kissed him. 'Thank you, Dr Curzon for making me the happiest girl in the world.'

'Blimey,' he said, 'and we haven't even started the honeymoon.'

They laughed, kissed again before Tom took control.

'Now your case and bits and bobs have been taken to the Honeymoon Cottage to join mine. So, it's a bit of a walk my darling but if you're ready, we can crack on and start our married life.'

Using her dramatic skills, she appeared concerned and spoke with a disappointment in her voice. 'You mean I have to walk? I thought you offered to carry me.'

For a moment he thought she was serious then grabbed her hand and led her outside. It was a good two hundred yards from the main house and Tom had inspected the possible routes yesterday. Arm in arm they walked in lock step, rounded the huge hedge and again bumped into Ernest Tharker the gardener.

He gave them a huge smile and his congratulations.

The summer house was a small but stylish bungalow surrounded by greenery. Tom stopped at the door and their eyes spoke cheeky messages. 'Now what's that business about me carrying you?'

She grinned then squealed as he swept her off her feet, struggled to open the door, did so then carried her inside. He pushed the door closed with his foot and, still carrying his wife, kissed her as she wrapped her arms around his neck. Plum's new life was off and running.

Chapter 20

Being married at 10am and choosing a honeymoon venue a few minutes' walk from the "church", meant the honeymoon started not long after noon. Louise had spent the little time she had between accepting Tom's proposal and walking down the second sitting-room aisle, in choosing her wedding night attire hoping it would prove satisfactory to her husband.

But slipping into her nightie in the middle of the day didn't seem the most romantic of manoeuvres. She wanted Tom to take control.

He did by taking her hand and giving her a tour of the summer house. 'This is the kitchen my dear where you will be expected to prepare fabulous food for the next ...' He checked his watch. 'Thirty-six hours.' She smiled and he gave her a peck on the cheek.

They turned around. 'You've seen this spacious sitting-room with seating for two and half people.' Another smile from Louise and another peck as Tom opened the bathroom door. 'Here madam we have the Queen Victoria water closet, hand basin, shower cubicle and multiple hand rails complete with one towel.'

It became a game with his descriptions becoming funnier by the room and his peck becoming less of a peck and more of an amorous invasion. They entered the bedroom. It was basic with a bed, two bedside tables and a wardrobe none of which matched.

'Now here we have the boudoir where the newlyweds will sleep.' He kissed her. 'And chat.' He kissed her passionately. 'And make love.'

She wasn't laughing. He pulled the curtains across the only window darkening the room a touch. He turned her around and unzipped her dress. She let it drop to the floor. He turned her around so they faced one another and he stared at her as he undressed. She kept staring at him as she moved the straps on her petticoat and pulled it down.

She knew her recently purchased nightie would not be required in the immediate future.

As he did at the front door, he scooped up his bride and then placed her on the bed. There was not a lot said for the next however few minutes it took for them to complete their undressing.

She thought she was naked and despite their passion realized she was wearing something.

'Tom, I'm still wearing my hat. Let me take it off.'

'Don't you dare,' he muttered examining her body in a way no doctor would ever examine a patient. 'Your hat turns you into a sex goddess.'

The years of their separation built desire within both their minds and bodies, and now those years of frustration were swept away. They celebrated their union and life could not have been better.

In the middle of the day they lay in one another's arms with Tom gently kissing the top of Louise's head.

'I love your new hairstyle, Mrs Curzon. Where did you have it done?'

'You won't believe me.'

'Try me.'

'Only if you let me remove my hat.'

He helped her. She reached over to place it on a bedside table and he stared at her body again. She turned back and saw him admiring her.

'I think I'm going to enjoy being married to you,' he said moving closer. She loved him and more so as he took control.

It wasn't usual to sleep during the day but after such strenuous lovemaking and a burning desire wanting to be together after so long apart, dozing and then deep sleep occurred naturally.

It was mid-afternoon when he woke and his movement caused her to open her eyes and meet his gaze.

'Is this how you plan to spend your entire honeymoon, Mrs Curzon?'

She snuggled into him. 'I hope so. What about you?'

He gave her a quick kiss and hopped out of bed. She watched him leave the room and pondered so many thoughts and questions.

My mother has no idea where I am or why. The SOE probably know I'm back in the UK but not that I'm married and on my honeymoon. What will Tom's family think of me? Where am I going to live? With Tom of course but where?

He appeared wearing an old dressing gown. 'Tea, my dear; I've forgotten how you take it if ever I knew.'

'Tea!' she exclaimed. 'My husband is bringing me tea in bed?'

'Start as you mean to go on,' he said. 'Milk, sugar, weak, strong?'

She threw back the bedclothes. 'I'm not going to have a slave for a husband.' She struggled to find a garment. He approached and opened his gown. She stepped inside his embrace. Another round of marital bliss appeared to begin until a whistling kettle called time on their smooching.

He vanished to make the tea as she found her robe and joined him in the kitchen. She hugged him from behind as he poured the boiling water.

'Careful, my darling, you want me as a lover and not a doctor.'

She squeezed him then stepped back to sit at the only table in the house. He placed two steaming mugs and a milk jug and sugar bowl on the table. She helped herself but wasn't sure if the sugar was real.

'I'm sorry about the missing Victoria sponge but I've been rushed off my feet all day.' He grinned and she stared at him as she sipped her tea joining in with his teasing.

'This is the best honeymoon I've ever had.'

He thought he knew her but now wondered if he underestimated this woman. He knew she was beautiful and clever but right at the beginning of their marriage he sensed there was so much more to Louise Beatrice Curzon nee Wellesley.

'I thought we might go into Southampton tonight and have a slap-up meal of spam fritters.'

She loved his sense of humour. 'That sounds wonderful. But I hope we'll spend our wedding night here in our little love nest.'

'Of course,' he said wondering if she had something special in mind for later. 'We can pinch a ride with one of the lads and find a cab coming home.'

'I know the perfect cabbie. How's your hair?'

He made a quizzical face and sipped his tea. 'Bags be first in the shower.'

'Oh?' she replied sounding miffed. 'Isn't there room for two?'

God he was glad he'd married this woman.

They asked for a lift into town and who could deny the honeymooners? With rationing in full flight, restaurants and cafes offered the shortest of menus.

They settled on the first they came across and ordered the special of the day. Where the fish were caught and when was never disclosed but the meal was of little consequence. It was their first together as man and wife and the conversation flowed.

'I know little about your family, Tom. Will they be disappointed they missed our wedding?'

'My sister, Gwen, will. I'm her baby brother and she cared for me when we were children.'

'How sweet. And your parents? What will they say?'

'About time and what took you so long?'

She didn't believe him. 'When can I meet them?'

'Whenever you like, my darling, but you'll need to travel alone for the foreseeable future.' She frowned. 'There's this special training for my unit and the full medical company is required.'

'Is it dangerous? Might you need a medic yourself?'

He dropped his voice. 'I shouldn't be telling you this so keep it under your hat.'

'I left that beside the bed,' she said with a twinkle in her eye.

'You've thrown me off the topic now.'

Their eyes met, well they'd hardly stopped staring at one another, and he didn't care. She continued not being able to stop.

'I'll go back to Farnham and Mummy and Ed. You can write to me there.'

'Explain the situation, me being on maneuverers and you off with ENSA.' He paused. 'I haven't asked you about your latest and next show. You must tell me all about your life these past few years.'

'I'm resting,' she lied and as he didn't know the term, she explained.

Ever since Tom proposed, Louise thought about what and when she would tell him about her other life, the one involving jumping out of aeroplanes, killing Nazis and climbing mountain ranges. With the war raging and her *Official Secrets Act* document signed, sealed and stored in an office somewhere, she chose to say nothing. The problem didn't go away and the longer her silence ruled, the harder it became to ever breathe a word.

They finished their wedding day meal and walked out into the Southampton evening.

'Let's find a cab,' said Tom.

'No, let's go for a walk.'

He became confused but she slipped her arm in his and led him a short distance to a certain terrace house.

He studied the location and his wife. 'You are a lady of mystery.'

They walked to the front door and she knocked. Fred answered it and his smile lit up the small front garden.

'Good evening, Mr Weatherly. This is my husband, Dr Tom Curzon.' The men shook hands.

From inside came a voice. 'Who is it, Fred?'

The cabbie ushered them in and Ethel worried then smiled. Louise moved to her and kissed the older woman.

'You look wonderful,' said Ethel before meeting Tom.

'We were wondering, sir,' said the bride with her sweetest smile, 'if we could hire you to drive us back to the camp.'

'But I thought you was married there this morning,' said Fred.

'We were but our honeymoon cottage is in the grounds.'

'Oh Fred,' gushed Ethel. 'It's their wedding night. Go and start the cab.'

Fred was delighted. Ethel loved the bride's hairstyle even though it had suffered a bit of wear and tear earlier in the afternoon. Tom added a generous tip and Fred drove home for a long conversation where Ethel asked the questions and he filled in the details.

It was dark in the summer house. Lights anywhere were banned. Tom closed all the curtains, found two candles, lit them and went to undress. He stopped when the bathroom door opened and his wife appeared. She had changed into her wedding night attire.

'Good evening, Doctor,' she said in a sultry voice.

He pursed his lips and blew air slowly. She brushed past him and stood behind the settee in the sitting-room. Their faces glowed in the candlelight.

'Sit,' she said and Dr Putty succumbed.

She moved and stood in front of him. Her black nightie covered the top of her black stockings, just. He found his mouth going dry.

Earlier, Louise had been nervous, not afraid but anxious. Tom's expert lovemaking gave her great joy and now confidence. She wanted to lead and he struggled to believe how exciting she made him feel.

The bed was never considered and their ability to please one another improved. Tom was still half-dressed when he helped Louise to disrobe completely. They became frantic and were celebrating their union when a siren exploded. It sounded like it came from the base. It *did* come from the base.

Louise was afraid.

'Air-raid,' snapped Tom reaching for his trousers. 'Come on, we need to go.'

Louise panicked. Her hormones kept racing while her brain screamed confusion. Tom snuffed out the candles and the flames being extinguished becoming a metaphor for the cessation of passion.

Tom was ready to fly. 'Louise, darling, let's go.'

'Tom, I'm naked.'

'Clothes won't help if a Jerry bomb lands in the garden.'

They hadn't been married 12 hours and yet Louise discovered disappointment. *Is this the action of the man I married?*

'Here,' he said wrapping her robe around her and leading her out of the summer house. The doubt about her husband vanished. They hurried through the garden running on grass with Tom knowing the way. 'In here,' he said ushering her down steps and into a bomb shelter. It was one of the cellars of the country house.

Many people were inside. In the dim light they stared at the new arrivals. Most were in uniform and so a woman in a robe was unusual and interesting. *Hang on, isn't this their wedding night?* The stares were less intrusive when the crunch of bombs sounded outside.

Tom wrapped his arms around his wife and kissed the top of her head. 'Bet you won't forget your wedding night,' he whispered and she never felt more in love with the man she married at 10am that morning.

Chapter 21

Portsmouth was the main target but after the raid, why carry excess bombs back to Germany? Bomb crews would often jettison their load on any nearby critical site with Southampton only a few minutes away copping the leftovers causing damage and death, and sorely interrupting the wedding night of Tom and Louise.

The all-clear was given and people left the shelter. Tom waited for the others to leave. Louise realized he was protecting her in her state of undress.

They walked back to the summer house hand in hand, laughing at their night's activities. 'If you ever tell anyone about our wedding night, Louise Wellesley, I will never forgive you.'

'I've changed my name, Dr Curzon or have you forgotten already?'

'Did I tell you your night dress nearly gave me a heart attack?'

'Good,' she said. 'I'll save it for the anniversary of our night in a bomb shelter.'

They stopped at the front door and kissed for a long time. He slipped his hands inside her robe and she reacted.

'I think we're better off indoors, sir,' she said. He agreed and they retired although sleep was not the first item on the agenda.

Their first breakfast together was full of touching one another between toast and tea. 'I thought we could go for a picnic today,' he said.

'Sounds wonderful,' she replied.

'I'll put the squeeze on the lads in the kitchen and we can hike along the trail by the River Itchen. They say the forest and wildlife are beautiful.'

'I did pack outdoor wear so I'm ready when you are, sir,' she said and saluted.

'Oh how disappointing,' he replied and tricked her again. She became sad but not after he spoke. 'I was hoping you'd wear your gorgeous little black nightie.'

She slapped his shoulder which became an embrace and a kiss.

'I'll find our lunch,' he said and disappeared.

She tidied the small rooms and changed into trousers, jumper and jacket with sensible shoes.

Tom returned with vittles. He packed them in a rucksack and picked up an umbrella as they set off. Wise man as an hour into their hike, the heavens opened and their walking hand in hand became clinging to one another beneath a brolly.

A crude shelter for ramblers proved a salvation from the constant rain. As it poured, their feast was consumed.

'So Mrs Curzon, how was your honeymoon? Flood or air-raid— which was your favourite?'

'I enjoyed getting to know my wonderful husband.'

They smiled at one another and while the rivers and streams of Hampshire rose and raced, the newlyweds kissed and delighted in their own company.

Tom became solemn. 'My darling, I've been thinking.'

'Oh dear, this sounds serious.'

'I think our divine honeymoon is soon to end.'

She became genuinely shocked. 'But we still have tonight and I still have your favourite little black nightie.'

'I must be mad turning down such a fantastic offer but I'm off in the morning at 6 and to have you and your little black nightie delivered safely to Southampton, we'll need to be up at 4 and there are no London trains till much later.' She loved him the more. 'I can take you into town this afternoon and you'll be back in your flat well before midnight.'

She kissed his cheek. 'Thank you, Doctor. I always knew you were a caring man.'

'Well you may not be correct there.' She studied him and worried. 'We haven't talked about starting a family and, in case you don't know, the way it usually happens is the man inseminates the woman which is what we did once or twice during our honeymoon.'

'Once or twice? Are you keeping score and if so, are you sure of the number?'

He threw back his head and roared. 'I love your wit, wife.'

'Only my wit?' she feigned disappointment.

'And your body, definitely your body and particularly your little black nightie.'

They kissed as the rain eased.

'Good, because I rather fancy your body too and yes, I would love to have a family with you as my husband.'

More kissing until Tom made the decision. 'It's home time, my wife. Let's have you back in London and, unless I'm much mistaken, down to Farnham to tell your mother your news.'

Louise couldn't speak and her eyes became moist. She'd had many terrifying, thrilling and heart-warming experiences in her short life but the last 36 hours proved more thrilling than all the others combined.

Back at the summer house, Tom helped Louise pack. In the garden they surveyed their little love nest enjoying the moment.

They had to wait before a ride into town became available. Tom carried her case to the station and bought her ticket, a single to London.

'When will I see you again?' she asked.

He grimaced. 'I can't say, my darling. This special training is to prepare for something much bigger and who knows when it will happen?' But I'll write to you at Farnham and telephone if I get the chance.'

'I have only one favour to ask of you, Dr Curzon.'

'Oh yes and what is that pray tell?'

'Promise me you will come home safe and sound.'

He said nothing but hugged her tight. He spoke softly into her left ear. 'I promise.'

The sound of an approaching locomotive announced the end of the play. It had been a wonderful and moving performance. Tom opened a carriage door and put his wife's case on the rack. He stepped outside while she stood the other side of the door with its window down.

Neither knew what to say. They kissed.

'I love you,' she said.

'I'm missing you already,' he replied.

The locomotive snorted and Tom stood back raising a hand as his wife, blowing a kiss, headed off to London.

144

She made two decisions. She would not go back to the flat in Maida Vale but would ring her mother before heading to Farnham. Turning up without warning would cause a shock, a happy one but still a shock. And to arrive and say, 'Hello Mummy, I'm married', would too be a massive surprise.

Mrs Crossley answered the phone. 'Miss Louise!' she exclaimed and Victoria was out of the sitting-room with her heart racing.

'My darling girl, is that really you?'

'Hello Mummy. How are you and Eddie and Mrs C?'

'We're fine. But where are you and how are you? We've been worried sick.'

Her chat was interrupted by a yapping sound.

'I can hear a dog?' cried Louise.

'Yes darling, we followed your advice. That's Larry the noisy one.'

'The noisy one! You mean there's a quiet one as well? You have *two* dogs!'

'Yes darling, and I'm sure you'll like them.'

'Tell them I'm on my way.'

Victoria stood in disbelief. 'Are you really coming home, Louise?'

'My train leaves in ten minutes. Bye Mummy.'

Louise hung up feeling her body surge with happiness. She couldn't wait to tell her family her news and their news about *two* dogs had her wanting to dance a jig.

The train pulled into Farnham and Louise was ready to spring from the carriage and walk—*dare I run?*—to her family home. She set off along the platform when a loud voice was heard.

'And where do you think *you're* going?'

She knew the voice, stopped and turned to see her big brother, Henry standing there with arms folded. Louise's case fell on the platform as she ran to embrace another man she loved with all her heart.

They embraced and kissed.

'What are you doing here?' she gasped.

'And it's nice to see you too, sister dear.'

He picked up her case, she slipped her arm into his and they set off for home.

'Just popped in to check on the mater and our war-hero brother.'

'How are you and your dear wife and however many children you now have?'

'Still the two thank you and we're all fine. But what about you, special secret agent sister of mine? Are you coming or going on another of your life-threatening missions?'

She stopped in the road forcing him to stop. There was no need to act as her serious nature slipped into top gear. 'Henry, you are the only person in our family who knows anything about my undercover work.'

'I know that.'

'You must never tell Mummy or even Eddie about what I've done.'

'*Official Secrets* old girl,' he said tapping his nose.

'And especially not my husband.'

Henry reacted as if he'd been shot. He dropped her case and his jaw. 'Your husband!?

They hesitated. She wanted to retrieve the bullet from her foot. He threw wide his arms and she ran to him.

'Bloody hell, Plum. You kept that quiet. Who's the lucky chap?'

She slapped his arm. 'Tom Curzon of course.'

'Of course. So when did all this happen?'

'About 24 hours ago.' He waited for the truth or the tag. She wasn't grinning. 'It was the shortest honeymoon in Hampshire history.'

He shook his head, picked up her case and they set off.

'You always were a show-off,' he said. 'Star of the show was little Plum. So what's happened about your career upon the wicked stage?'

'Lots but if I tell you now I'll only have to repeat everything when we get home.'

He laughed and they both wondered about their mother's response to the baby of the family getting hitched.

'Here they are,' said Mrs Crossley when she spotted the siblings coming through the back garden. She opened the door and two cocker spaniels raced outside barking and whipping the air with their tails.

Louise dropped to her knees and the dogs gave her the best of greetings. The canines had been told Plum was coming and their expectations were sky high.

The human had trouble patting and greeting both frisky hounds. One barked with excitement. 'You must be Larry, the noisy one.'

Larry confirmed his name by barking even louder.

She turned to the other canine. 'You have to be a lady, so quiet and gentle. What's your name?'

Henry had forgotten. He couldn't forget the names of his children; sadly as he considered them awful, the names that is.

'She's Lily,' called Mrs Crossley, 'and we're all inside.'

Calling the excited dogs, Louise headed inside with her brother being the butler. She kissed the housekeeper.

Her mother stood in the living-room, so excited to see her only daughter. Edmund relaxed in his wheelchair. Henry and Mrs Crossley held back. Louise entered.

Victoria threw open her arms and the women wept in one another's arms. Neither spoke as their hearts fought to have the louder and busier thump.

Louise broke away and hugged and kissed her other brother.

The housekeeper made an announcement. 'Why don't you all sit down and I'll fetch the tea.'

Mrs Crossley was a war widow from the last big bash. Her husband died in France, his body never recovered. She was hired as a young widow when the Wellesley children were young and Louise a toddler. Her name was Enid but only Victoria ever used it.

Louise sat beside her mother with Victoria holding Louise's right hand in both of hers.

'You look wonderful, my darling,' said Victoria. 'I don't think I've ever seen you so serene.' She asked her sons. 'I'm right, aren't I?'

'You've scrubbed up all right, old girl,' said Edmund.

Henry stood and observed. His mother wanted her older son's response. 'Henry?'

'She's a picture of beauty and happiness and must be in love.'

Louise died inside and her mother wondered if she'd missed something. Henry stared at Louise and she knew why. It's time, Plum.

'Mummy, I have news. Please don't be upset.'

'What's happened?' asked Victoria holding her breath.

'Yesterday Dr Curzon and I were married.'

Edmund roared, Mrs C clapped and the dogs went crazy and they didn't even know the groom. Victoria's hands went to her face and then to her daughter. The women embraced for the second time.

Edmund pointed at his brother. 'You knew!' he challenged Henry.

The others studied the now patriarch of the family. 'Only ten minutes ago,' he stated in his barrister-stance defence.

The buzz, the excitement settled and Louise wondered if her family thought she was rude and cruel and disrespectful to not invite her family to her wedding. She explained.

'I was touring in Southampton and overheard a soldier talking about his unit which I knew was Tom's. I asked him for directions and Tom was based in a lovely old home out of town. I went there and asked if I might have a word and he came flying down this magnificent staircase and we kissed in front of all the office staff. Then we went walking in the garden and he proposed and I said, "Yes".'

'Of course you did,' said Edmund who was shushed by the mater and housekeeper.

'Tom leaves for a training camp at 6 o'clock in the morning so rather than wait, the army chaplain married us and we went for a 24 hour honeymoon in the summer house. Tom wanted me home before dark so he put me on the London train and here I am.'

More sighs from the females and "Jolly good shows" from the males. Louise knew how to deliver a powerful denouement. She removed her left glove revealing her new wedding jewellery. The women gushed and the men nodded their approval.

Phew.

A massive feeling of relief swamped Louise. She thrilled to the happiness her news gave to her mother and the others but especially Mummy. The worrying thought her wedding might upset her mother faded. She knew how her mother would have thrilled to be in the local packed church with her daughter in a stunning white wedding dress being escorted by her barrister brother, Henry.

So to not have the traditional white wedding and worse, to not be there or even know the event was taking place, Louise reckoned might hurt her mother and to do so was the last thing Louise wanted.

But happiness reigned and Henry's lips were stitched together when it came to speaking about Louise and her SOE activities. And anyway, he too was working privately for intelligence and was not allowed to speak of his activities.

Louise moved into her old room, Henry went back to his snobbish wife and their badly-named offspring. Louise entertained the others with tales both true and embellished about her ENSA performances and spent ages walking the fields and lanes of Surrey with her two new friends, Larry and Lily.

She knew Colonel Buckmaster would want a report on her last unauthorized trip to Belgium and France and so after a week, told her mother she needed to see theatre people up in London.

'I'll stay at the flat, Mummy and be home tomorrow.'

'Take care, my darling,' said Victoria.

'And if my husband rings, tell him I've gone out on the town.'

'I'll do no such thing,' said the mater in a serious voice.

64 Baker Street took on the status of an old school week when she entered the reception area. They all knew Sister Claudine, Plum, Sherlock and Louise Wellesley. No-one knew Louise Curzon.

Buckmaster received the news and asked the agent to come upstairs. Louise climbed thinking she was either heading to the headmistress's office to be expelled or was about to kneel beneath the guillotine for the loss of one's head.

Vera Atkins stepped out to greet the young woman. They always hit it off with Louise reckoning the expression "still waters run deep" applied perfectly to Vera.

'I hear you've been busy, Plum,' she said.

Louise didn't know what to expect from Colonel Buckmaster. 'Is he upset?'

'Come in and find out.'

He wasn't upset with Louise but desperately worried about missing SOE agents in France.

'So Sister Claudine, what have you been up to?'

She started with a field in Suffolk and a chance to jump aboard a Lysander heading to Belgium. She finished with a French sub surfacing off the coast of the Isle of Wight.'

Two other SOE officers had arrived to hear the tale. All were impressed with not a word spoken until she finished.

'I do apologize, sir, for acting as I did.'

'And so you should. Now have you left out anything we need to know about?'

Louise paused and then announced. 'I got married last week, sir.'

'We knew as soon as you arrived wearing new jewellery.' She had unconsciously been handling her new rings. 'And by the way, many congratulations.'

'Thank you, sir,' she said as the others joined in.

'Now what are we going to do with you, Mrs ...'

'Curzon, sir; my husband Dr Thomas Curzon is an Englishman serving in the US Army.'

Buckmaster knew all about Tom Curzon. 'We discussed the possibility of you training new agents before they head off to France.'

'Yes sir.'

'In fact you could already be doing so if you hadn't headed off on your latest trip we called a Plum jaunt.' Louise smiled at the expression. Buckmaster continued.

'Why don't you have a break from all your killing of Gestapo and double agents and we'll draw up a proposal and have you back in a week or two?'

She agreed, thanked everyone and left.

In Baker Street, she set off for the office of her theatrical agent, Richard Graves. Calling on him always gave her heart a kick. She longed to perform and he was her ticket to success.

Without an appointment, she entered his office where his secretary perked up whenever her boss's much-admired client arrived.

'I'll tell Mr Graves you're here.'

From inside his voice was clearly heard. '*The* Miss Wellesley, the star of the Welsh valleys and beyond?'

He appeared with a smile and extended hand. 'What an utter delight, my dear young lady.' They shook hands.

'I apologize for not calling ahead, sir.'

'Apology irrelevant and forgotten,' he said ushering her into his office and calling, 'Tea please, Miss McCauley.'

'First, how are you and second, what on Earth have you been up to? I lost track after your adventure in Wales.' He waited with genuine interest.'

'I joined a tour with an ENSA concert party but then did a most unprofessional thing and ran away—again.'

'So I heard and you are making a bit of a habit of disappearing.'

She worried. 'Am I ruining my chances of becoming a professional actress?'

'I shouldn't think so. My information is many in your concert party were both jealous and angry they hadn't done the same. And of course I guess you ran away to serve your King and country although I don't know anything about that.'

They exchanged knowing smiles. He it was who recommended Louise for a life in undercover intelligence all those years ago before the war even started.

'There is one other bit of news.' She paused. 'I'm married.'

Graves threw up his hands and exclaimed, 'Wonderful!' as the secretary appeared with tea. 'Tea, Miss McCauley! We should have champagne!'

Louise held out her hand and Miss McCauley gushed.

They settled and Louise put her cards on the table. 'I know the war has ruined many theatres but I wish to say I have taken a vow to never abandon a show again. Mr Graves, if you ever find an opening for me, I will give it my immediate and earnest consideration.'

'Excellent.'

'Although what I mean is, I'll say "yes" before you've finished the phone call.'

He laughed and asked about her husband. They chatted and he promised to be in touch as soon as a suitable role came along.

In the street, she remembered her third task for the day—ENSA. The decent thing, the proper and right thing to do was to attend the Theatre Royal Drury Lane in person and apologize for her behaviour in again acting in a most unprofessional manner.

She turned coward, went to her Maida Vale flat and wrote a long letter to the ENSA founders doing what she should have done face to face. She didn't exactly quit but stated how having failed the company twice she believed she could no longer continue performing for ENSA finishing with wishing the two men and the company the very best of British in their superb goal of entertaining the troops. She posted the letter knowing she was a coward.

She spent the night alone in London thinking about her future, possibly with the SOE, hopefully on the stage, and how she missed the man in her life. She fell asleep reliving her wedding and honeymoon.

She headed back to Farnham and found coincidences do happen as she alighted at the station to be met again by brother Henry.

'There's no need to chaperone me anymore,' she said kissing him. 'I'm a grown-up married woman.'

He indicated his case. 'One in, one out, Plum. Spot of business in Winchester so I popped in to check on the mater and Eddie and now I'm off home.'

His train was not due for a few minutes. They sat on a bench.

'I think my days of shooting Nazis abroad are over, brother.'

'So they should be. It's no job for a lady.'

He was teasing and she didn't bite.

'What about you? Are you still in intelligence?'

He nodded. 'I understand you not telling the mater and Ed but what about your husband?'

She stared at her brother. 'I've told him nothing and now feel if I do, he could be upset.'

'But why? You're due a medal, medals from France and here. Why be ashamed of your heroism?'

'I'm not ashamed but why didn't I tell him years ago? If I do now he may think I don't trust him.'

'Rubbish. Yes the Act says you can't tell him but the man is head over heels in love with you. Your decision, old girl but you could concentrate on being a film star and giving the mater a bonnie wee babe who actually is brought to see her.'

Louise was pleased Henry even hinted at his odd wife. His train approached and they stood and kissed.

'Send me a photo of you and the Doc on your wedding day.'

He boarded the train. She waited and waved then headed for home where the dogs gave her an enthusiastic welcome; after all they were old pals now.

Chapter 22

Louise settled in the family home sleeping in the room of her childhood. The other three human inhabitants watched her being happy walking the new dogs but all her acting experience couldn't hide her profound sadness at missing the man she loved.

Victoria would watch her daughter whenever the postman arrived. Louise would approach full of hope and when nothing from Tom arrived, her shoulders would drop.

'Thank God for the dogs,' said Edmund to his mother.

And thank God for the first letter which arrived from Tom. Louise opened the envelope in the garden, again being watched by all inside. The dogs skipped around their new mistress and shared her happiness as she read and re-read the news.

'Letter from Tom, my dear?' asked Victoria as her smiling daughter bounced inside.

'Yes and he sends his love to you all.'

'Does he say when his training will end?' asked Edmund.

'He's not sure but it sounds like they're preparing for this invasion people are talking about.'

'Well as he's a doctor, darling, it's most unlikely he'll be anywhere near the front lines.'

Victoria immediately wished she hadn't spoken as it clearly triggered thoughts Louise so often pushed to the back of her mind.

'I'll write a thank you note to Tom then pop down to the post office.'

'You could take the dogs,' called her brother to his absent sister. Then he spoke in a soft voice, 'for their third walk of the day.'

The expression on Victoria's face warned him about going easy on his sensitive and troubled sister.

Mrs Crossley handled the purchase and preparation of food for the family with great expertise. Their vegetable patch was working flat out but there was nothing she could do about the atmosphere inside the home. You would think she was making omelettes then dropping egg shells on the floor. People trod or wheeled with delicate moves.

Louise knew she was to blame for the tension, hated bringing her worries to others and even thought about moving out and going to live in London.

She raised the matter with her brother as they enjoyed sunshine in the garden.

'Stop blaming yourself, Plum. You waited years before marrying Tom and now, when all your hopes have come true, the happiness is ripped away because of this damn war.'

'Thanks, Eddie, I needed that,' she replied with sincerity.

'And be practical. Living in London you'll have to do everything for yourself. Here you have Mrs C to fill your belly, your best friends Larry and Lily to play with and even a boring old fart like me to talk to occasionally.'

'I like boring old farts.'

'And besides, Mummy adores having you here. She'd be mortified if you left home, at least not until hubby comes to collect you.'

They watched the dogs and embraced the warm sunshine.

'So what's on the agenda for you?' she asked. 'I can't believe you're going to retire to sleepy Surrey for the rest of your life.'

'Henry's a brick. He's pushing me to hop back on the horse again.'

'Fantastic, good old Harry.'

'He reckons I could move to criminal law and work on briefs being a fresh pair of eyes before a case goes to trial.'

'Would you like that?'

He nodded. 'I've been mulling it over and he told me there's a chambers in the city willing to give me a trial.'

Louise reacted with joy. She hugged her brother but stopped when the housekeeper called from the back door.

'There's a telephone call for Miss Louise.'

The actress panicked. 'Is it Tom?'

'It's Mr Graves.'

Louise ran with the dogs loving the game.

'Hello, Mr Graves, it's lovely to hear from you.'

'Good morning, Miss Wellesley. Are you well?'

'Thank you I am and all the better for hearing from you.'

'We never discussed your change of name. I would recommend you maintain your previous stage name of Miss Louise Wellesley. How do you feel about that and will it upset your husband?'

'Nothing seems to upset him. I'm lucky to have married such an understanding man.'

'Jolly good. Well to business. There's a part which might suit you although not on stage.'

Louise was hooked anyway but doubly so with his last remark. *Not on stage* suggested out in the field, even in enemy-held territory.

'Are you recruiting for the government, Mr Graves?'

He produced his usual gentle laugh. 'No, I'm referring to the world of motion pictures.'

Louise froze. *The movies.* She couldn't speak.

'Are you still there, Miss Wellesley?'

'Yes, yes, I'm here. You did surprise me, Mr Graves.'

'No doubt you've heard of Mr Alfred Hitchcock.'

Another slap in the face for Louise. Who hadn't heard of the famous film director? *The 39 Steps, Rebecca* and *The Lady Vanishes*.

'Yes, of course I have.' She wondered if her voice displayed the excitement she sensed coursing through her body.

'He's directing a film about the French Resistance set in the south of the country. The script is in French and you would be perfect in two ways.'

A touch of panic set in. Travelling to war-torn France would not win her husband's approval.

Her voice oozed regret. 'I'm not sure travelling to France would please my husband.'

'Oh good Lord no, Miss Wellesley, I wouldn't dream of putting you in harm's way. The filming is here in a studio in London.'

Louise suffered relief and embarrassment in one hit.

'Of course, how silly of me.'

'As well as a small role, you would be ideally placed to understand the setting and the war.' Then he stopped. 'Of course, you may not wish or be allowed to mention your other experiences.'

'Thank you for your kind understanding.'

'Mr Hitchcock is auditioning tomorrow and I've booked you a spot at 11. Are you interested and available?'

'You've asked two silly questions, Mr Graves. Where should I go?'

155

He gave the details and when she hung up, she struggled. This was a totally different genre, medium or activity. Put her on a stage and she was like a duck taking to water. But a film set? To her it was foreign territory.

She found her mother in the sitting-room. Mrs Crossley was with her with the housekeeper knitting for her great niece.

'Everything all right, my dear?' asked Victoria.

Before she could speak, Edmund pushed himself inside wanting to know what his talented sister was about to announce. They were all ears.

'Mr Graves has arranged an audition in London tomorrow.'

'No need to audition, Plum. The part is yours,' declared her brother.

'How wonderful,' said Victoria hoping a name such as Dame Sybil Thorndike would be part of the new company.

'It's not for a play, it's for a film.'

The women gasped and the man yelled his approval.

'The director is Alfred Hitchcock.'

The room, already alight, caught fire. Congratulations and questions flowed freely. Louise needed to be so careful. The film featured the French Resistance but there was no way Louise could even hint at her involvement with the SIS and SOE.'

'I think Mr Graves thought of me because the script is in French.'

'What did I say,' said Edmund. 'The part is already yours.'

Louise bubbled inside with the only sad news being she couldn't share it with Tom. She couldn't share anything with Tom and physically yearned for his touch.

She wondered if his lovemaking expertise was due to his being a doctor or if his expertise came from experience with another woman or women. She knew he was once married and his wife died. She knew only one thing for certain; she loved him madly.

Over the evening meal, much discussion was had about the films directed by Alfred Hitchcock. Edmund got personal.

'I said you were a star, Plum after the performance you gave in the church hall with that Nightingale chap. What was his name?'

'Beauford,' she said and wondered what he would think of her career to date and where he was today. He moved and no-one knew his address.

Next morning, Louise was up and out apologising to the dogs for their short walk as she left for London. She found her way to the audition address and waited outside in a corridor lined with chairs. She reckoned being early would be appreciated then groaned inside discovering all the chairs were taken. A woman spoke.

'Louise?' This young woman moved to her. She'd been in the pantomime *Cinderella* and Louise knew her face but couldn't remember her name. 'Susan,' she said and Louise smiled.

'It's lovely to see you after all this time. What have you been doing?' asked Louise.

'Oh bits and bobs. And you?'

'The same but this is a first for me. I know nothing about film.'

Susan's expression changed to serious. 'Tell me, what happened after Windsor Castle? You disappeared and even the ENSA chaps were perplexed. It was as if you were kidnapped or worse.'

Louise laughed. 'Not so dramatic, I'm afraid.' Liar!

Inside she started shaking. When the IRA grabbed Princess Margaret and the pantomime's leading lady, life became serious, potentially catastrophic. The ENSA big-wigs were hopping mad and sent one of their assistants to demand an explanation. Louise was saved from having to explain when a couple of gents took an interest in the actress. Those gents, the King and the PM, carried a bit of weight and their words and actions put the ENSA chaps well and truly back in their box.

But this was different. Louise was confronted by a witness to her disappearance. She could hardly refer the matter up to Buckingham Palace or to Number 10.

What will I say?

As she scrambled for anything vaguely credible, a woman opened a door and called, 'Susan Fleetwood.'

Plum's luck held; she was saved by the casting director's assistant.

'Break a leg,' whispered Louise and breathed a deep sigh of relief.

When Susan stepped back into the corridor only a few minutes later, her face of thunder spoke volumes. She'd lost interest in Louise's vanishing act and grumbled as she left.

'The whole thing's in bloody French. I'll kill my agent.'

After others came and went, the assistant spoke the magic words. 'Louise Wellesley.'

There was a corridor to negotiate and then a room to enter. Louise would naturally smile which gave her an advantage in most situations.

'Mr Hitchcock, this is Miss Louise Wellesley.'

The great man stood and offered his hand.

'How do you do, Miss Wellesley and thank you so much for coming.'

'Good morning, sir.'

He indicated another man. 'This is my colleague Monsieur Clermon.'

'Bonjour, Mademoiselle.'

'Bonjour, Monsieur.'

The director invited Louise to sit. 'As I hope you have been informed, the screenplay is in French. Will it be a problem for you?'

'No sir,' said Louise then realized she would need to prove her claim as M. Clermon questioned her in French. She replied speaking naturally in the same tongue.

'Have you ever been to France, Mademoiselle?'

'I have, sir, several times.'

Hitchcock decided there and then the face, speaking voice and her command of French meant this woman was required for his film. The men allowed the conversation to continue simply because they wanted to watch and listen to the beautiful and intelligent actress.

Clermon had already given "the signal" to the director meaning the auditionee's French was perfect. Hitchcock took over and explained the plot of the film he called *Aventure Malgache*. It was a propaganda war film praising the work of the French Resistance in Vichy-controlled France.

'I see here your stage credits are admirable but not so your experience with film.'

'You're correct, Mr Hitchcock but one must start somewhere.'

He smiled. He liked the young woman. 'We do not expect the film to be released until 1944 but much of the planning has already begun.' She nodded thinking *if they don't want me, surely I would have been excused already.*

'Unlike a play, we film in sections or scenes and you would only be required to attend when your scene or scenes are being filmed.'

She chose bravery and decided to risk it. 'Am I to understand you are offering me a part, sir?'

The great man smiled without displaying any teeth. He stood and offered his hand.

'You can expect a contract in the near future my dear and I shall eagerly anticipate the time when we can work together. Au revoir.'

She smiled, shook the hand of both men and left. The line-up of hopefuls in the corridor stared at her. She offered an inscrutable face and left. Who'd be an actor?

In the street she wanted to cry with both happiness and sadness. Winning the role was wonderful. Being unable to tell her beloved husband was torture.

Her family was thrilled and the dogs never more proud. The catalogue of questions dealt with her audition but most were about the small man with the glum expression and thinning hair, the famous film director. Everyone had been to the cinema to see at least one of his films.

Louise went upstairs to write to Tom. She kept it brief explaining her latest success and spent the other half expressing her love and enquiring about when they could be together again.

She didn't need an excuse to walk the dogs but posting a letter to the man in her life was perfect. *Come back into my life, Tom Curzon.*

He did when a letter arrived. It gave Louise a blast of joy and doubly so when he told her the special training would end soon, the unit would return to Southampton and best of all, he has been given leave to spend Christmas with his wife.

Her news about working with Alfred Hitchcock thrilled Tom and he spent all his spare time boasting about being married to a movie star.

The other Farnham residents took delight in seeing Louise back on form. She first tried but failed to tell her mother about Tom Curzon on the night her father collapsed, and then introduced her to the man she fell in love with when he attended to the family patriarch, Charles Wellesley on Christmas Day 1938.

Brother Edmund got to know Tom when recovering from his horrible Dunkirk wounds.

For Louise to wait five years before she could marry took courage and to have the couple separate a day after their wedding meant her emotions stretched to breaking point. Now things were on the up.

'You might have Christmas here, Plum,' said her brother, 'but you can't spend all of Tom's leave stuck with us.'

Louise saw his point. 'We could spend a few days in London.'

'Yes; lock yourself away in Maida Vale. Think of your poor old husband. He wants to hold your hand and give you a hug and a kiss.' She saw the twinkle in her brother's eye and smiled. Inside she went all mushy.

The film contract and a screenplay arrived and Louise read same with a mixture of excitement and more excitement. Her role was small but the payment she reckoned to be large.

The waiting dragged. She wanted Christmas and Tom to be back in her life so having lines to learn helped relieve her boredom. Filming would start in the New Year and typical Louise, she would arrive line perfect.

As if the film, Tom and the dogs were not enough to keep her busy, a letter arrived from an anonymous source. *It can't be Dickie Graves*, she thought. *He knows I've accepted the film.*

It was from Maurice Buckmaster who had written to Louise care of Maida Vale and received no reply. He tried again and avoided a phone call knowing how important it was for Louise's history to remain secret. If anyone saw the letter, there was nothing to suggest the real nature of the sender.

It was a request to discuss a training project for a typing agency. She comprehended the vagueness of the letter and when alone in the house, telephoned the SOE.

Vera Atkins took the call. 'We wondered if you've given any more thought to the training proposal we discussed.'

'To tell the truth, Miss Atkins, I've been rather busy. I've been cast in a film to be directed by Alfred Hitchcock.'

'Oh how marvellous, congratulations.'

'Thank you. It's about the French Resistance in Vichy France and the script is in French.'

'Well if your acting ability wasn't enough, your SOE experience would have clinched the deal.'

Louise became sick. 'But my family know nothing of my history.'

'Of course they don't. I'll tell Colonel Buckmaster your news and I'm sure he'd like to hear from you when life is a little less hectic.'

'Thank you,' said Louise.

'And how is married life?'

Louise hesitated and Miss Atkins thought horrible thoughts including about death in time of war.

'I'll be honest, Miss Atkins, it's bloody awful. Tom's away on special training but will be home on leave over Christmas.'

'Well good luck with the ... oh no, I'm not supposed to say that.'

Louise laughed and they parted on a happy note. And her happiness climbed as another letter arrived from the doctor she married.

This time his news gave her a start.

'Is it from Tom,' asked Victoria. 'Nothing sad I hope?'

'Not sad but challenging. Tom's parents want me to visit them.'

'Of course they do. They want to meet their new daughter-in-law. Do they say when?'

'Tom says whenever I'm free. He suggests I telephone.'

Victoria studied her daughter. 'There's no time like the present, my darling.'

Louise returned with her mother anxious for news.

'Well?'

'Mr Curzon will meet me at the Henley-on-Thames station tomorrow at 10.'

'I'm so pleased. How did he sound?'

'I spoke mainly with Mrs Curzon. She was friendly and said the whole family is looking forward to meeting me.'

'I'm sure they are. It's another exciting part of being married. You gain an instant new family. What will you wear?'

'I thought my wedding dress.'

'Perfect.'

Chapter 23

Mr Ralph Curzon was easy to spot when Louise alighted at Henley-on-Thames station. Being a week day with summer long gone, passenger numbers were low. The retired stockbroker was nudging 70 and his son was, if not a spitting image of the old man, then pretty darn close.

'Louise,' he cried having received a precise description of his daughter-in-law from his son. He walked the faster and kissed her on both cheeks.

'Hello, Mr Curzon,' she said unsure what to call one's father-in-law.

'It's wonderful to meet you and to welcome you to the family.'

'Thank you.'

She took his offered arm and they set off walking to the Curzon home. He couldn't stop talking about how happy he and Mrs Curzon were to have their son married and to such a beautiful and talented young lady. There wasn't a lot Louise could say. She didn't get much of a chance. Praise and compliments were nice but these kept on coming.

The impressive home was a short walk from the station and Tom's mother, Esther, opened the door as they approached.

'My dear,' said Ralph, 'meet our lovely daughter-in-law.'

'Hello Louise,' said the well-preserved woman.

More name selection problems from the visitor who chose none.

'Hello.'

The kissing and smiling went on until they entered the sitting-room. There was nothing cheap in this house. A younger woman sat on a settee beside two children, aged 7 and 9. They were either perfectly behaved or glued to the furniture.

'Children,' said the younger woman, say hello to your Aunt Louise.'

The offspring spoke in unison in a singsong voice. Their rehearsing paid dividends. 'Hello Aunt Louise.'

The grandparents smiled and Louise became less anxious, smiled and spoke. 'Hello nephew and niece.'

Grandma intervened. 'Louise this is Thomas's sister, Gwendoline and her children Carter and Amelia.'

'It's lovely to meet you all,' said the visiting relative.

The lady of the house wore an invisible badge with the word CAPTAIN thereon.

'Do sit, Louise, please.' The skipper doubled as traffic policeman and indicated the chair chosen for the visitor. Everyone sat in their assigned places and stared at their new arrival.

The women were examining the outfit, hat, accessories, shoes and make-up being worn by Aunt Louise. The father-in-law and children were just staring.

'How was your trip?' asked Esther.

Louise loathed the obligatory small-talk and replied in kind.

'It was all right especially in these difficult times.'

Louise was expecting the next comment to be about the weather so was shocked when her father-in-law jumped the queue.

'I must say, Louise, we were jolly surprised when Tom wrote to say he was married. He'd never mentioned meeting you or being engaged so it came right out of the blue.'

Esther didn't like her husband not sticking to the script but now her curiosity was off the leash. She hung on Louise's response

'Well my family met Tom years ago so it wasn't so much of a surprise to them.'

Esther fired off her first question. 'Tom told us you're an actress.'

'Yes, it's how we met. He was staying with your sister and her husband in Cambridge.'

Esther's jaw dropped. Her family met her daughter-in-law and I wasn't told. *I'll be on the phone as soon the younger Mrs Curzon is gone.*

Louise kept going. 'I was performing in a play in the local church hall and Mr and Mrs Bird were in charge of supper for the audience. I remember Tom called his aunt, The Cake Queen of Cambridge.'

Esther kept taking mental notes.

'Are you from Cambridge, Louise?' asked Ralph.

'No I was studying at the university. My family are from Farnham in Surrey.'

The impressive news kept coming. *She must be clever if she went to Cambridge University.*

Gwendoline fired off her first question. 'We thought you must have only just met Tom.'

'No we met briefly before the war when Tom came to Cambridge. The next Christmas my father suffered a stroke and we took him to the local hospital, it was Christmas Eve, and the doctor caring for my father was Dr Tom Curzon.'

For a family fascinated about their new relative, her revelations were stimulating and they wanted more.

'Then during the war I joined ENSA and performed in shows on tour for the troops.'

'How wonderful,' said her father-in-law.

'My younger brother escaped from Dunkirk but suffered terrible injuries. Tom was working in the hospital where my brother received treatment and a few months ago I was home on a family visit and Tom arrived to check on my brother. We've had these serendipitous meetings for a few years.'

Serendipitous thought the family. The children were in raptures.

Then a fortnight ago, I finished a tour in Southampton, discovered Tom's unit was based there and went to say hello.' She had her audience in the palm of her hand. 'Apart from saying hello, he asked me to marry him and the next day we wed and went on our 36 hour honeymoon.'

Her in-laws were stunned. Esther could normally talk under water but even she struggled. Her questions were many and had the following lined up.

What did you wear? Who was at the wedding? Where did you spend your honeymoon?

Fortunately the luncheon gong sounded and the ration-weary food was served. After lunch, sister-in-law Gwendoline volunteered to show Louise the garden. Gwen had little interest in plants but far more interest in her brother's choice of wife.

'I can see why Tommy chose you.'

Louise wondered what was coming.

'He had his choice of pretty young things but he always liked women with a brain.'

'I see,' said Louise.

'Mind you your dazzling beauty obviously helps.'

'Thank you,' said Louise thinking her first impression of Gwendolyn may not be correct.

'You're lucky because our mothers are already grandmothers so the pressure to conceive won't be as great.'

Louise studied her relative. 'Are you the voice of experience?'

'I am indeed, so good luck with the baby business.'

Gwendolyn's smile prompted Louise to smile and they continued to gossip before they went inside where Louise said her goodbyes.

The hugs from her niece and nephew were heartfelt. She wanted to play with the children, tease and challenge them and they were busting to be let off the leash. Hopefully in the future.

Back home, Mrs C and the others were all ears wanting to know about the in-laws. Louise was guarded in her response.

Victoria cut to the chase. 'Did Tom's parents mention Christmas?'

'They said they hoped to see me and Tom when he's on leave. No plans were made. Should I have said something?'

'Of course not,' said Victoria hoping the couple would be in Farnham on Christmas Day.

Edmund had the answer. 'Why don't you have lunch here then spend Boxing Day in Henley.' Louise liked his suggestion. 'To save having a long trip, you could have a stopover in London at the flat.'

Louise liked his suggestion even more and saw her brother give a tiny wink. The older females chose not to react.

Christmas couldn't come soon enough. Tom's next letter gave Louise his dates. She replied asking if he would come to Farnham for Christmas lunch and suggested they go to his family for lunch on Boxing Day. She made no mention of a London stopover.

He replied giving her suggestions his hearty approval and immediately Mrs Crossley began planning. Having a guest for Christmas meant her wizardry with food rations required an even greater bout of inspiration and juggling.

It was as if Louise had an advent calendar on her wall as she marked off the days until her husband would appear. How many days till Christmas? How many days would they have together? Where would they go? What would they do? Well, the last one was a bit silly.

Louise discovered the truth of the saying, "absence makes the heart grow fonder". *But how does Tom feel?* She learnt her French film lines, walked the dogs and counted the days.

Henry came for the day and after lunch he joined Louise on her dog wanderings. She loved her family but Henry was an exception. He alone knew all about her secret life as she did about his involvement working for Intelligence. It was such a relief she could say anything when alone with big brother.

'When is this invasion happening?' she begged. 'I can't stand not knowing and especially if it means Tom will be off to France.'

'The planning is well established. The venues and times are still being sorted but my guess is the middle of the year, around June.'

'Do you think Tom will know?'

Henry shrugged. 'Listen, you need to stop worrying, old girl. Whatever will be will be. You're young and healthy and married. Enjoy life. Who knows what tomorrow brings?' He paused. 'Bloody hell, I sound like a philosopher.'

They laughed. She changed the subject becoming serious.

'Forgive me prying, Henry but why don't you bring your family to Farnham. Have you ever had a Christmas here?'

He gave a pensive grin. 'Do you need to ask those questions, Miss Wellesley?'

He put an emphasis on her former name to state the bleeding obvious. When Louise first met Henry's wife, Georgina, never Georgie, she addressed Louise in a formal way calling her Miss Wellesley. The sister-in-law had every skerrick of wit, humour and irony surgically removed at birth.

Louise took his arm as they turned for home.

'Well I'm doing the reverse. We're off to Tom's parents on Boxing Day.'

'Bully for you.'

The forecast for Christmas was fine but cold with snow unlikely. Tom rang from his base the day before. Louise tried to stop breathing like a teenage girl in love for the first time. Their call had to be short with a queue of impatient American servicemen waiting their turn.

'I love you, my darling,' he said pinching Louise's line. 'There's no need to meet me at the station in this cold weather.'

'You just try and stop me,' she replied and they ended with words of love.

Louise was out of bed and making sure she had the right colour and amount of lipstick. There were simple presents to give and receive with the dogs wishing Christmas happened every day.

She decided not to take the canines to the station. She wanted her hands free to embrace her lover.

His train arrived and Louise stood in the middle of the platform. He was one of the last to appear and with so many passengers Louise scrutinized them from left to right. Then she spotted him and moved. His smile was wide as he dropped his kit bag and threw his arms wider.

He loved her smile but it was her lipstick which made him excited. They embraced with feeling but as wonderful as it was, standing still in the cold made no sense so with an arm around his wife, the doctor walked her home.

Apart from the canines, he knew all the inhabitants and the greetings were warm with Victoria giving the doctor a hug with extra feeling. Coats off, they sat around the blazing fire.

They knew the Wellesley version of the proposal, wedding and honeymoon—although not the air-raid siren and what it interrupted—so Tom was "instructed" to give his version of events.

Louise worried. *Surely he won't mention the air-raid.*

Though lacking his wife's dramatic and storytelling skills, Tom's sincerity made the listeners emotional with not a dry eye in the sitting-room.

Louise disappeared and returned with a well-wrapped gift.

'I have a present for my husband,' she announced, bent to kiss him and said, 'Merry Christmas, Dr Curzon.'

He was delighted and remained the centre of attention as everyone watched him unwrap the present and hold aloft a pair of socks. Much laughter as Tom stood, kissed Louise and then mimicked her.

'And I too have a present for someone special.' He searched his bag.

'Me?' said Edmund. 'Tom, you're too kind.' More laughter ensued but stopped when Tom produced a wrapped item which was certainly not a pair of socks and handed it to Louise.

'Merry Christmas, Mrs Curzon.'

Again all eyes were on the recipient. What had Tom given his wife?

She removed the wrapping and gasped. She blubbed and put a hand to her mouth. She handed the gift to her mother and embraced Tom with a ferocity he found surprising.

Victoria gasped and Mrs Crossley and Edmund moved to see.

'Wow!' exclaimed Edmund. 'What a fabulous gift.'

'Is it your wedding?' asked Victoria close to tears.

It was a framed portrait of the couple at the reception soon after they were wed.

Tom won the award of son-in-law of the year. 'I have two the same. There's one for you Mrs Wellesley and another for my parents. But you, Mrs Curzon, that one's for wherever we make our home.'

Boy, did his comment stir emotions. The lunch was successful. Where Mrs C even found the ingredients was a mystery as was how she made them into such visually appealing and delicious-tasting creations.

The afternoon turned dark and Edmund played his role to perfection. 'What time is your train, Plum?' he asked giving the couple a reason to make tracks.

The farewells were as emotional as the arrival. The dogs were all over the new man in the family and wondered if Louise would be back soon for their next walk. They needed counselling when she didn't appear.

Arriving in London in late 1943 was still a scary experience. Germany might be in trouble elsewhere in Europe but still found time to drop bombs around the UK. Last January a primary school in Catford in London was bombed resulting in dozens of deaths.

The couple caught the Tube to Maida Vale and walked to the flat.

'I did tell you it's small,' she said.

'You did and your point is?'

'It's only a single bed.'

'No problem, we can take turns.'

He confused her. *Is he joking? What does he mean?*

'I'll sleep on you and then you can sleep on me.'

She slapped his thick army coat before he finished the sentence.

They dined magnificently on Welsh rarebit and weak tea then spent serious time trying to fit two adults into such a small bed.

Their trip to Henley on Boxing Day took longer than expected due to track damage. Louise worried if being late would upset her mother-in-law. But no, she was full of sweetness and joy greeting Louise as warmly as her son.

Gwendolyn and her children were there along with Gwendolyn's husband and Louise met her new brother-in-law, Oliver.

The room was buzzing but exploded when Tom performed his magic trick presenting his mother with the wedding photo. His family wanted to see what the bride was wearing and both the women knew Louise had worn her wedding outfit on her first visit to Henley.

Louise was biased but reckoned Mrs Crossley's spread outdid Esther's commendable luncheon. The conversation flowed both at the table and later over coffee.

Where did that coffee come from? thought Louise.

Later, Gwendolyn waited outside the lavatory and buttonholed Louise when she appeared. 'Just to let you know,' whispered Gwendolyn, 'you scored top marks from your in-laws.'

'Oh, how nice,' said Louise, embarrassed.

'As you now know, my mother is picky but winning high praise from the Captain herself is no mean feat. My father of course was besotted as soon as you stepped off the train.'

The women exchanged smiles and joined the others.

Louise wondered how she and Tom would make their move. He took control. 'Well, family dear, it's been a special Christmas and I hope the first of many with our new family member.' He smiled at Louise who counted another reason why she'd been so lucky in love.

'Hear hear,' said the other males.

Nine year-old Carter couldn't help himself. 'Hear hear,' he said, not understanding but in such an endearing voice, his grandmother was silenced until Tom took control.

'Thank you, Mother for a splendid meal and everyone for welcoming Louise into our family but now I must gather my lovely bride and bid you all adieu.'

Esther wanted details. 'Have you far to go, Thomas? It's nasty weather you know.'

'We're heading back into town, Mother and then tomorrow we're off on the honeymoon we never had.'

Esther again wanted more details but her husband was helping Louise with her coat and Tom was farewelling his sister and her family. The time for idle chat was over.

The whole family stood in the bay window of the front room and waved with Tom and Louise smiling and waving back.

They reached the station in good time and sat close inside the carriage. Tom already knew his wife was a hit with his family and moved onto another topic. He spoke intimately aware of other passengers.

'I'm not so sure about the heating in your little flat, my dear.'

'It's actually *our* little flat. Edmund kindly gave it to me and as I understand the institution of marriage, what's mine is now ours.'

He kissed her. 'How wonderful but getting back to the heating.'

'I thought you could keep me warm. Didn't you know? It's why I married you.'

'Again I'm grateful and glad but one question remains. Will it be too cold for you to wear your little black nightie?'

She found another reason to love him and they hurried onto the Bakerloo Tube and alighted at Maida Vale.

It was cold even inside the flat but the proposed supper of another round of cheese on toast was suspended in lieu of keeping warm in a single bed. It was tricky but they managed—several times.

Their honeymoon was to wander around London despite the weather, dine out in the cheapest of cafes and spend time together. There were no foreign sights or skiing activities to stop it being the best of times.

Louise wanted to ask questions about Tom's army future. The more she delayed, the more her anxiety levels rose. On their last night as they lay entwined in the single bed, he broached the subject.

'I'm worried,' he said.

'Oh, and what about?'

'I'm worried my wife won't ask me about my future in the US Army and if she doesn't ask, I'll be unhappy.'

She hugged him even more. 'Thank you,' she whispered. 'I'm scared. I love you so much I can't bear to think anything horrible will happen when you go with the invasion force.'

'Invasion force?' he sounded surprised. 'What would my brilliant actress wife know about war and especially in another country?'

Louise shuddered inside. Her secret life kept coming back to haunt her. Tell Tom and hurt him for not taking him into her trust. Not tell him and feel guilty again and again.

'All I want is you to be safe. I know you can't tell me where you're going or when but I'm not sure I could bear it if I lost you.'

He knew she suffered. He kissed the top of her head. 'I promise I will be as careful as possible and when we win this damn war, I'll send you a photo of me waving a flag from the top of the Reichstag.'

It was a hollow promise and both knew it. They tried to forget tomorrow and lived instead for the moment.

Louise tidied the flat while Tom showered and shaved. He was off.

They would travel to the city together and separate, he to Southampton and she to Farnham. Their conversation was limited and mostly banal. Neither wanted to say goodbye and Louise reckoned she was ready to burst—her tears had formed a reservoir.

She went with him to his station which was packed with troops heading back to their units after Christmas and New Year.

He tried talking about anything other than his departure. 'I want a full report on my wife the movie star.' She smiled. 'I'll write whenever I can and if you can spare the time, a line to my parents I'm sure would be much appreciated.'

A stationmaster's voice rose above the chatter and clatter of a busy London station.

'My train, my darling.' They kissed and she struggled. 'Give my love to your family and the dogs.' She managed a weak smile as he picked up his bag and walked to his train. She waited. It started and she moved close. He fought with other troops to find a space by an open window. He blew her a kiss and she waved and wept in unison.

The smoke and steam blocked her view and she turned to start her journey back to Farnham.

Will I ever see my husband again?

Chapter 24

The world and its mother knew the Allies were preparing to invade Europe. There seemed to be more Americans in Britain than there were in the United States and they weren't there on holiday. A serious game of bluff or cat and mouse was being played.

The Allies wanted to fool the Germans as to where and when the invasion would take place. The Germans tried every spying trick they could to discover the truth.

With the date and venues decided, Tom and his unit were given instructions. Specifics were verboten but the training the troops rehearsed involved leaping from landing barges and scrambling up beaches. Of course an army doctor wasn't an infantryman meaning such activities were not for him.

He and his fellow doctors would bring up the rear.

Louise knew that but being a veteran SIS and SOE agent knew too how booby traps, misdirected bombs, collaborators and friendly fire were often daily events in a world war.

When the filming of *Aventure Malgache* began, she had something to take her mind off her husband's safety. Her role was small, the experience fascinating and possibly life-changing. Dickie Graves had encouraged her to try different ventures.

'You never know what you'll learn from a new project and what it might lead to in the future.'

The film was created in a London studio and Louise based herself in her London flat. Being line perfect, her short scenes were never held up because a performer forgot or stumbled.

During a break, Anna the woman who dealt with performers at the audition, sat beside Louise and they shared a cuppa.

'This is your first film,' said Anna knowing that already.

'Is it so obvious?' replied Louise.

'Not at all, you're the consummate professional and Mr Hitchcock admires you. But you probably don't know all your good work may come to nothing.'

Louise was shocked and her face showed it.

'Broadly speaking the three stages of making a film are preparation, shooting and editing. After filming, the director and editor will spend time putting the film together and then decide if changes are needed. Scenes or bits of scenes may be cut and your excellent work could finish up on the cutting-room floor.'

Louise's stomach dropped. *I will have my family and friends come to the cinema expecting to see me on the huge screen and instead, I'll not be there. How embarrassing would that be?*

Anna patted Louise's arm. 'But don't worry. Whatever the final print may be, you have one pretty impressive credit on your CV.' Louise wasn't so sure. 'You've been directed by one of the world's best.'

Back in front of the cameras, she continued to perform. She needed to be told how stage acting usually if not always required projection. On a film set, the microphone above her head could capture even her breathing.

Mr Hitchcock hopped out of his chair and stood close to Louise. 'I think you may be trying too hard, my dear,' he said. 'You're a natural actress. Be yourself and let the words carry you along. Forget about the chap sitting in the back of the stalls. Speak to the person in the camera.'

Louise thought she knew the routine and the scene was shot again.

'Much better,' said the director, 'in fact perfect. Thank you, ladies and gentlemen.'

As Louise walked off the set, she saw Anna who winked.

Her next filming, her last, was not until next week. Louise went home to Farnham with Mrs C, Victoria and Edmund all keen to hear what happened. To them Louise was, well, Louise. They'd known her all her life but working in the world of movies with a famous director didn't diminish their fascination with her new career.

'Mr Hitchcock gave me sound advice today although Anna his assistant made me sad when she told me about editing and the cutting-room floor.'

No-one followed so she explained. Edmund reacted angrily.

'But that's nonsense. You do what's required and then they wipe you.'

'That's the movie business, Eddie but at least they pay me regardless of my screen time.'

Next morning, despite the cold, she rugged up and the dogs were their usual tail-wagging excitement machines.

'Be careful of the ice, Louise,' called her mother.

'I will,' she called back. 'Come on you two. Larry, that's not how a gentleman behaves.'

Being young, the dogs had more energy than sense and when she let them off their leads they tended to run anywhere. The country lane was hard due to the winter temperature. Having seen a rabbit, Larry dived into a hedge. The bunny disappeared leaving Larry confused. He tried to return but couldn't. He yelped and Louise naturally went to his aid.

'Stop struggling, Larry.' The pup grew more agitated. Louise struggled and trying to grab the dog she slipped. Her shoulder hit the ground and it hurt. She managed to kneel and then she vomited.

Lily was by her side and Larry managed to wriggle free. He saw the vomit and decided it would make a tasty snack.

Louise yelled. 'Larry, no! Get away.'

Both the dogs were not used to their mistress being on the ground or worse, yelling with a serve of anger in her voice. She stood, kicked snow over her vomit, put the dogs back on their leads and headed for home.

'What's happened to you?' asked Mrs Crossley with concern.

'Nothing, except Larry needed catching.'

Victoria arrived and saw her daughter a tad scruffy as if she'd had a fall. 'Oh Louise, I warned you about the ice.'

'I'm all right, Mummy. I need to keep Larry on lead until he becomes a bit less silly. Now if you'll excuse me, I have a letter to write to a certain man in my life.'

'I'm here,' called Edmund. 'No need to write.'

In her room she knew what to say to Tom including all the film-making events minus the cutting-room floor episode. Falling over

174

outside and being sick were minor matters and she knew he'd worry and want a more detailed diagnosis, symptoms and remedies. He had enough on his mind so she settled for telling him how much she loved and missed him.

Coming downstairs, she announced her latest move. 'I'm going to post a letter to Tom.'

Her mother came after her. 'Louise, no, you've already hurt yourself. Stay and keep warm.'

'It's all right, Mummy, I'm not taking the dogs.'

Victoria knew her daughter was in a difficult place. She was so in love and yet separated from her husband with him facing the prospect of going into a war zone.

She posted her letter and walking along the High Street glanced across the road and spied the surgery of the local doctor. She had first been treated by Dr Peoples when a toddler. She crossed the road and entered the reception area.

'Miss Wellesley,' said Mrs Peoples, the doctor's wife and receptionist.

'Good morning, Mrs Peoples.'

'We haven't seen you for ages. How is your family?'

'We're all well, thank you.' Before she could continue with family news, the elderly doctor came into the room.

'Miss Wellesley, the famous actress; how lovely to see you my dear.' They shook hands. 'My wife and I went to the performance in the church hall all those years ago and we were thrilled with your performances.'

'We were,' said his wife. 'Dr Peoples still talks about that night.'

'You're both awfully kind and I wonder if I could make an appointment please.'

He gestured to his room. 'It's made on the spot, now please step into my surgery.'

She did and the room brought back memories of all those activities like a thermometer in your mouth, a stethoscope on your chest and, horror of horrors, a needle being pushed into your arm. Louise remembered crying so well she thought a prize would be forthcoming.

'Now, my dear, what seems to be the trouble?'

'Walking the dogs this morning, I had a fall, Doctor and have a small bruise or two but I vomited.'

175

'I see. Anything like this happen before?'

'No, Doctor.'

'Any other pains or changes to your health?'

'I've had a change to my lifestyle. I'm married.'

The medical man's face lit up with a sparkle in his eyes. 'How wonderful and many congratulations. Tell me about him.'

'He's like you, Dr Peoples, Dr Tom Curzon and he's away serving as an Army Doctor.'

The medical man wagged a finger. 'Well you tell him from me, he's a very lucky man.'

'Thank you, Doctor. May I ask if you could examine me please?'

'Of course but let's talk about your health first. Have you missed your monthly period?

'Yes.'

'Just the one?'

'I think so. I mean my next is due this week.'

'Determining if a woman is pregnant is an ancient art. One rather quaint method involves injecting the woman's urine into a frog.'

She thought he was joking.

'It's true,' he said, 'but after 50 years practising medicine I still rely on observation. If you have missed two periods and certainly three, your chances of being pregnant are high. If you add morning sickness and a bulge in your abdomen, I think the term is "London to a brick".'

'Why did I vomit this morning?'

'It may well be because you are in the early stages of pregnancy.' He paused and wasn't sure about asking his next question. 'How do you feel about that?'

She put her hand to her face as tears formed. 'I think I have never been so happy and can't wait to tell my husband.'

He enthused then gave her a basic check-up. 'Why don't you come back in a fortnight and we can monitor your progress. I'd wait until then so as to be sure it's not a false alarm.'

He smiled and escorted her back to reception.'

'My dear, wonderful news as Miss Wellesley is now Mrs Tom Curzon and her husband is a doctor.'

'Oh congratulations, my dear and I can recommend a doctor for a husband.' All three laughed, Louise made another appointment then went home with a spring in her step.

She joined her mother in the sitting-room. 'You were a long time, my dear.'

'Yes Mummy, I went to see Dr Peoples.'

Instantly serious, Victoria dropped her magazine. 'Why?'

'I'm fine but he wants me to return in a fortnight.'

The mother spoke in a soft but clear voice. 'Are you pregnant?'

Louise hesitated. 'Possibly.'

Victoria moved to sit beside her daughter. She held Louise's hand and they studied one another. Louise rested her head on her mother's shoulder and quietly, both shed a tear.

They agreed to say nothing. Edmund reckoned something was up and Mrs Crossley was sure she knew.

A fortnight later she sat in the surgery with the local doctor.

'I told my mother, Dr Peoples but no-one else.'

'Well done and what's the latest news?'

'I missed my second period, I've been feeling sick and I'm sure I have a small swelling.'

'Well let's have you on the bed, my dear.' He examined Louise. 'I guess I've only examined about a thousand pregnant women in my career as a doctor and on such a basis, I'm prepared to say you are expecting your first child. Congratulations Mrs Curzon.' He helped her to stand.

'To be sure of your diagnosis, I was wondering, if you have any frogs in your cupboard?'

He roared with laughter and his wife and two patients outside wondered what on earth was so funny.

'Now there are certain rules for you, young lady. No heavy lifting, plenty of sensible eating and sleep and no alcohol. Take life easy.'

'Is walking the dogs all right?'

'Of course, keep moving but don't let the dogs walk you. Are you able to see your husband?'

'I'm hoping soon because I fear if this invasion we're all hearing about happens, he may be posted to somewhere in Europe.'

There wasn't much Dr Peoples could say about the war. 'When you become bigger, I'll make house calls to see you're okay.'

'Thank you ever so much, sir.'

'You're welcome, my dear. Now you take care.'

She smiled at Mrs Peoples who gazed expectantly. When Louise nodded with a smile, the elderly lady gave a busy soft clap of her hands.

Tom opened the latest letter from his wife and shouted.

'Good news, buddy?' asked his colleague from Arkansas.

'Great news, my wife is expecting.'

'Hey, congratulations man. Is it a boy or a girl?'

'She doesn't say but the little one is due in September.'

'And where will you be when the babe arrives?'

The conversation stopped. Tom worried he'd be in France in a field hospital up to his elbows in blood as wounded men were carried in missing limbs, blinded or dying on a stretcher.

Tom wrote to Louise telling her of his excitement and joy. He promised he would try to get leave and certainly before any major move took place with his unit. He thought about adding a so-called joke, "Do you know who the father is?" but decided against it.

She loved his note and settled in a special chair recommended for expectant mothers. Victoria and Mrs Crossley sat opposite both knitting small items of clothing.

It was a time of waiting.

Chapter 25

BRITISH Intelligence worked its socks off to convince the Germans the invasion would be at Calais, the south of France, even Scandinavia, anywhere but the Normandy beaches. Movie studios built fake tanks and aeroplanes which were housed in Kent. British spies pretending to be German spies sent all manner of reports to steer the Abwehr in the wrong direction. Newspapers printed false reports of American troops fighting over women in pubs located in areas where troops would disembark for Calais. The aim was to have as few Germans and as few tanks as possible near Normandy when the invasion took place.

One lucky break occurred on the day of the invasion. Hitler was having a lie-in and his underlings knew he hated being disturbed. So as the allies stormed ashore at Normandy, the German dictator was snoring away and it took hours before his tanks were ordered south.

Originally the D-Day landing was set for June 5, 1944 but the chap in charge of the weather forecast overruled all those heads of state and 3 star generals and D-Day became June 6.

Tom was granted leave not so much because his wife was expecting but more so because he was about to be a part of the largest amphibious landing in military history.

Louise received his letter about coming to Farnham and told the wee one inside her womb, 'Your Daddy's coming on Saturday. You must be on your best behaviour.' And as if to indicate understanding and agreement, he or she gave mother a polite but definite kick.

Victoria put her foot down when Louise announced she would go to the station. At nearly six months, her body shape clearly announced she was expecting, and even walking around the house and garden was no easy task.

'Don't be silly, darling. Tom will be unhappy if you do such a thing. He's a fit young man and the most important person is your baby.'

Louise surrended and, on the appointed day, sat in the garden in the summer sunshine waiting for her husband.

She heard the front gate and went to stand. 'Wait!' said Edmund sitting beside her and both the dogs froze.

Tom knew to use the back door, stepped into the rear garden, threw his bag on the ground and hurried to his wife. He helped her to stand, kissed her briefly then admired her bump.

'So it really is true,' he said laughing then kissed her properly.

'Don't mind me,' said Edmund and Tom greeted his brother-in-law. Then Victoria and Mrs Crossley came outside and more greetings of delight took place.

At lunch, the mood was bitter sweet. Louise, was thrilled to have Tom at home yet knowing he was probably going into the lion's den across the Channel allowed a cloud of sadness to hover above the table.

'Now this invasion, Tom, what can you tell us?' asked Edmund.

'Even if I knew anything, I'm not allowed to say. All the troops and officers feel we're like mushrooms being kept in the dark. But with the mass movement of troops and the visits from the top brass to address them, I'd say it's sooner rather than later.'

The cloud of sadness sunk lower.

Tom had only two days leave and because of Louise's condition, they opted to go nowhere other than trips around the garden. In her room at night, she lay in his arms.

Do you want a girl or a boy?' she asked.

'I want a healthy child and a safe delivery for you,' he said and kissed her gently on the head.

'What about names? What are your favourites?'

'How about Buttercup for a boy and Caractacus for a girl?'

She wanted to slap him but didn't have the energy. She found she slept longer these days.

'When the baby comes, how can I contact you? *Can* I contact you?'

'Well there won't be a postman on a bicycle but there's always a way to get messages through.'

She hesitated. 'Do you remember your promise?'

'Of course but which of the one hundred and three do you mean?'

She loved the way he teased her. He knew she worried and tried to make light of what might be a frightening and catastrophic future.

'Go to sleep, Mrs Curzon and I'll wake you when it's time for your morning sickness.'

She loved him and loved having him home.

He said goodbye to Victoria, Edmund and Mrs Crossley first then walked with his wife to the front gate. You didn't need any stirring and emotional music to set the scene. They both knew they may never see one another again. If Tom is killed, Louise would be bereft and their child would never know its father.

Their kiss was short but their embrace went on and on. Tom released her, kissed her forehead, picked up his bag and left. At the bend in the road, he turned and waved. Of course she was still there and waving. Then he was gone.

Once the invasion began, the press embargo was lifted and the newspapers and wireless were full of it. The Farnham family listened to BBC reports then read and re-read newspapers.

Tom's letter arrived after the invasion saying he was off in the morning. That was several days ago. His news was old and there was nothing anyone could do to communicate.

The invasion was successful but not without cost. The Americans at Omaha copped a fearful pasting with thousands of casualties. Louise wondered if Tom was helping those poor men.

She kept growing. Dr Peoples dropped in to check on her progress and the date of her delivery drew ever closer.

'I'll have Mr Hazelmere give you a call Mrs Wellesley and he'll come with his odd-looking taxi and take your daughter to hospital.'

The senior doctor knew everyone in and around the town.

Victoria was to travel with Louise, and Mr Hazelmere arrived on time. She was so large her brother asked if she was having twins.

The ladies arrived at the hospital, the same one in which Charles Wellesley died attended to by a young doctor named Thomas Curzon.

With Louise settled in the maternity ward, Victoria kissed her daughter and went to find the taxi driver to go home. Two hours after she arrived, the phone rang and Victoria struggled to speak.

'What do you mean she's had the baby?' Edmund and Mrs Crossley dropped everything. The nurse explained.

'It's a girl, Mrs Wellesley, and mother and baby are well. The little girl is 7 pounds, two ounces.'

'I can't believe it,' gasped Victoria staring at the others who came into the hallway. She put her hand over the receiver. 'It's a girl, 7 pounds 2 ounces.'

'Would you like to know her name?' asked the nurse.

'Of course, I mean, yes please.'

'It's Victoria Jane Curzon.'

This time Victoria really was speechless.

'Feel free to visit any time before 8, Mrs Wellesley.'

Victoria gathered her emotions. 'Thank you, I will. Goodbye.' She replaced the receiver. 'She's named the baby Victoria Jane.'

Mrs Crossley twigged. 'That's you and your mother.'

'Well done, Plum,' added Edmund.

Victoria fussed. 'I must ring Mr Hazelmere and change my dress. She left in a hurry. Having changed, she booked the taxi and then rang her first born.

'Henry, it's your mother.'

He panicked as his mother rarely rang. 'What's wrong?'

'Louise has had a baby girl, Victoria Jane.'

Henry relaxed and copied his brother. 'Well done, Plum.'

'Can you find a way to contact Tom?'

Tricky because apart from his sister, no-one in his legal chambers knew he worked in military intelligence. In fact he'd been a part of *Operation Fortitude* designed to mislead the Germans as to the D-Day landing sites.

'He's in the US 1st Infantry Division isn't he?'

Victoria knew. 'Yes, he is.'

'I could try a few contacts but I can't make any promises, Mother.'

'Please do your best, Henry. This is your new niece we're talking about and your brother-in-law surely needs to know.'

'Leave it with me and give my love to Plum.'

He rung off and went to see a colleague he thought knew someone in the War Office who might be able to help. He did and eventually Henry was given a name and address in London. He reckoned asking such a favour over the phone wouldn't work so set off from his office.

'He crossed London and entered a building used by the US Army. He showed his MI6 ID and was sent to a room where uniformed people worked at desks and was directed to the man in charge.

Henry went through his story which he considered perfectly simple. 'My brother-in-law's a British doctor serving with the US 1st Infantry Division. He's become a father. Can you please get a message to him with the news?'

The man with a badge showing the name Lieutenant Cradle on his jacket appeared sheepish.

'Is there a problem?' asked Henry more serious than worried.

'We've had reports of an incident involving that Division, sir.'

'What sort of incident?'

'It was a serious raid with casualties.'

'Jesus,' breathed Henry feeling sick. *My baby sister becomes a mother and a widow all on the same day.*

'My brother-in-law is Major Dr Thomas Curzon. Now can you please check the casualty list and tell me if he's on it?'

'We don't have a complete casualty list as yet, sir. Things were pretty chaotic out there.'

'What happened? Germans got lucky?'

Officer Cradle turned a whiter shade of pale. 'We believe it was a case of friendly fire.'

Henry lost it and screamed. 'Friendly fire?' Everyone in the room stopped to observe. 'Dr Curzon was born in the US to English parents. He's lived most of his life here. Your mob asked him to serve as a medical officer in the US 1st Infantry and he agreed. He goes to France to save the lives of your men and you repay him by dropping a bomb on him the day he becomes a father for the first time.' Now he raged with his sarcasm and anger in freefall. 'Any tips on what I should say to his wife? Sorry Missus, your old man joined an army that can't read the map of a fucking drop zone.'

Cradle sweated. 'We'll have the casualty list by tonight, sir.' Henry boiled. 'In the meantime, sir, I must ask you to say nothing of the incident.'

Henry produced his MI6 ID. 'I signed the *Official Secrets Act* Sunshine before you enlisted.' He put his business card on the desk and scribbled his mother's telephone number on it.

'I expect a call to that number the moment you have a complete casualty list from the American cock-up in France. Are we clear?'

Cradle nodded. 'I'll see to it myself, Mr Wellesley.' He re-read the card and hurriedly corrected himself. 'I'm sorry, I mean, My Lord.'

Henry stared at him and the others and stormed out.

Back in his office, he rang his wife and explained about her sister-in-law having given birth. Georgina could not have been less interested.

'I'll be working through the night so please give the children a kiss from me. Goodbye.'

He collected the always packed overnight bag in his office and set off for the next train to Farnham.

It was getting dark when he knocked on the back door, opened it and called. 'It's only the prodigal son.'

The dogs were most interested. His mother, brother and the housekeeper appeared.

'Henry,' exclaimed his mother instantly anxious.

He kissed her. 'Nothing to worry about, Mother. I've come to check on my new niece.'

He didn't sound convincing and they retired to the sitting-room. A cup of tea magically appeared. 'Thank you, Mrs C.'

'Henry, something's wrong, I can tell you're hiding something. Please tell us what is wrong.'

'You're right, Mother. This is what I know. There was an incident with Tom's unit and they think he's been wounded.'

Victoria and Mrs Crossley gasped.

'How badly?' asked Edmund himself a victim of war.

'They're still trying to obtain full details. I've given the Americans this number and told them to telephone me here. I'll stay the night if necessary. I'll tell Plum once we know the facts.'

'What happened?' asked Edmund, 'or can't you say?'

Henry's expression told Edmund all he needed to know.

The older brother had still not recovered from the friendly fire news and tried to keep his cool for the sake of the others and certainly for his baby sister.

'So Plum and the baby are both doing well and the little one's named after mother and grandmother?' he asked.

That decision thrilled Victoria but all she could think of was her daughter and the possibility she was a mother and a widow.

The phone remained silent and Henry took control. 'There's nothing to be gained sitting here in the dark. Go to bed, all of you, I'll nap on the settee and if there's news, well, you'll hear the phone.'

They did as it rang. Henry was up and ready for whatever news was to be delivered. Heart beats increased. He lifted the receiver.

'Hello? Henry Wellesley speaking.'

'Henry?'

Shock hit him. 'Plum?'

The others died.

'What are you doing in Farnham?'

Henry needed to think fast. 'I was in the area and heard I've become an uncle. Well done, old girl, absolutely top hole.'

'And I'm glad I've caught you. Any chance you could make enquiries about how Tom is getting on? Surely there must be a way to tell him he's a father.'

'I'm happy to help, old girl. You take it easy and here's Mother.'

He placed a finger to his lips ordering his mother to say nothing about the real reason he was in Farnham.

Victoria spoke. 'Hello darling. How are you and little Victoria?'

Off went Louise talking about every minute change which had happened in the last three hours. 'What a wonderful surprise to have Henry drop in. Is he staying?'

'Yes but only overnight.'

'I'd love to see him. Tell him he must come to the hospital before he leaves.'

'I will my darling. Now you get some rest and I'll see you in the morning. Good-night my darling.'

She hung up and the room fell silent.

'Henry, she wants you to visit her in the hospital before you leave.'

Now that could be tricky. The young mother is on a high, thrilled her big brother's in the area not knowing he'll be coming anyway; and with a message.

Chapter 26

It was nearly midnight and in the Wellesley household no-one was asleep. In each bedroom, the occupant listened with one ear. Who could sleep? Henry stirred fitfully on a settee. Mrs C had given him a blanket. Then the phone rang. Henry ran and the other three residents arrived with the women pulling on their robe.

'Henry Wellesley speaking.'

All the others could hear were Henry's comments.

'That's all right, thank you for calling.' ... 'So definitely wounded?' ... 'And you're absolutely sure it's Dr Thomas Curzon?' ... 'When will it happen?' ... 'I understand.' ... 'Thank you Lieutenant, I appreciate your work.' ... Goodnight.'

'He's alive,' he said and the combined sigh sounded loud. Victoria silently wept.

'I'll make tea,' said the housekeeper and disappeared.

The others hung on Henry's words. ''It might actually be good news if being wounded in battle is ever good; apologies Eddie. Tom copped fragments from a shell far from the front line.'

'How?' demanded Edmund. 'Behind the lines he should be safe.'

'Don't ask. He was hit in his left shoulder and has already been operated on.'

Victoria still suffered thinking of her daughter. 'How can it be good news?' she asked.

'There's a good chance he'll be sent home. A doctor with only one working arm might do more harm than good. Patients needing life-saving surgery don't want a quack with an arm in a sling and a bloodied bandage round his head.'

'His head?' exclaimed Victoria.

Henry raised his hands. 'Not literally, Mother. They may, *should* send him back to Blighty for rest and recovery.'

'He could stay here,' said Victoria her hopes soaring.

'I'll come with you in the morning to see Plum, Mother and let me do the talking.' The tea arrived.

Mother and son entered Louise's ward and her face lit up. She extended her arms as they got close and Henry gave her a hug and kiss.

'Who's a clever little Plum, hey? Well done you, old girl.'

'Good morning, darling,' said her mother kissing the new mum. 'Did you sleep well?'

'I did only because your granddaughter is a little angel.'

'So where is she?' asked Henry. 'I've come all this way so she can meet her favourite uncle.'

'She'll be here soon. She's due a feed.'

'Right,' said an uncomfortable Henry. 'I'll love you and leave you.'

'No you won't,' said Victoria. I'll visit the babies while you and Louise have a chat.'

He sat on her bed. His smart sister's instinct raised a red flag. 'What's wrong?' Her heart raced and she stared at him.

'There's a little bit of bad news and some absolutely brilliant news.'

Louise trusted Henry. 'Tom copped a bit of shrapnel in his left shoulder.' Louise gasped and tears formed. 'He's been operated on and is resting and they think he'll be sent home to recuperate.' He let her take it in. 'That's it, Plum. By the time you and the bub are home, the father of the century may already be there waiting for his wife and daughter.'

Louise couldn't stop the tears. The shock then relief knocked her sideways. He hugged her. A nurse arrived to see if help was needed.

Henry whispered. 'She's just heard her husband may be coming home earlier than expected.' Henry produced a handkerchief for his sister.

'I can't believe you would keep anything from me, Henry; you would never be cruel and not tell me the whole truth.'

'Cross my heart and hope to die. The rest of his handsome body is in fine working order including his undercarriage.'

She wanted to whack him but stopped as Victoria arrived pushing the crib with her namesake on board. Henry made an inspection.

'Blimey, she's as beautiful as her mother and grandmother combined.' He went to Louise. 'I'll be off old girl. I'll chase up Tom's situation and ring home with all the news.' He kissed her.

'Thank you, Henry, thank you for everything.'

He kissed his mother, blew a kiss to his niece and slipped away.

To say it was a day of high emotion would be an understatement.

Dr Curzon was shipped home looking worse than his injuries were. Co-incidentally, his father-in-law was wounded in the first War and both men could have swapped yarns about buried treasure; shrapnel lodged within their bodies.

Henry contacted the local Home Guard who acted with pride forming a guard of honour at the Farnham station, carried Tom's luggage and helped him aboard a local farmer's cart with its one horse power motor.

At the Wellesley home, they helped him alight. There was a nip in the air so his wife and daughter waited inside. Victoria and Edmund formed the family greeting party. They negotiated his arm in a sling then led him to the front door.

'The front door,' he said. 'I *am* honoured.'

Mrs Crossley opened the door, greeted the returning soldier then stood back as Tom walked into the sitting-room where Louise stood with a small bundle in her arms.

The young mother cried while her daughter slept.

Tom stopped in front of his new family. 'Hello Mrs Curzon and hello Miss Curzon.'

With a little difficulty, he held back his arm in a sling, leant in and kissed his wife then bent and kissed his daughter. It was a grand sight.

'Everybody sit,' ordered Edmund wheeling himself inside.

Tom wanted to know about the birth of his daughter. Louise wanted to know about the injury to her husband. Victoria purred with Edmund acting as referee.

Over lunch, Victoria tapped her cup. Everyone stopped. 'I have made a decision, two actually and I will brook no argument.' No-one dared speak. 'I am to move to Louise's bedroom and Tom, Louise and little Victoria will move to mine.'

'Mummy,' protested Louise.

'Plum, she said to brook no argument,' reprimanded Edmund and the matter was settled.

'Thank you, Mrs Wellesley,' said Tom, 'you are most kind.'

'Most sensible,' said Mrs Crossley. 'Now you mentioned two matters, Mrs Wellesley.'

'I did and for the life of me I can't remember ... oh yes, to avoid any confusion, I have decided to call my granddaughter Vicky which I do not expect any of you to follow.'

'Perfectly fine, Mother,' said her son. 'I'm thinking about calling you Mum.'

That comment broke the ice and laughter took over.

Everyone became involved in the room switch. The disabled males did their bit with private teasing. 'I never expected to have to manage my mother-in-law's wardrobe,' said Tom.

'Welcome to the Wellesley family, old man.'

'What's happening with your mobility?'

'I think I'm low on the list. Chaps are being smashed in Europe, as you well know, so fresh victims have priority, and rightly so. And yourself? Is it a case of physician heal thyself?'

Tom laughed. 'Like you, the military take responsibility for their members. I'm going to have to go up to London for my ongoing repairs.'

'If it's not dramatic surgery, why don't you pop along to a local doc? Our family chap has taken care of us for half a century.'

His comment got Tom thinking. He nodded. 'Thanks Eddie, I'll have a chat to the boss.'

Edmund smiled at his brother-in-law and they laughed as one.

'That'll get back,' he said, and they continued to pack items.

The new bedroom was far better for the young family. Baby Victoria's bassinet stood near the bed on Louise's side and the bed itself was spacious having served Louise's parents for decades.

Tom had to sleep on his back and Louise treated him with care. She snuggled into his non-wounded side.

'I'm sorry about your war wounds, Dr Curzon, but I'm thrilled to bits to have you home. And Vicky agrees.' She called to the sleeping infant. 'Aren't you darling?'

'Some men shoot themselves in order to escape the war.' She lifted her head with fear on her face. 'Not me, my darling. I was stitching a sergeant's hip wound when the bomb exploded.'

She kissed his cheek. 'Henry told me you didn't sustain any other injuries.' She was probing.

'He's right.' Tom turned his head to kiss her. 'You can take a peek under the bonnet if you like.'

'Stop it,' she whispered. 'You concentrate on getting back to your old self. Now there are rules about our new bed. If Vicky wakes, I'm the one who wakes. Okay?'

'So we're going with Vicky now are we?'

'I like it and Mummy wants it and it's her house so why not?' Louise turned off the lamp on her side of the bed. They lay there in darkness.

'Eddie suggested I see your local doctor about my shoulder?'

'Will the US Army allow that?'

'It's mainly dressings and Farnham's a lot closer than London.'

Louise thought about it. 'I told Dr Peoples all about my husband.'

'Did you now?'

'I said you were the best doctor in the world and would soon become the best father.'

Tom groaned. 'You need to wind back the rhetoric, Vicky's mum, although I agree with you as I too am thrilled to bits to be home.'

With baby Vicky in her new pram, Dr and Mrs Curzon set off for town as Louise had an appointment with the midwife. Two days a week the woman dealt with expectant and new mothers in a room as part of Dr Peoples' surgery.

The new family entered reception and Mrs Peoples came alive. She adored the baby but was delighted to meet the man with his arm in a sling. Dr Peoples appeared with a patient and finally met the new father and fellow physician.

'I'm delighted to meet you Dr Curzon. I feel as if I know you already thanks to your dear wife.'

The midwife appeared, met Tom then took Louise and Vicky away.

The two doctors chatted. 'I'm being treated by Army doctors up in London but my brother-in-law suggested, as I'm recuperating and only need dressings changed and a new bandage and sling, I should consider asking a local doctor to take over my care.'

'I'd be delighted but what would your employer say?'

'Why don't I ask them?'

'Excellent,' said the senior physician. 'Come and have a seat in my surgery and tell me about your situation.'

When Louise and baby appeared, the reception area was vacant.

'Your husband's having a chat with mine, dear. You know how men are such terrible gossips.'

They laughed and Louise took a seat. Tom arrived and with fond farewells to all, they headed out into the High Street. A few locals came up to Louise who had the task of introducing her baby and her husband. He stood back and admired the way his wife reacted to people. He reckoned her sincerity was natural.

They stopped outside a shop or two.

'Window-shopping, my dear?' asked Tom. 'What's that all about?'

'I'm choosing Christmas presents for our daughter. I can see you have a lot to learn about parenting.' Her reprimand was followed by a smile.

'Okay, it's my turn to push the pram,' he said and with only one free arm, did so all the way back home.

Louise received a letter from Dickie Graves. He enquired about her availability and if she was open to considering offers or willing to audition. He added his best wishes for the coming festive season and New Year.

She replied informing him about her newborn daughter and a wounded husband home from the war in France. "At the moment, Mr Graves, as much as I would love to be back performing, my family duties simply don't allow. Merry Christmas to you and yours and I wish you a happy and most importantly, a healthy 1945." Her letter made her agent sad. He believed audiences had yet to see the best of Miss Louis Wellesley.

She felt the same about her time with the SOE. She chose not to accept Colonel Buckmaster's offer of helping female recruits before they left for France. She certainly had the experience for the job but lacked the enthusiasm. When marriage and motherhood came along, any SOE activity faded from view.

Tom received a letter from the US Army requesting he attend a medical. He told Louise. 'I don't want to go. Dr Peoples did a first-rate job.'

'You don't want to go because they might pass you fit and send you back to war.'

She was spot on. 'Yes but it's a war which will be over next year.'

She gave him a gentle reminder and the week before Christmas he went up to London for a medical.

'This is an excellent job,' said the American physician. 'I can't believe you changed the dressings yourself, Doctor.'

Tom grinned. 'I'm flexible, sir.'

'So how's the shoulder?' he said gently moving it.

It was a change for the American to have a doctor as the patient. Tom gave a self-assessment. 'The wound has healed and the collarbone seems to have fused nicely. The only issue is stiffness and a bit of pain on cold mornings when the shrapnel comes out to play.'

The examining colleague listened but performed his own examination. 'How did a Limey get to serve in the US Army?'

'It's a long story.'

'Raise your arm above your head.' Tom did and winced at the top. 'How do you feel about being assessed as ready to resume service?' Tom went to speak. 'Don't answer. You need another month. Any questions?'

'No sir.'

'Get dressed. So what will you do once this damn war is done?'

'What I trained to do; help old people who are dying, pregnant women bringing new life into the world, and children who fall off a pony or out of a tree.'

The American signed the paperwork. 'Sounds great; good luck.'

All the residents at the Wellesley house were anxious for Tom's news. In the morning would he be off to France with its murderous bombs and bullets? Louise in particular struggled. Her tummy ached and she reckoned she could vomit on command.

'Officer on parade!' called former soldier Edmund spotting Tom coming through the garden. 'Stand by your beds!' Nobody laughed at Edmund's attempted humour or even moved when Tom stopped in the doorway.

'So what's for Christmas dinner?' he asked and relief exploded.

Louise moved to kiss him. 'What happened?'

'They've given me another month. You and Vicky will not be getting rid of me quite so easily.' More palpable relief interrupted by a baby crying. 'You'd think she'd be pleased Daddy was staying.'

Supper had an extra serve of happiness. Later, in their big bed in their big bedroom with Vicky sound asleep, her parents embraced one another. With his arm no longer in a sling, Tom found it easier to make love to his wife. She found it easier knowing he was getting better.

As they lay still, Tom calmly spoke. 'I've been meaning to tell you, I'm starting a new job tomorrow.'

'What?' Louise broke her rule of being quiet once the baby was asleep. Now she spoke softly but with fire. 'What new job?'

'I'm going to be a doctor?'

'Where?'

'In Farnham?'

'What!?

'My darling, may I suggest you remain still and quiet while I whisper the full story.' She forced herself to not speak. 'Dr Peoples has asked me to join his practice as a junior partner. I will work on Tuesday and Thursdays for a trial period of six weeks after which we will reconsider the arrangement.'

She leapt at him, kissing and hugging. 'Brilliant!' she said.

'My shoulder,' he whined and she instantly pulled back.

'I'm so sorry, Tom but it's the most wonderful news. When did all this happen?'

'Over the last few weeks. He's planning to retire and wants to do so gradually. He likes the fact I'm a local man.'

'Not to mention a brilliant doctor.'

'Thank you, now can I have that in writing?'

She snuggled in beside him. 'I have only one question.'

'Oh yes?'

'Can I be one of your patients?'

Chapter 27

Christmas Day, 1944 was cold, damn cold. Iceland gave generously of its icy winter donating chill winds to the United Kingdom. Mrs Crossley had a roaring fire going well before dawn.

This was the first Christmas for young Victoria Jane and my was she the star of the show. Lying on the floor, her favourite present was the wrapping paper and ribbon which once adorned the outside of the box which contained her new doll. She was a lot like her mother in so much as her acting took over. Vicky had no nerves or hesitation about performing. Who couldn't adore the newest member of the family?

Henry rang to wish his family a Merry Christmas. Tom rang his family and promised they would be there tomorrow. Mrs Crossley continued to work her magic in the kitchen.

Edmund proposed a toast. 'Here's to Christmas 1945 with the world at peace and when we'll enjoy the biggest plum pudding ever!'

Unanimous support greeted the toast. Lying on her rug, baby Vicky seemed to be trying to clap her hands. Clearly she was her mother's daughter.

The trip to Henley-on-Thames had to proceed. The Curzons had only ever seen photos of Vicky so with more wrapping around her than a room full of Christmas presents, the trio set off for the station.

Of course she was a hit in Oxfordshire. Vicky's cousins were still wearing straitjackets with their mother and grandmother on guard duty. The luncheon was pleasant but afterwards, when Vicky was placed on the floor and again became the centre of attention, Louise encouraged her nephew and niece to play a gentle game with their cousin. The youngsters seemed reluctant to come out of their shells but the clever actress teased and challenged them.

It was a joy to see hesitant youngsters become carefree and excited children. Their grandfather celebrated internally and encouraged them for all his worth. Oh dear, the genie was out of the bottle.

Going up to London, Tom nudged his wife. 'Getting Carter and Amelia to play was a work of genius.' He kissed her. 'Thank you. Now tell me; when is my wife returning to the stage?'

Louise had worried thinking by doing what she did with the children she was criticizing Tom's family. Then her mind went into a spin. *Is he encouraging me to return to acting? Is he serious?*

Tom's two-day working week worked like a dream. Patients admired him. Dr and Mrs Peoples knew they had chosen a perfect partner and the only problem was Tom being recalled to active service.

He discussed the matter with his boss. The elderly doctor decided to take a risk and, without telling anyone, wrote to the US Army. He fudged the truth. He pointed out how he was delaying his retirement until a replacement doctor was found. Dr Curzon was the perfect replacement and the hundreds of patients Dr Peoples had cared for since 1893—many of course had dropped off his list, permanently— would not have to travel far to see a doctor. Dr Curzon was their man.

Tom wondered why he'd not been called into London for his next assessment. Louise asked him about it. 'I don't know, my darling but I'm not going to chase them.'

When he mentioned it to Dr Peoples, the elderly man came clean. Tom wanted to hug him.

'There is a cost,' said the senior partner. 'You'll have to double your days at the practice.'

There was much rejoicing over supper in the Wellesley home when the news was shared. 'You're getting to be part of the furniture around here, old man,' said Edmund who rejoiced at the decision.

Hitler's madness explored new depths. Winning made him hop with joy. Losing saw him explode. The Russian and North Africa results were crucial. The Wehrmacht retreating back to base Berlin invoked insanity in their leader. Asking young boys to join the fighting troops was the final pathetic gesture of a tyrant.

On the day VE or Victory in Europe Day was declared, Vicky had progressed to her high chair and Louise was feeding her daughter when the news was announced on the wireless.

Edmund was working, assessing the brief of a Crown case in a forthcoming criminal trial when he heard the women in the house screaming and crying. In solidarity with her elders, a now frightened Vicky Curzon joined the howling and was consoled by everyone.

Tom returned a patient to the waiting-room where other patients and Mrs Peoples were hugging. He discovered the news and joined the celebrations.

Those expecting food and fuel to magically become available in copious quantities would be sorely disappointed but the silent guns produced tears of joy and mugs of beer throughout the land.

During the summer, the first since 1939 when peace last ruled the land, big changes were afoot. "Is Your Journey Necessary?" posters disappeared. People could travel. Closed theatres re-opened. The Old Vic needed major surgery but others were ready to raise their curtain straight away. The world had changed.

Dr Peoples was ready to hang up his stethoscope. Tom knew the retirement was coming but was surprised when the old man came into Tom's surgery. The younger physician tried the humorous line.

'Good morning, sir and what can we do for you today?'

'I think you well know, young man.' He pulled up a chair. 'I would be honoured if you would give an old doctor a quick once over before he becomes a patient in his former practice.'

Tom's heart beat faster. He was the one feeling honoured and took pride in examining his colleague making notes after each test. When finished, Tom sat at his desk.

'I know,' said the old man. 'My heart is slowing, my lungs are struggling and I can assure you my urination is getting slower and more tricky.'

Tom noted the patient's comments but said nothing of two other possible worrying signs he discovered. Today was not the day.

'Now my wife has ordered me to invite you and your good lady for Sunday lunch this weekend right after the morning service.'

'You're very kind, sir and over lunch you can reveal confidential stories about the family Wellesley.'

Tom smiled and Dr Peoples laughed with vigour.

A new routine settled in for families everywhere and most certainly in the Wellesley home. Tom became the busiest doctor in Farnham, Edmund buried himself in his room as a working-from-home barrister, Vicky found herself seated in a high chair and the only fly in the ointment was a minor clash between Victoria and Louise. Vicky didn't need two adults to care for her.

Victoria adored her namesake but as Louise was a full-time Mum, Grandma was surplus to requirements.

'Would you like me to feed her?' asked the grandmother.

'Thank you, Mummy, I can manage,' replied Louise.

The penny dropped for the actress. She was frustrated because she wanted to perform, to return to treading the boards. She had a live-in babysitter who adored helping raise the little child.

'I'm sorry, Mummy, she said. 'Of course you can feed Vicky.'

Should I explore the new world where theatres are opening and plays are being staged?

She wrote to Dickie Graves. He didn't reply but rang the next day. Louise's excitement kicked in, an excitement she knew well but had not experienced for an age; was it years?—the thrill of a new role.

'Thank you for your letter, Miss Wellesley. I was delighted to receive it and to learn you are coming out of retirement.'

She knew he was teasing.

'I will make it my business to find a role which suits your many talents.'

'Thank you, Mr Graves but please don't feel I should be given preferential treatment over any of your many talented clients.'

'Now that will never do, Miss Wellesley. I thought I explained when we first met how actors need to develop two things—a thick skin when rejection and sniping critics come along, and a cut-throat attitude driving you to walk over broken glass in order to win a part.'

She loved his continuing way of giving advice in the guise of a joke, thanked him and went back to check on a now sleeping baby. Studying her daughter, Louise wondered why she had not fallen pregnant again and at night asked her husband.

'There is no magic formula, darling girl. Fecundity can be elusive.'

She'd never even heard the word before and loved his explanation and him. She paused then popped the question. 'What would you say if I told you I was thinking about returning to the stage?'

'I would say, what took you so long?'

She experienced feelings of guilt not having been open with him but showed her gratitude by hugging him while not saying a word.

Vicky's first birthday loomed large. Being an only child meant she was in danger of being spoilt rotten. She *was* spoilt rotten. Only a week before her birthday, Louise and Victoria were both able to witness Vicky's first step. Step singular as she wobbled and collapsed causing her mother and grandmother to dissolve in tears.

Tom took a call at his surgery and worried. Why would his wife telephone in the middle of the day? When told his daughter had taken her first step, his celebration was internal but no less satisfying.

The father missed out on the first word as well. In fact it was Uncle Eddie who struck gold. Nearly a month after her much-celebrated birthday, the now mobile child, holding her grandmother's hand, appeared in the doorway of Edmund's bedroom cum office.

'Hello Vicky,' he said glad of a break from his work.

'We're having our morning walk,' announced Victoria.

'Excellent so why not come and have a chat to your favourite uncle?' He slapped his knees and Vicky didn't need a second invitation.

He picked up his niece, placed her on his lap, and nodded to his mother who left pleased to share the load.

Vicky was in the "grab anything not nailed down" stage and tried to pinch a pen. Edmund placed it out of range and, to distract the little one, reached for a framed photo on his desk. It was one of the three Wellesley siblings taken when his sister was a young lass soon to start boarding school.

Edmund pointed. 'There's Uncle Henry, and there's Uncle Eddie and there's your Mummy; there's Plum.'

Vicky entered the world of speech. 'Plum,' she said and Edmund nearly fell out of his wheelchair. He called, 'Hello. Anyone there?'

Victoria hurried thinking something awful may have happened. She saw all was well and now wondered why Edmund called as he did. 'Come closer, Grandmother,' he said and Victoria did so.

Holding the photograph, Edmund pointed to his sister and spoke to his niece. 'Vicky, who's that?'

There was a pause before the child thrust a finger at Louise and said, 'Plum'.

Grandma put a hand to her mouth and wanted to cry. Her slight unhappiness at her son teaching Vicky a nickname Victoria never liked was swamped by her joy at her now verbal granddaughter. Another generation educated in the family lingo.

Victoria called to her daughter and housekeeper. Both came quickly anxious to know why.

Edmund repeated the routine for all three women. As if knowing what the cue was, Vicky repeated her "speech" on demand.

The child was kissed and praised and Edmund explained how his first identification was Mummy which morphed into Plum. 'One syllable words are easy to learn. I think I'll now be Ed and Henry can be Hank.' The women were too busy praising the child to notice Edmund's attempt at being funny.

Vicky's father received another call at work and, apart from serious pride; his immediate response was to laugh.

The little girl took centre stage with news of her development the talk of the family. The Curzons were kept informed of her progress and Uncle "Hank"—you can imagine how his wife took to that bit of family news—laughed long and loud.

But it was Vicky's mother, the one forever to be known as Plum, who took her daughter's limelight with a call from Dickie Graves.

'I have a brilliant way for you to return to performing, Miss Wellesley,' he said with his listener starting to shake. 'The BBC are to record a radio play and there's a part I think which is ideal for you.'

Louise struggled to respond. 'That sounds interesting,' she said striving to keep a lid on her excitement.

It's obviously not a long run, you don't have to memorize your lines and you'll only be away from your family for a day or two.

'It sounds perfect.'

'Can I put you forward for an audition?'

'Please do, Mr Graves. I'll take whatever day and time you suggest.'

'Jolly good. The play is called *The Dark Tower* written in verse by the Irishman, Louis MacNiece. I'll call back with your audition details.'

'Thank you so much, Mr Graves.'

The news was wonderful, a clever and apt suggestion and any new challenge was always welcome. Excitement flooded her body and built to a crescendo.

Chapter 28

Travelling up to London, Louise kept moving her tongue to moisten her mouth. They weren't interested in her face or hands, but her voice. Finding the BBC building was easy and she ended up being met by an assistant who turned being unpleasant into an art form. The man was offhand, rude. What happened to "Good morning, I'm So-and-So?" He handed her an audition form.

'Fill this out and wait there,' were his only words. Charming.

'Next,' came a voice over a tannoy and the rude assistant took off with, 'This way.'

The change in manners could not have been greater as the writer of the play; Louis MacNiece stood and greeted Louise.

'Welcome Miss Wellesley, I'm Louis MacNiece and this is Mr Benjamin Britten who has composed the music for the play.'

Louise smiled and made a mental note of another famous person in the arts she'd been fortunate to meet.

'Here's your audition speech,' said MacNiece handing her a sheet and indicating a music stand which stood beneath a microphone. 'Have a read through and when you're ready, please favour us with your audition.'

Louise studied the text written in verse. Despite her years of performing in school plays, Parisian clubs and touring in the Welsh valleys, this was new. Her voice alone was being assessed. She thought about asking for advice on an accent but didn't.

They haven't mentioned an accent so here I go.

She placed the page on the music stand, took a deep breath and spoke. Remembering advice from Beauford Nightingale about tempo and pitch, she gave it her best shot. She finished and waited for a response from the two listeners. The playwright stood and smiled.

'Thank you so much, Miss Wellesley. We'll let you know.'

'Thank you, gentlemen,' she replied and headed for the door where Mr Rudeness stood. Louise stopped when the composer spoke.

'I see you've been touring with Tyrone Guthrie,' said Mr Britten.

'Yes,' replied a surprised Louise. 'It was Shakespeare in Wales.'

'How did you find the great man?'

Louise was thrown. 'Oh he was a wonderful director and a huge help to a young actress.'

'Good show,' said Britten and smiled his goodbye. Assistant Sourpuss suffered a Pauline type conversion. Tyrone Guthrie, hey?

She went out to Maida Vale to check on the flat and collect clothes then headed for home.

Coming through the back door, Louise was greeted by her mother holding Vicki's little hand. The granddaughter came alive when her Mummy arrived and called with excitement, 'Plum.'

If that wasn't enough to make the actress's day, it turned instantly better when Victoria spoke. 'Congratulations, darling.' Louise didn't understand. 'Mr Graves rang to say you've been awarded the part.'

It seemed like an age since Louise last performed. Her family were pleased, Victoria loved being in loco parentis, and Tom saw a new energy in his wife who couldn't wait to start rehearsing, and life seemed close to perfect.

Travelling up to London, she saw signs of the country re-building with the first serious Christmas decorations since 1938.

The BBC recording studio was crowded with people—actors, instrumentalists, technicians. Louise met the cast and caught the buzz, the excited atmosphere as instruments were tuned, arpeggios performed and actors rattled off vocal exercises with *me me me me meeeee* being a favourite.

'Quiet please,' called Mr MacNiece. He welcomed one and all, wished them success and left for the control room. His next words were via a loudspeaker.

The recording engineer spoke about where to stand, a few microphone tests were made, the importance of keeping quiet was repeated, and then a light appeared and Mr Britten raised his baton and conducted the opening of his score.

There was no live audience but the tension was real for the actors, for everyone. When it was not your turn, the pressure to remain silent was enormous.

When it ended, the collective sigh pushed the needles on the desk in the control room to new heights. It was like the curtain falling at the end of an opening night. Actors who barely knew one another hugged with people clapping and offering congratulations.

After Mr MacNiece told the company how delighted he was with the recording, he reminded them to listen on January 16.

Many prepared to head to a nearby pub to celebrate their work with Louise politely declining. She was ribbed for her reluctance by males who were keen to see her become tipsy.

Olga Lindo, the experienced actress who played the female lead, took her aside. 'Take no notice of them, love. Bunch of stage door Johnnies and a few fellas in the orchestra pit *are* the pits.'

'Thank you,' said Louise. 'I have a little daughter at home and I'd rather be with her.'

The leading male role was played by Cyril Cusack who in years to come would be the patriarch of a talented acting family. He interrupted and held Louise's hand. 'It was lovely to meet you Louise and I hope to work with you again.' He kissed her hand. 'Safe home.'

She did arrive safely home with her family keen to hear all about the play. 'You can hear it on the radio in January.'

Edmund butted in. 'Last year you said you were a star in Mr Hitchcock's movie. I blinked and missed you.'

The laughter didn't cover the thinking that Louise Curzon a.k.a. Louise Wellesley was now a serious performer recognized by professionals involved in theatre, film and now radio. How far would, could she go? And how many people in the world of entertainment knew about her life jumping out of planes in occupied countries, stabbing and shooting Gestapo officers, blowing up railway tracks and killing Nazis? Would the world ever discover her other career?

Christmas was joyous not only because peace ruled the world but because little Victoria was up and about and learning and speaking new words at a rapid rate. In the New Year, the whole family sat around the radio on January 16 to listen to Plum's performance. Vicky cuddled with Tom who kept putting a finger to his lips and whispering, 'Shhhh" as his chatterbox of a daughter was yet to understand her mother's other life.

When it was over, the family congratulated the actress. Edmund was effusive. 'Bloody marvellous, Plum and I still can't believe that was my little sister.'

'You were excellent, darling,' said Victoria and Tom put down his daughter who ran, yes ran to her mother.

1946 was off and running with the War beginning to fade in the distance. Louise had loved her taste of being back performing and now wanted more.

In bed at night, Tom heaped praise upon his wife. She waited until he finished, paused and then spoke.

'Tom I know you support me seeking more performing opportunities but I'm not sure about the practicalities.

'What's the problem? Your husband puts food on the table, your mother is the best children's nanny in England, and all you have to worry about is remembering your lines.'

She smiled in the darkness.

'But what if I'm in a show which is late finishing? There may not be a train to bring me home.'

'Spend the night in the flat and if you do come home, I'll be at the station to meet you off the train.'

A tear slid down her cheek. 'Thank you,' she whispered and made a mental note to telephone her agent in the morning.

Tom wasn't finished. 'Have you ever thought about teaching?'

He shocked her. 'Sorry?'

'You could give elocution lessons to young ladies wanting to speak well. Didn't you once tell me you went to finishing school?'

'I *did* go to finishing school. It's where I met Matilda.'

'Well there you are. Pop a notice in the High Street—*Mrs Curzon Elocution Lessons*. It'll give you something to do between acting jobs and you can make a little pin money on the side.'

This time Louise shed more than one tear.

She took her husband's advice and because she had become a notable Farnham resident—locals remembered her youthful performances but now her fame spread. The Farnham newspaper published an article with a picture about a local resident appearing in a BBC radio play.

'Miss Wellesley?' folk said. 'You mean Mrs Curzon the doctor's wife.'

So it was no surprise when would-be students responded to her notice in the post office window and soon she was teaching locals to project, pronounce and perfect their vowels, consonants and diphthongs.

Victoria had her hands full when the youngest member of the family wanted to help Mummy with talking.

Tom would come home to tales of the day's students. Most were young ladies seeking skills without having to travel to the continent and pay a fortune to a finishing school.

'Have you thought about giving French lessons?' asked Edmund.

She hadn't and with a waiting list for her elocution lessons, French never appeared on the agenda.

Louise enjoyed her teaching days but it didn't replace her love of acting. Vicky kept growing and it was in the summer when Richard Graves telephoned.

Finally she had a chance to audition for a play to open in the West End. The play was *An Inspector Calls* by J. B. Priestley who was a good friend of the actor Ralph Richardson. Unsurprisingly Mr Richardson was cast in the main role of Inspector Goole.

Louise went up to London to audition. Dickie gave her advice. 'You know the director, Basil Dean, but never as a director.'

'Mr Dean from ENSA?'

'That's the one. They say he calls a spade a spade but I have no concerns as you are such a dab hand at auditions. Just think of Mr Dean as one of those chaps you encountered in your other career and, of course, I wish you all the best.'

Basil Dean's reputation went before him. His bark was worse than his bite although that packed a punch as well. He welcomed Louise.'

'Miss Wellesley, it's lovely to see you again.'

He sounded sincere but Louise sensed the man remembered her as the actress who went AWOL from ENSA productions *twice*.

'And you, Mr Dean,' she said.

She met the playwright and leading man, Mr Ralph Richardson.

Louise was handed a page of dialogue and studied it while the panel waited. Dean couldn't hide his impatience. 'When you're ready, Miss Wellesley; there are others.'

She ignored his rudeness, moved closer to them as if to say, "If that's your best shot, try this on for size".

The moment she spoke, the trio and an assistant were hooked. Being beautiful obviously helped but the way she used her voice suggesting the character in the play for which she was auditioning, Sheila, grabbed her audience. They knew what they wanted in this role and Louise Wellesley was it.

She ended and stood there waiting. All three men huddled and whispered. Louise could only understand the odd word but knew they were discussing her audition. The conflab ended.

Priestley and Richardson stood and enthused, thanked her, and asked if her details were held by the assistant. Basil Dean, the director, was abrupt and told her they'd be in touch.

Travelling home, she remembered her last audition for the BBC radio play. She hadn't reached Farnham when Dickie Graves called with the news of her success. Would history repeat itself?'

It didn't and it was a week before her agent rang.

'I've bad news, Miss Wellesley. You missed out on the part I'm afraid but I heard you were most impressive.'

Victoria watched her daughter end the call and knew the result. 'Do they say why you missed out?'

'No, Mummy. Rejection or failure are two constants in the theatre. Some you win and some you don't.'

When Tom came home and heard the news, he kissed Louise and admired her stoicism. He knew she was unhappy inside but loved the way she didn't let the result drag her down. She had an ability to remain positive.

Up in London, rehearsals for *An Inspector Calls* began and the director was soon ruffling feathers. His nickname of Basil Bastard was well chosen although experienced actors like Ralph Richardson and Alec Guinness stood their ground or even hit back. But the young actress given the role Louise auditioned for became upset.

Two of the older actresses found the poor woman in tears.

'Now, now, dear,' said one. 'He's a bully but you mustn't let him get under your skin.'

'He said I can't act,' sobbed the lass.

'Well he doesn't know what he's talking about. You won the role because of your ability. Now don't let Basil Bastard grind you down.'

He did and two days later the director again exploded in the rehearsal shouting, 'No, no, no, I told you how to say that line. Why can't you remember a simple note?'

That did it. He'd broken the actress's spirit and self-belief. She made a dramatic exit and left the production with a vacancy.

Louise was listening to a young lady saying, "How now brown cow" when the phone rang and her mother answered. She interrupted the elocution lesson. 'Forgive me, my dear but there's a Mr Basil Dean on the phone.'

The brown cow wandered off to pastures new and Louise picked up the receiver. 'Louise Wellesley speaking.'

'Ah, Miss Wellesley, we've had a spot of bother with rehearsals for *An Inspector Calls*. Are you available to take the role for which you auditioned?'

Shock hit. 'Yes, yes I am, sir. Are you offering me the part?'

'Well I haven't rung to wish you Merry Christmas.'

'Of course not and especially as it's still only September.'

Basil realized his audition mistake. He went against Richardson and Priestley in rejecting Louise. He held a grudge believing she insulted him by twice going AWOL from ENSA and used the King and PM to back her. He hated her. She was clearly the best auditionee and now displayed her gumption unlike the unfortunate actress who ran away. Actually the runaway was a fine actress but Dean's brutal rudeness would damage many a young performer.

'You'll be required for 10 in the morning. Don't be late.'

Click. The line went dead.

Victoria appeared with granddaughter and Louise gave a forced smile. 'I need to pack, Mummy.'

Tom was thrilled but when they were alone gave his advice. 'I know acting is in your blood. Oh, and I reckon it's worth bottling.' He winked and she smiled. 'But work should never impact your health; badly I mean. Take on any challenge you want but never let it harm your body or mind.'

She kissed him.

206

In the morning he walked her to the station. Rehearsals were in the day and until the show opened, she would be home for supper.

The big losers were her elocution students. They were disappointed their teacher was absent and lessons cancelled but thrilled to know she would soon be performing in a London theatre.

She went out of her way to be early. She entered the theatre to be greeted by a shouting match. In the middle of the set, Brutal Basil, a new moniker, attacked the playwright and star.

'What is the point of having a director if he can't have the final say on all matters including the set? Well?'

'It's a consensus, Basil,' replied Priestley. 'Ralph and I have a vision which sees the whole thing being realistic.'

'Oh so now it's you *and* Ralph. It's two to one and I have to direct a play in a set I loathe. It's not a democracy, it's a benign dictatorship.'

Richardson saw Louise and moved downstage. 'Miss Wellesley?'

'Good morning,' she called from the stalls.

'Do come up.' The actor and playwright collected her and led her onto the stage. An assistant approached handing her a script.

It had the crossed-out name of the actress who quit and was filled with her entrances, bits of business, and what appeared to be tears.

'You've saved our bacon, Miss Wellesley,' said Priestley who couldn't stop smiling. 'Mr Dean believes the whole production will be better now you've joined us.'

Dean interrupted. 'I'll give you a week to hang on to your script.'

'A week!' exclaimed Richardson. 'We've been rehearsing for a month, Basil. Give the girl a break.'

Dean mumbled and other actors arrived and were introduced to the new girl. Dean made a speech welcoming Louise in which he included a jibe about her ENSA career. The man bore a grudge.

Rehearsals began and the former secret agent, nun and mountaineer, clutching her script, spoke her lines on time. Dean went to correct her pronunciation on a particular word and the glares he got from others meant his note was never given.

Chapter 29

What a month. On week days Louise went up to London adoring the challenge. The other actors were thrilled with their new colleague. She put down her script after a week impressing everyone. Brutal Basil Dean was pressured into thanking her in front of the entire company. Opening night raced towards them.

Tom was there with his parents as was Henry sans wife. Dickie Graves was there although his wife sadly was in a care home.

Louise received flowers and the dressing room she shared with other females resembled a small florist shop. Her nerves came out to play. "Break a leg" became a common expression. The ASM knocked on doors calling, "Beginners on stage please" and as the actors entered the wings they were met with the unmistakeable buzz—the sound of an audience before the first-act curtain.

The house lights dimmed, the stage lights came up, the curtain rose, and the British premiere of *An Inspector Calls* began.

Louise loved it. Playing with her daughter and giving elocution lessons were wonderful but the thrill of a live performance when working with fellow professionals was the spark in Louise's life. She wanted more. Once this play was over, she decided she wanted another audition and then another.

The audience seemed pleased. It was a long play, three acts, and the applause for the curtain calls was solid if not rapturous.

In her shared dressing-room, Louise accepted kisses as she removed her stage make-up. Many years ago, she enjoyed people congratulating her after she stepped in at the last minute to perform for the amateur theatre group, the St Peter's Players in Cambridge. It was an unknown play so badly cast it stood little chance of success. When most of the audience had gone, a man spoke behind her. It happened again about 8 years later, tonight. It was the same chap.

The foyer was crowded with friends and family members. Louise thanked people she didn't know until a man spoke behind her. 'I can recommend the cakes,' said Tom and his wife turned to be embraced.

'You remembered,' said his wife to be surrounded by Dickie and her in-laws. Graves stood back allowing Louise's family to have first dibs. They were effusive with her father-in-law already her biggest fan, kissing her with more energy than he ever kissed his wife.

Esther was beginning to warm to her son's choice of bride. How could she not? Louise was if not a star already then surely would be in the future with Esther hoping her daughter-in-law's fame might rub off on her.

The in-laws left and Tom met Dickie Graves. The agent used simple words describing Louise's performance in glowing terms. He didn't know how to gush. He kissed her and slipped away.

Henry sneaked in, kissed his sister, whispered, 'Brilliant,' and disappeared. Tom stood back as Louise accepted an endless stream of compliments. The director appeared and gave Louise an air kiss on each cheek.

He knew how to gush. 'Darling Louise, you were brilliant. I knew I was so right to cast you in the role.'

Louise ignored his balderdash.

'Mr Dean, may I present my husband, Dr Tom Curzon.'

Basil recoiled slightly. *She's married to a doctor!* The three chatted briefly on a shallow level before the brute slipped off to accept the fawning of anyone wanting to impress the man with power to make or break a career; or so he thought.

Tom gave his wife a one-armed hug and whispered in her ear. 'I'm sure it's past your bed time, Mrs Curzon.' She studied him and he spoke with his eyes.

They left with as little fuss as possible and took a cab to Maida Vale. Entering the flat, Tom despaired. 'Darn, I forgot to bring my pyjamas.' She laughed and they prepared for bed. Memories of their second honeymoon came flooding back. They were not as keen this time but often the older wine tastes better, much better.

Breakfast was basic as Tom started work at 9 and they needed an early train. Louise would have liked a lie-in because she was dog-tired after opening night and besides, the man with whom she shared the small bed was her absolute favourite.

They walked together from the Farnham station. Tom went to his surgery but Louise wanted newspapers. She resisted the urge to read the notices in the High Street and went home.

The greeting from two females named Victoria, an older brother, the housekeeper and two dogs took an age. Finally, finally she sat at the dining-room table and read the notices. Oh dear. Several critics attacked. One reckoned the script could be cut in half. Another declared only his self-control kept him from groaning declaring Mr Richardson to be a pitiful sight parading like some dummy.'

Not all reviews were negative and *The Times* opened with "Bang! Bang! Mr Priestley lets drive with both barrels.' Louise needed Dr Livingstone to find any mention of her good self. Still, as Mr Graves repeated, "Today's newspaper is tomorrow's fish 'n chips wrapping".

Tom rang home to see if his wife was taking it easy. She was in the garden with Vicky and the dogs and Victoria was told to convey doctor's orders meaning rest for his wife before going back to London.

The play having three acts meant if Louise was caught up talking to people after certain performances, she would find it difficult to catch a train and Tom insisted she stay overnight at the flat.

The play settled into its run. Louise was preparing in her dressing-room when a loud voice was heard. Alec Guinness sounded angry.

He came out of his dressing-room shouting. 'Who did this? Come on, own up. Who put my shoes in a bucket of water?'

No actor wants their costume or props damaged and to have anything go missing is a disaster. Alec's shouting continued.

'All right, all right, keep your shirt on,' cried Ralph Richardson.

'I might have known it'd be you.'

'Well I did warn you, old man. Those shoes squeak and the whole world can hear you walking across the stage.'

The actor with the wet shoes pointed at the leading man. 'You haven't heard the last of this.' But in fact he had. Richardson and Guinness were pals but there were consequences for Guinness as he missed two performances and needed to be treated for pneumonia.

Even the best actors are at times out of work. Louise had built an excellent CV with fine reviews from prominent directors and actors happy to sing her praises. Nevertheless she didn't step from one production into another. Her fall-back position was her teaching with no shortage of students all of whom were delighted to learn from the talented actress.

Vicky had an advantage in mastering speech. She was allowed to sit in with Mummy when Louise was teaching, provided Vicky sat still and remained quiet. Her doll received the same instructions.

'Daisy will be very quiet, Mummy,' promised the younger Victoria.

So here was a toddler in the early stages of speech development picking up new words, rapidly expanding her vocabulary and, at the same time, learning to pronounce the jolly things.

Of course many, probably most of the words meant nothing to a small child but the human brain is a wonderful receptacle and when your mother is intelligent and apples don't fall far from the tree, little Victoria Jane Curzon enjoyed a spectacular foundation to her education. Was this the foundation for an acting career?

The family was greatly entertained by Miss Curzon when she gave her rendition of "How now brown cow" although she did struggle with "Peter Piper picked a peck of pickled peppers."

Not everything Louise touched turned to gold. She joined the cast of the musical *The Nightingale*. She and the rest of the cast loved the show but unfortunately the theatre-going public did not. It closed after a few weeks whereas other shows, *Annie Get Your Gun* and *Oklahoma* ran for years.

Life went on and building and rebuilding became the norm. Britain played host to the 1948 Olympics and theatres badly damaged in the war were rising from the ashes. The Old Vic, absolutely smashed by German bombs underwent a remarkable revival. The venue announced a new artistic director with a specific goal.

Guthrie Tyrone declared he intended to stage every Shakespearean play over the next five years.

When Louise read the news, a shiver ran up her spine. That man directed her in a modest Shakespearean tour of Wales during the war. She was in the bus travelling with Mr Guthrie.

Would he remember me? Would he cast me in another play or plays by the Bard?

She contacted Dickie Graves who said he had already put out feelers and she was most definitely on his list.

Not only were theatres being rebuilt but the content was being changed. Kitchen sink drama was the label being applied to these new works replacing the glittering, upper-class drawing-room settings. Would the gritty plays attract an audience? Would people prefer catchy tunes, dancing girls and a happy ending to arguments and swearing by characters in grubby trousers and soup-stained vests?

A further test would come with the expansion of television. Another channel and more programmes. Why go out in the cold and wet when you can sit by the fire and watch a play on the telly?

Vicky, approaching another birthday and her first year at school, announced she wanted to be a performer simply by performing. Victoria and to a lesser extent Edmund, remembered Louise at Uncle Crispin's house full of cats doing her interpretation of Shirley Temple before the famous child performer was even born.

Talk about life imitating life. It was like mother like daughter and as the young child grew older, so too did her family. Well Mrs Crossley was as much a part of the Wellesley family as anyone.

Victoria took Tom aside. 'I'm worried about Enid,' she said. 'Will you have a word with her?'

'Of course.'

'Please don't make a fuss as she's a proud and private woman.'

Tom picked his moment and waited until the housekeeper was alone in the kitchen.

'Ah, my favourite housekeeper, how are you dear lady?'

'I'm well, Doctor and thank you for asking.'

'Forgive me for saying so, but I thought you appeared a bit off colour yesterday and ...'

'Mrs Wellesley has put you up to this, hasn't she?'

Tom smiled and surrended. 'She has but I do think it will be good if you have a check-up, prevention being better than cure.' She nodded. 'There is a lady doctor at the practice; she's there on Wednesdays and Fridays. How about I make an appointment?'

Mrs Crossley smiled and nodded. She wasn't well, hated making a fuss and was secretly grateful she was being pushed into taking action.

Dr Constance McBride examined the housekeeper and was so concerned she called an ambulance immediately to convey the woman to Farnham hospital. There she was subjected to various tests and the senior consultant declared her heart to be in danger of collapse.

Alas the range of treatments for heart disease was limited at the time—morphine for pain and bed rest or alternatively, bed rest. Tom and his mother-in-law came to visit their housekeeper. She of course was apologetic.

'I'm so sorry to be such a nuisance,' she said.

Victoria, always a woman of polite behaviour and restraint surprised Tom with her response being angry.

'Enid, stop all this nonsense. Your heart is unwell and you will come home and spend your time resting. On sunny days you will sit in the garden and knit. Now the matter is done and dusted.'

The patient wanted to protest and ask about the cleaning, cooking and laundry. Victoria declared how she and Louise would manage between them although the rest of the family, including Louise, reckoned such a move was doomed to fail.

It was and a notice was placed in the High Street seeking applications for a housekeeper. She would not reside in the home and would work from 1pm until 5pm weekdays. The pay offered could only be described as generous and Victoria had the task of selecting from the many applicants.

Miss Harriet Mummery was offered the post. She rode her bicycle from the family's farm about a mile away. Victoria chose her because her cooking skills seemed outstanding; she cared for her elderly father and two brothers and was physically strong. Her tasks were cleaning, laundry and preparing the evening meal. She'd be cycling home by the time the Wellesley residents sat down to eat.

Mrs Crossley would come from her room and with Edmund in his wheelchair, the dining-room reminded Tom a little of a field hospital with the walking wounded.

Vicky found the fierce and solid Miss Mummery frightening calling her Miss Mummy until it was agreed she would be Miss Harriet.

Life rattled along until Louise wanted to have a chat with her husband. He was constantly on call and his surgery had never been busier. She had enthusiastic would-be elocution students on a cancellation list and waited until she and Tom were in bed.

'Doctor Curzon,' she said.

'Oh no, here's trouble.'

'I think I'm pregnant.'

In a split second he stopped joking and switched on a bedside light. He gently touched her abdomen. 'And what's been happening with your periods?'

'I've missed two.'

'Well we don't need to tell anyone, even your mother until we're sure. And you must stop any difficult tasks. Miss Harriet is paid to do those. Do you understand, Louise?'

He was serious.

'I do.' She paused. 'Are you pleased?'

'He took her in his arms. 'Pleased? I'm over the moon' he said and the way he kissed her proved it.

Louise knew all her acting ability might not be enough to keep a secret from her mother and she was correct as Victoria sensed the situation. After her daughter's final student left, Victoria came into Louise's room. She said nothing but stared at her daughter. Louise knew she knew.

'How can you tell, Mummy? Will I have such a gift when Vicky is married?'

Victoria hugged her daughter. 'I'm so happy, my darling.'

'Tom thinks we should not say anything until we are sure.'

'Of course you say nothing but don't do anything silly.'

A few days later, on a Thursday when Miss Harriet had gone home, Victoria, Mrs Crossley and Vicky were in the garden. Edmund heard a scream, not terribly loud but certainly a cry of pain or distress.

'Plum, is that you?' No reply. He pushed himself through the house to the rear. His sister was kneeling on the floor in the laundry. 'Plum!' he cried and stopped beside her.

'Ring Tom,' was all she said obviously in distress. Edmund hesitated, unsure, himself distressed. 'Now, Eddie!'

He pushed himself back to the phone. 'Mother,' he yelled as he dialled the surgery. Victoria hurried inside her face wanting answers.

'In the laundry,' said Edmund. His mother vanished and he asked to speak to Tom.

Twenty minutes later the doctor and father ran into the house. Louise had been made comfortable on the laundry floor. Vicky had been kept outside with Mrs Crossley. The child saw her father and wanted to follow. The former housekeeper used her wits to keep the child in the garden.

Tom knelt beside his wife. He didn't need a detailed examination, he knew. His wife had miscarried.

Chapter 30

It took weeks before the tears were finally put away. Louise became doubly sad. The loss of the baby in itself was heartbreaking. To have probably contributed to the miscarriage by doing her laundry, was an additional punishment.

She received tremendous support and love from her family which in some ways made it worse. Too much love seemed to increase her guilt.

'We can try again, my darling girl,' said her husband.

'You're still a young woman,' said her mother.

'You've always been a fighter, Miss Louise,' said Mrs Crossley.

Of course Vicky was told nothing and her performing tricks and inquisitive mind continued to bring joy to Louise and her family.

Elocution lessons helped but Louise was dragged out of her sadness when an offer of a film part arrived. Dickie Graves rang with the news.

'It sounds wonderful, Mr Graves. When and where is the audition?'

'I didn't make myself clear. There is no audition; you've been offered the part.'

Louise gasped. 'No audition; but how?'

'Your fame precedes you, Miss Wellesley. The producer, Michael Balcon has seen your work and convinced the director, Basil Dearden to cast you. It's not a major part but as you've already discovered, one role can lead to another and work is work.'

It was the perfect news to lift her spirits, to take her out of herself. Not only was she back performing, she didn't have to audition. Her family saw her body come alive and rejoiced in her happiness.

The film, *The Blue Lamp*, was set in London after the war and Louise knew the locations, the time and even the characters in the screenplay.

The actors were new to Louise but salt of the earth people with whom she got along famously. Towards the end of her schedule, she was relaxing with cast and crew between scenes when an assistant told her there was a chap outside who wanted a word.

The others laughed and teased her. 'Sugar daddy on the set,' they ribbed her.

'Did he give a name?' asked Louise.

'No, he said he was one of Plum's friends.'

Louise was up and off in a second. In the foyer of the film studio she burst in and saw her brother Henry reading a poster.

'Henry!' she cried and they hugged and kissed.

'I've kissed a movie star,' he said over-acting and grinning.

'What are you doing here?'

She knew he wouldn't turn up at her place of work to say hello. He pretended otherwise.

'I heard you were up in town and thought I should take my baby sister out for a cream tea before she becomes too famous.'

She scoffed, reckoned he was lying but happily agreed.

Two hours later he collected her and they went off arm in arm.

In 1945 as one war finished, another began. It became known as the Cold War where two super-powers—Russia and the USA—threatened one another with what amounted to empty warnings. "My dad can bash up your dad" sort of thing. Spying became an art form.

The nuclear weapons were ridiculously dangerous forcing both sides to lock their armoury with at least two keys. But both the Ruskies and the Yanks were happy to let their friends, those much smaller satellite countries engage in wars with other equally tiny neighbours provided each only used conventional weapons.

In Cambridge, before the war, a group of like-minded students discovered a mutual interest in politics of the Communist variety. Nothing wrong with that but when said students graduate and find a job, and one working for the British government, to then start nicking British government secrets, military secrets and supplying same to the USSR, well, actually that's *not* all right.

The fact the British spies escaped capture for so long revealed the appalling incompetence of the British Intelligence services.

As Louise restarted her stage career, her daughter kept growing and the British Intelligence services started sniffing around those

Cambridge graduates and their treasonous activities. Sadly their sniffing resembled the Keystone Cops.

Sitting in a quaint tea-room, Henry and his sister went through the small talk about family matters. It saw Henry's dearly beloved's whacky personality mean that she and their children were estranged from the rest of the family. Victoria despaired as her other two grandchildren were strangers and to think Henry's son would one day inherit the family title, how weird it was the boy and his sister never knew the grandmother who lived less than an hour away. Mrs Henry Wellesley had some serious sway.

"All happy families are alike; each unhappy family is unhappy in its own way," according to Mr Tolstoy.

Louise knew this wasn't a cheer-up-little-sister social visit. She wanted Henry to get to the point. He did, eventually.

'You know we're unique members of the family Wellesley.'

What's his plan?

'You and I working undercover in intelligence.' He paused causing Louise's curiosity to rise. 'Do you remember your first job working with the Secret Intelligence Service?'

'I do, Henry and what is this, Plum's History Quiz?'

'It's now called MI6 or Military Intelligence, Section 6.'

She knew there was more to come.'

'And?'

'How would you like to go back to work?'

Wow, his question floored her. Whatever she was expecting, it wasn't that.

'Henry, the war's over. It finished years ago.'

'Ah but there's a new one, old girl and it's called the Cold War.'

'Henry, I have a husband, a daughter, dozens of students and a life as an actress, and you want me to pretend to be another person and jump out of a plane in the middle of the night?'

He shook his head. 'No parachutes, no weapons or explosives and any and all assignments will be in London or thereabouts between acting gigs.'

She examined him with a spark of curiosity beginning to catch alight inside. Her immediate response of "Go away" or "Forget it" turned into, "Tell me more." He sensed her interest.

'I can't or won't tell you all the details until you tell me you are definitely interested.'

'I can't say *definitely* but I would like more details.'

'More tea,' asked the waitress interrupting their classified conversation.

'We're fine, thank you,' said Henry sending her away.

'You want me to spy?'

'Not me, old girl, my MI6 masters. They believe there are many respectable Englishmen here in London, passing military secrets to the Russians and there are many respectable Russians here spying for their Motherland. The service needs a person to unmask Russian spies living here in London working as trade or artistic emissaries. Your history, acting skills and beauty make you a perfect operative.'

He stopped speaking. She sipped her tea. He selected a small cake from the collection on their table.

'Tuck in, Plum. The government's paying.'

On the train going home, Louise thought only of her brother's visit and his offer. She knew he wasn't the boss but had obviously recommended her and been sent to sound her out. The most frustrating thing about this possible new career involved a minor matter of *The Official Secrets Act*. It meant she could discuss it with no-one. Her husband, the perfect sounding-board, was off limits.

If she chose to break the Act, there would be trouble indeed, but would also open a can of worms. Obviously Tom would ask her why, and then would come tales of the years living in peril killing Nazis and risking death. Alas, she must think and decide alone.

Henry rang two days later and his mother answered the phone. She would always ask after her other grandchildren. Henry asked after his siblings, niece and Mrs C then asked if he might have a word with his sister. Out came the fib. Daughter of a colleague in his chambers, where Henry spent little time due to his MI6 commitments, wanted an autograph of the famous actress.

'Hello big brother,' said Louise.

'Can you speak?'

'Yes.'

'Can you come for a chat with the firm next Friday at 4?'

'Oh that sounds lovely,' she said for the benefit of anyone listening.

'I'll meet you off the ten past three train at Waterloo.'

'Okay and please give my love to Georgina, Hester and Cuthbert.'

She said the names of his wife and children to remind him of their continued absence from his former family home.

Her first introduction to the SIS, now MI6, was in Baker Street where she met a man, Major "Bunty" Bunting with half a leg missing. The person accompanying Louise was a Mr Richard Graves, theatrical agent and part-time dabbler in matters of military intelligence.

This time Henry was Dickie and he took his sister to another London location and the man she met sported four healthy limbs.

He was a MI6 operative calling himself Gordon Hetherington.

'It's lovely to meet you Mrs Curzon or should I call you Miss Wellesley?'

'I answer to both,' she said blunt and to the point. Henry blanched. His baby sister was no chip off the block of their mother.

'Well I assume your brother has told you a little of the work we do.' She said nothing. This was not the naive young university student who in 1939 was introduced to the world of spies and secret agents.

'The Nazis are no longer the enemy, it's the Russians, our former allies in the previous punch-up. It's called the Cold War and is a bit like the Phoney War of 1940.'

Henry could see Louise was bored. She was an intelligent woman and the MI6 chap was waffling. She saved Henry and spoke first.

'Do you have a job offer for me, Mr Hetherington?'

Her metaphorical face slap jolted him. He didn't like being treated like a fool and certainly not by a woman. He paused and gave her the evil eye.

'We need a woman who can mingle with the Russians here in London to discover who is spying and how. If you can discover what they are after and, God forbid, what they have already taken, that would be a bonus. Someone like you, in the world of theatre and film would be an easy fit at receptions, first-nights and parties.' He paused. 'Does the position appeal, Miss Wellesley?'

'Will you have listening devices and other fancy items I can use even secrete on my person?' Neither man expected that question.

'When working with the SOE I had access to many intriguing gadgets.'

'I think you'll find, madam, our boffins have made significant strides in the development of espionage devices and you will be given all manner of technical support. Today's cameras have to be seen to be believed.'

Louise remained silent.

'Are there any other questions?' asked Hetherington.

'I require the contract with full terms and conditions, details of my handler, my salary, and details of the insurance payout for my family in the event of my death or disappearance.'

Henry struggled to believe not just the words coming out of his sister's mouth but the way she spoke. It was as if she was running the meeting and he and the MI6 officer were being interviewed by the actress.

Hetherington produced a smug smile. 'I'm sure we can provide detailed answers to all your questions, dear lady. Now, is there anything else?'

'Do you expect me to sleep with my targets?'

Henry nearly fell out of his chair and "H" as the MI6 man was known, swallowed. 'The government would most certainly not make such a request. How an agent behaves is entirely up to them.'

Louise stood. 'Thank you, sir. I shall await your formal offer.' She turned to her brother. He stood as if being controlled by her. 'I have a spot of shopping to do, Henry. We'll no doubt talk soon.' She stood on tippy-toes, kissed his cheek and headed for the door. Both men raced one another to be first to open it. In the corridor, a woman assigned to escort Louise from the building smiled and led her away.

Louise decided she would take the job because it did not involve leaving home. Of course she knew there were dangers but not in a foreign country and not when her country was in a state of war.

The fact her performing career could continue was another factor. In fact the more successful she became through theatre and film, the better her chances of being involved with Russian spies.

Her one and only stumbling block was the secrecy. Not being able to tell Tom raised the fear of possibly hurting him, damaging their rock-solid relationship and upsetting others particularly her family.

How would they react if even any or God forbid, all of her past undercover adventures became known?

Henry telephoned to advise the paperwork was available and they made a time to return to MI6 HQ where she read and re-read the contract, thought about taking it to Dickie Graves for his input, decided against same and signed.

Mr Hetherington thanked and congratulated her and pointed out her responsibilities under *The Official Secrets Act*.

'Do you have a preference for a code name,' he asked.

'Call her Plum,' said Henry.

Louise shrugged and Plum it was. From the SIS to the SOE and back to the SIS now MI6, the actress was back in the business of spying. Break a leg, Plum.

Chapter 31

The excuses Louise developed for heading up to London were as follows: initial audition, call-back audition, meeting with Mr Graves, costume fitting for film, opening night of film or play, lecture in elocution at the Royal School of Speech and Drama, launch of new play, book launch, spring clean of Maida Vale flat, lunch with Henry, lunch with old friend from ENSA and anything else believable which came to mind.

It took all her acting skill to make such excursions sound low-key. If the function was late afternoon or evening she would stay the night in London. So far, exposing Russian spies was easier than hiding her latest secret life from her family.

Everything was secretive including another bank account into which her salary was paid. She needed a way of communicating with her handler, a retired field operative, Fanny Poplin. For a dead-letter drop, they used the personal touch. Fanny's niece, Penelope became one of Louise's elocution students and payment for lessons, in a sealed envelope, would pass to Mrs Curzon when required. For Louise, there was an under the counter box in a florist's shop off Sloan Square where the owner had government connections.

But first came the training. Louise had to memorize faces and their names. Mikhail Antonovich was the number 1 suspect. He was second in charge at the Russian Embassy, married to society princess Vika, and the man MI6 suspected had found a way of obtaining classified material before sending it back to Moscow.

Mikhail's offsider, in reality his bodyguard, was Vladimir Gribanov, and a NKGB officer not slow to use violence. To tackle Mikhail, Louise would need to pass Vladimir. Tricky.

Two other suspects were Dusa Yenin from the Russian Arts and Culture Academy and Dima Durov, a member of the Russian Sports Association. To MI6 they were Dusa and Dima, the terrible twins.

After disjointed but intense training, Louise was ready to begin. She wasn't an unheard of cabaret performer or an unknown pretend nun; she was a successful and well-known actress.

The one command or piece of advice given to her was to let the Russians come to her. She was never to seek an invitation to one of their events or request an audience with any Russian official. Let them come to you. Of course if you're at the right parties, social events and cultural activities, you'll be seen. Let them come to you.

'You do know, Plum,' said Henry, 'MI6 have chosen you not only because of your SOE training, your experience in France and your ever-increasing popularity in the world of theatre and film, but because of your beauty.' She could tell he was sincere. 'The Ruskies like to surround themselves with rich, famous and beautiful people.'

As she prepared to perform her new undercover role, Dickie Graves rang to ask if he could put her name forward for a role in the relatively new world of television.

'The BBC are to record a series of one-off plays to be screened on Sunday evenings. Mainly drama and there will be a call for experienced thespians. Does it appeal?'

Of course it appealed and more so if it raised her profile making her more widely popular and thus hopefully more likely to catch the eye of the relevant Russians.

'It appeals greatly, Mr Graves. I'll await any audition details.'

Her life became hectic. Apart from auditioning for roles on stage, film and now television, she continued to teach and look for ways she could become involved with those foreigners MI6 believed were spies for Russia in Britain.

But her life continued and at times with sadness. Victoria made a point of always popping in to say goodnight to Enid Crossley and this night found her lifeless. Tom was called and pronounced the elderly housekeeper dead. The family grieved. Telling Vicky was tricky.

The Wellesleys organized Enid's funeral and paid for her burial plot and gravestone and life moved on. Her bedroom was given a major renovation and little Vicky, who was no longer so little, now had a proper room of her own rather than the makeshift room in her mother's dressing-room. The child was thrilled and the dogs loved their new sleeping headquarters.

Penelope, the handler's niece, arrived for an elocution lesson with the envelope and the "fee". The payment was a ticket to the opening night of a play performed by a visiting Russian theatre company.

It seemed a dream start. MI6 were behind the move having obtained the ticket from the Arts Minister who'd been given several.

Knowing the importance of her appearance in this new role, Louise arranged to have a suitable range of outfits and accessories stored at Maida Vale. Within reason, MI6 agreed to cover her expenses in acquiring appropriate items knowing the importance of embellishing her natural beauty.

When she left Farnham she was smartly dressed although not glamourous. When she arrived at the theatre, Cinderella was definitely en route to the ball.

She wondered if a photograph in the social pages of a newspaper might be seen by her husband and family or his family and if so, how she might explain her makeover. But then hiding her secret life was a role she'd performed for years and at which so far she was pretty darn good.

The theatre foyer was buzzing with a few genuine theatre lovers and far more social butterflies and "gosh-look-at-me" society social climbers. Louise turned heads in her stunning gown and simple accessories oozing class. An actress she vaguely knew called her name and joined her. People gravitated to Louise.

She admired the play and production, caught up with the actress she'd met before the first curtain and then it happened. An MI6 operative working in the Ministry of Arts approached through the masses in the foyer after the show. 'Miss Wellesley, I'm Myles Fortesque-Wright from the Ministry. May I introduce an admirer of yours, Mr Dusa Yenin from the Russian Ministry of Arts and Culture?'

Dusa's head had been chiselled from a block of granite and his teeth needed work. He took Louise's hand and held it close to his lips. His accent punched those in close proximity and the man was in need of many elocution lessons from the woman in front of him.

'Miss Wellesley, I have seen you perform upon the stage and was enchanted by your performance.'

'Thank you, sir.'

'It is a great honour to have you attend a Russian premiere. Did you enjoy the performance?'

She wanted to tell him to never ask that question but instead smiled effortlessly and replied. 'Enjoyed and admired, sir, your countrymen and women are outstanding professionals.'

The Russian public servant and possible spy grinned with delight exposing those teeth which were a terrible advertisement for Russian dentistry.

'I am trying to persuade Mr Fortesque-Wright to send a company of English actors to tour my country. Muscovites would be overcome with joy to see such a performance.'

'We're considering Mr Yenin's suggestion,' added the Englishman.

'Dare I suggest you might consider joining such an illustrious company, Miss Wellesley? I would count it an honour to welcome you to my country.'

'You are most kind, Mr Yenin. I've heard so much about the wonderful culture of your homeland.'

Fortesque-Wright was already writing a report on Louise and giving her tick after tick.

There were more meetings and greetings but none from Russians. Still a contact had been made and Louise remembered her training and the comments about the spy game being often long and slow. Let them come to you and learn to play the patience game.

Weeks went by and her next opportunity surprised her. A woman she worked with while performing in the ENSA pantomime at Windsor Castle landed a role in a new musical *Guys and Dolls* and invited Louise to opening night. Surprised and delighted, Louise accepted. She hadn't seen the woman for ages but with a free ticket, what's not to like?

Again when she left Farnham, she dressed sensibly but without glamour. In her flat in London she changed and entering the packed foyer felt a twinge of envy or sadness; both. She missed the dressing-room, the make-up and the chance to perform.

People she knew wanted to grab her and those she'd never met tried to get close. People gossiped about her being alone.

'Isn't she married?'

'Yes but to a doctor who I think was wounded in the war.'

Her former ENSA colleague arrived after the show and was mobbed by her friends and family. She spotted Louise and came over. Her over-the-top greeting may have been down to the high she was on following a great opening night.

'Louise, we must catch up. There's a party the producers are giving. Do come.'

'Thanks Elaine but it's for the cast and crew.'

'They'll bring their friends. I'll bring you. Please,' she begged.

With the alternative being an early night in the flat, Louise agreed.

It was in a wealthy person's home with the décor and furniture seemingly as expensive as the real estate. Louise was introduced to one of the musical's backers who could bore for England. Dying to leave, Louise was grabbed and ushered away.

'Darling, why haven't we met? And where in God's name did you find your dress. It's divine.'

Louise's new "best friend" was a woman dressed to the nines and who made over-the-top people seem like wallflowers. Her clothes smelt of old money and she looked like her occupation; a trophy wife.

'I'm Vika, darling and you and I must become the best of, how you say, bosom buddies.'

A light bulb pinged in Louise's head as she recognized the woman as the wife of Mikhail Antonovich, the top but one official at the Russian Embassy and MI6's best bet as a definite Russian spy.

Has my luck finally turned?

'I'm Louise Wellesley ...'

'I know, I've had you checked out. You must know we Russians are famous for investigating our friends and foes alike.'

'Vika, what an interesting name.'

'Yes in English it means Victoria.'

Louise joined the game. 'Oh my daughter's name is Victoria.'

'See?' said Vika. 'We were meant to be friends. We can have long lunches, gossip for hours and discuss our many lovers.'

She studied the actress who showed no outward reaction intriguing Princess Russia. 'Please give me your number, darling and I will call and arrange the first of our many meetings.'

Louise remembered this situation in her training. Be honest, be open. Let them see you have nothing to hide. She took a card from her expensive handbag and, using an expensive fountain-pen, underlined her Farnham number. The card disappeared into Vika's even more expensive handbag before she kissed Louise and wafted away with a wink for good measure. Louise's heartbeat took off.

Next morning, travelling home, she wondered about her new job. Her success or failure didn't cause concern. What did concern her was wondering if it might damage her marriage, upset her family or prevent her being close to Vicky as she grew.

Tom Curzon loved his wife and could read her moods. 'I'm no psychologist, my darling, but methinks you are not yourself.'

She expected this response and had an answer ready to go. 'You know how much I would love another child but if it's not to be, I will keep on loving you and Vicky while finding whatever acting roles I can. These BBC Sunday night television plays sound promising. But I've found having the most wonderful agent is not enough. I need to promote myself which is why I'm going to opening nights and events where I can meet people and let them know I'm available.'

'For acting you mean?'

She hugged him then gazed into his eyes. 'I think it's impossible to love you any more, Dr Curzon.'

They continued staring then kissed with feeling. In her heart she hoped he had no idea of her secret life. He knew two things. There *was* a secret in her life and she could never love him and their daughter any more than she did right now.

The phone rang. Victoria and Harriet were discussing domestic matters allowing Louise to take the call.

'Darling, it's Vika. Let's have lunch tomorrow. My husband has an account at Harrods. 12.30 in the restaurant. I can't wait. Oh and how are you?'

'Thank you, I'm well. Lunch sounds wonderful.'

'True but the gossip will be better. Till tomorrow, darling.'

She rang off as her mother appeared. 'Another audition, my dear?'

'No it was a woman keen to have an English theatre production tour in Europe.'

'Europe? You're becoming an *international* star.'

Louise arrived at the fashionable department store on time, mentioned her companion's name and was about to be shown to the table tucked away in a corner when Vika's voice bounced around the restaurant.

'Darling,' she called and waved. Other diners stopped sipping their Margarita or Manhattan to observe.

The women exchanged air kisses—Vika was a three-time girl—Louise settled and the conversation flowed in hushed tones. This trophy wife was a professional gossip assuming Louise was like her—popular, wealthy and self-centred. It took the actress's best performance to carry off this role. She tried to play it straight.

'But being in the theatre, you must have used the casting couch. Tell me, which of the famous actors have you slept with?'

'Now, Vika that would be telling.'

The Russian's eyes sparkled. She liked being teased. As they lunched, Louise wanted to say but didn't, "I wonder what the poor people are having for lunch?"

The maître d' came a-fawning. He knew the Princess from Belgravia well. She scribbled a signature on the bill and then announced they were to have coffee at her residence. Louise had no say in the matter.

The "company" car appeared and obviously knew the destination. Vika was the leading trophy wife in London. The Wellesley family home near Farnham was no two-up two-down but Vika's shack was special. The grounds were wonderful but the pad screamed wealth.

'Come inside and meet my children,' said Vika having doors opened and closed by staff.

Louise was confused. *Children? She never mentioned offspring.*

An interior door opened and three French poodles, groomed and manicured scampered towards their Mummy. They ate better than half of London's children.

Being an old hand with dogs, Louise handled their enthusiasm with ease.

'Ah,' smiled Vika, 'you are a dog lover, darling.'

Coffee appeared as if by magic with Russian routines set in stone. Louise changed the topic. 'I need to powder my nose.'

'Of course,' said Vika and spoke to a woman in black wearing a short white apron. 'Ludmilla.' No further instructions were needed.

Louise followed the servant along a corridor where a door was indicated. Louise entered what must be London's largest bathroom. Powdering complete, she stepped into the corridor to find a former wrestler wearing a suit a size too small glowering at her.

'Good afternoon,' said Louise including a delightful smile.

'I'm Vladimir Gribanov and if you have any business with Mr Antonovich, you speak to me first.' She knew who both men were.

'Thank you but I'm a friend of *Mrs* Antonovich.'

'Ha,' he grunted and whispered, 'bitch.'

'If that's all, sir, I'll return to my coffee and gossip.'

She wandered off feeling the glare of his stare on her back.

'*There* you are,' said Vika juggling dogs and coffee.

The servant stepped forward and poured Louise's coffee.

'Now darling, I am having a party at our country estate in two weeks and you absolutely must come. I need you beside me to help persuade those powerful men in the arts to have you perform in Moscow, and I will not take no for an answer.'

What could Louise say? 'You're very kind, Vika.'

'Wear something sparkling and daring. I will give you the best bedroom with the largest bed in the house—apart from mine.' She made a face suggesting debauchery to Vika and infidelity to Louise.

The actress was glad to go home and when she did Vicky ran to her, hugging her and calling, 'Mummy's home, Mummy's home.'

Louise greeted her mother and brother with Vicky refusing to let go.

'Someone's missed you,' said Edmund without sarcasm.

Louise discerned his true meaning and after supper with Vicky asleep in her new bedroom complete with dolls and dogs, the family held a meeting. Louise was right to sense danger. Victoria started.

'Darling, I think you should know your daughter misses you terribly.' Louise grimaced. 'She comes home from school and after playing with the dogs, the one question she asks is, "Where's Mummy?" or "When will Mummy be coming home"?'

Tom remained quiet but Edmund had his say.

'I'm neither judge not jury, Plum, but is being a professional actress more important than watching your daughter grow up?'

It was a rhetorical question and the others waited for her to speak.

'I would like to audition for these new plays being filmed by the BBC. If I'm offered a role it will be a one-off. But whatever happens, I think it's time I concentrated on elocution lessons and taking Vicky to and from school.'

Great relief escaped into the room.

'Whatever you decide, my dear, I'm sure we'll all support you,' said Tom and his comment received a mixed response.

'I do have a weekend in the country where decisions are being made about English actors performing a one-off tour in Europe but that will be it.'

She thought quitting her MI6 role would not go down well in Intelligence circles but if the choice was to upset her family and particularly her growing daughter, then so be it—family comes first.

A serious boost came when Dickie Graves arranged an audition for Louise with the BBC. It was hard for producers to ignore her stage success, her radio play work and movie roles including one directed by Alfred Hitchcock. She was offered a role in one of the BBC Sunday Night Play series.

She telephoned Vika crying off the weekend in the country because of rehearsing and filming her latest television performance.

'I will forgive you, darling but only if you come next month when I will have even more powerful men you can impress and even seduce.'

Louise was glad to agree knowing the weekend trip and suggested seduction would never happen. She placed a note for her handler in the Sloane Square florist's shop pointing out, in code, how her main target was protected by a brute in the form of a concrete wall and Louise had nothing to report due to spending all her time on petty social activities with a frivolous wife.

The television play was a hit with Louise taking a main part and being praised by viewers and critics alike. One declared she had blossomed into a mature and brilliant actress and predicted a long and successful career. Another reckoned a call from Hollywood was surely on the cards.

Staff at Farnham station treated her like royalty. 'Good morning, Mrs Curzon,' they said opening carriage doors for her. Yes, she might be the town doctor's wife but they knew her as their movie star.

Having seen the television play, Vika gushed and insisted on Louise coming to the country estate for a weekend of fun and political manoeuvring. 'I will get you to Moscow, darling, if it kills me,' she said and Louise sensed the walls closing in.

'It's for one Saturday night,' she told her family, 'and I think, I'll be back to elocution lessons the next week.'

'You think?' asked her mother.

'No, Mummy, I've decided. I want to be here as Vicky grows up.'

Louise stuck with the MI6 instruction to be herself and chose not to be collected at her Maida Vale flat. 'I'll take a cab from the station and meet you in Belgravia,' she said to Vika.

'Wonderful, darling. We'll leave around 3.'

They did and the vehicle was not the kind Muscovites, if they were one of the very few lucky enough to own a car, would ever be seen driving in around Gorky Park.

'You have a tiny case, Louise. I hope you haven't neglected one of your gorgeous gowns,' said Vika in the foyer of her home.

Louise smiled and switched to her sincere self. 'I want to help you, Vika, to have English actors perform in your magnificent theatres in Russia.' The women hugged as Louise's heart thumped while at the same time her stomach dropped.

Chapter 32

Their trip to Buckinghamshire took about an hour and the driveway seemed as long as the trip from Belgravia. When they reached the end of the tree-lined drive, the Georgian mansion appeared in all its glory.

'Our little hideaway, darling,' said Vika. 'This can be a place for you to enjoy as long as I am in London.'

'You or your husband?'

Vika laughed. 'He dare not leave without my say so. You will meet him this weekend. I have told Mikhail all about you and I can tell he is interested.'

So too was Louise wondering if and how she might discover anything about his alleged spying.

There were members of staff on tap to open doors and carry cases. Vika was correct about Louise's bedroom and the size of its bed. She unpacked and went downstairs for afternoon drinks. There were no teetotallers to be found.

About a dozen other house guests were already there and they all turned when Louise entered because Vika announced her arrival.

'Darling,' she cried balancing a glass of champagne, the best, with a long cigarette holder and performing air kisses with panache.

'Everyone, in case you don't already know—where have you been hiding?—this beautiful lady and wonderful actress is Louise Wellesley.'

She smiled, others greeted her and a tray with glasses of bubbly appeared at her side. Champagne cocktails were not served in Farnham but playing her role, Louise took a glass. Hors d'oeuvres appeared as if by magic.

A woman introduced herself. She was the wife of a member of cabinet in the Clement Attlee government who wanted to befriend any woman likely to improve her husband's prospects of promotion.

The conversation was one-sided and Louise breathed a sigh when a man took her arm. She stared at the face of Mikhail Antonovich.

'Do excuse us, Lady Thornhill,' he said and turned Louise to face him. 'My wife tells me you are the most beautiful and talented actress in London.'

'I believe she may be biased,' said Louise.

'On the contrary, madam, she has seriously understated your stunning appearance.' He kissed her hand. 'I do hope we can become better acquainted this weekend. I always find intimacy the best way to establish a friendship. Do you agree, Louise?'

His eyes did the talking and Louise now faced a predicament. Is sleeping with Vika's husband the only way to discover his spy status?

'You pose an interesting question, sir.' He liked her answer.

Guests were given an hour or two to repair to their room, change into formal wear before the first of several courses would be served in the dining-room. Louise lay on her massive bed and pondered her situation. Her country wasn't at war; well, not officially. She was unarmed although she couldn't believe the likes of Vladimir, the bathroom attendant, could not possibly be without several firearms and blades.

A thought popped into her head. *Has Vika adopted me as a friend for her husband? Is Mrs Antonovich procuring women of beauty and class for Mikhail's pleasure? Will she be a participant?*

The dinner gong sounded and Louise, having slipped into her only gorgeous gown, checked her hair and make-up and headed downstairs. Her miniature camera lay hidden inside her handbag.

More drinks in a reception room before guests were summoned to sup. Louise was placed beside Mikhail and a Russian oligarch who spent part of his fortune financing films.

The appetizer had barely been served when Louise sensed a slight rubbing on her lower leg. She went to glance down but instead turned to the host. He smiled as if to lay down a marker, speaking without words: *The night is young madam and the matter of intimacy will begin whenever both parties are free.*

She opted to play the woman of virtue which the Russian took to mean "Yes". She wanted to ask, "If no means yes, what is the word for no?" Her other fellow diner prattled on about the movies he'd invested in and how he could help her acting career if she was interested. Was there a Russian version of nudge nudge wink wink?

234

'What would I have to do to be cast in one of your films, sir?' she asked with the straightest of straight faces. She confused him.

'*Is she dumb?*' he thought. '*Like one of those Hollywood tarts?*'

She kept him guessing all night. When the ladies retired, Vika took Louise aside. 'What did you think of my husband, darling?'

Now Louise was confused. *What sort of reply should I give?*

'Most interesting as was the gentleman from the world of film.'

'Oh god, I'm so sorry. I don't know how he was placed next to you. Come, let me show you the house.'

Louise was glad to be away from sleazy men and glad to see behind the scenes. A trip inside Mikhail's office was doubly interesting. She surveyed the room for possible places to find incriminating evidence but reckoned being able to search here or anywhere would be impossible. They had security for their security.

They stepped from the office to be confronted by the gorilla.

'It's all right, Vlad,' said Vika in Russian. 'I'm giving Miss Wellesley a tour of the house.'

Vladimir grunted, entered the office and closed the door.

Louise's main worry now was how to survive the night. If push came to shove with requests for sex, how would she respond? She was a long way from home and all alone.

Downstairs in the kitchen, Louise performed. Puffing out her cheeks, she slumped against a kitchen bench. Vika reacted with concern.

'Louise, what's wrong?'

'Sick,' she gasped. 'I'm going to be sick.'

Vika took control guiding Louise to one of the several sinks. 'Not on the floor, darling.'

Bent over the sink and on the upstage side of the hostess, Louise stuck two fingers down her throat and forced herself to gag and then vomit. Not difficult after all the food and drink she'd consumed.

Vika put an arm around her speaking words of comfort.

'I'd like to lie down,' said Louise and Vika walked her upstairs and into her room.

'What can I bring you, darling?'

'I have water. I think a good night's sleep will do the trick.'

'What a pity because I know there are certain gentlemen who are keen to get to know you a little better.'

'Perhaps tomorrow,' said Louise and lay on her bed.

'Come and see me if you need anything,' said Vika removing Louise's shoes. 'Get some rest, darling.' She blew a kiss and left. Louise worried her sigh of relief could be heard downstairs.

She drifted asleep lying there still fully dressed. She woke when someone tapped on her door. It took a few moments to establish where she was and the time—12.48 am.

She didn't respond but in the moonlight saw a piece of paper slide under her door. Quietly, she tip-toed to collect it.

The message was simple. *My office in five. Mikhail.*

'Bloody hell,' whispered Louise. 'What now?' She remembered the interior. There was a Chesterfield sofa and a floor to ceiling mirror.

She put on shoes, brushed her hair, fixed her lipstick and gently pushed her tiny camera under the top of her stocking on the inner thigh of her left leg.

What's my alternative? she thought. *Stay here and discover nothing. Take the opportunity and give myself a chance? Is Mikhail passing British secrets to Russia?*

She opened her door. The house was dark and, as far as she knew, asleep. Louise crept towards Mikhail's office on the thickest of carpets. This mission featured no Nazis, crazy Resistance fighters or collaborators but she could feel the danger. And she was alone.

Getting closer to the office, she heard footsteps and backed into an alcove. She saw Vladimir the statue give a certain tap on the door.

Mikhail opened it being surprised expecting a certain female. He and his colleague spoke Russian leaving Louise none the wiser. Mikhail was given a message and left. Vladimir entered the office, remembered something and ran after his boss.

Not hesitating, Louise scampered inside the office and hid under the desk. Vladimir returned, closed the door and headed to a painting on the wall. Louise crawled out and peered around the corner. She saw Vladimir open a safe and sort papers. The ones he selected were placed on a table after which he closed the safe.

With his back to Louise he didn't see her approach. He sensed movement and spun around. Louise was a good six feet away.

'Bitch!' he hissed and reached for his gun. It was withdrawn and about to be pointed at Louise and fired when she kicked and her right shoe smashed into the Russian's left kneecap.

He dropped the gun and went to clasp his knee. Exquisite agony flooded his body which Louise helped remove when she chopped his Adam's apple rupturing his thyroid cartilage and killing him. It was messy.

Out came her camera and all the documents removed from the safe were photographed. She put the camera back in the top of her stocking and pushed the barrel of the stolen pistol under her bra on her back. Then a sound gave her a reason to panic.

The key turned in the door and Mikhail entered and froze.

'You! How did you get in?' He saw his comrade on the floor not moving. 'What happened?'

Louise fell back on her acting prowess. 'I knocked as you asked and he let me in. Then he attacked me, groping and trying to kiss me. I told him to stop. He wouldn't so I pushed him and he fell and hit his head on the desk. I didn't mean to hurt him, it was an accident.'

To Mikhail it sounded plausible. His comrade treated women with contempt. The English actress oozed beauty. What Vlad missed, Mikhail would enjoy. He moved towards her.

She knew if he put his hands on her body, on her back or between her legs, the gun and camera or both would be discovered. She needed to at least knock him unconscious if not kill him and flee.

His hands gripped her shoulders. He pulled her to him and kissed her mouth with brute force. She needed to act fast. As she poised to move, the door opened and the crude sexual preliminaries were interrupted.

'Ah,' said Vika, 'you have started without me. She entered wearing a silken robe and opened it to reveal her exotic lingerie. She moved to her pending playmates. The husband grinned and the visitor froze. As Vika reached them, her eye caught sight of the body on the floor and the documents Louise photographed.

She screamed, lost interest in the sex, and stared at her husband. 'What are these doing out of the safe and what happened to Vlad?'

Mikhail's mind was fixed on one thing, sex with his wife and her friend. He struggled to explain. 'Vlad removed the plans then attacked Louise. I was ...'

Vika underwent a personality change. 'You fucking idiot!' Gone was the ditzy trophy wife replaced by an angry killer dedicated to the Motherland. Louise reacted as if shot. The men were the minions and the woman was the boss, the top spy. Her cover fooled MI6 and Louise.

Dressed for seduction not slaying, Vika strode to the desk to retrieve a gun. Louise produced hers. 'Don't,' she snapped and, like her ladies-who-lunch friend, Louise's pleasant personality changed in an instant.

Vika saw Louise's weapon pointing at her. 'Interesting,' she said. 'And what happens now, Miss Wellesley? Have you a rescue team hidden in the garden?'

Good questions as Louise tried thinking on the spot. Concentrating on Vika she didn't expect Mikhail to play the hero. He kicked Louise's shin which threw her attention elsewhere. Vika ran and as Louise re-focused on her best luncheon friend, Mikhail grabbed Louise's gun and they fought with the weapon pointed towards the ceiling. Releasing one hand, she stabbed a knuckle in his left eye and the shock and pain caused him to drop everything. She chopped his throat and he collapsed gasping.

Louise set off after Vika with Louise's shin complaining. In the corridor she listened, heard Vika and followed the sound. Leaning over the bannister, the Russian wife called quietly but desperately for either of the two guards on duty. With no response she moved to the top of the stairs.

'Don't,' said Louise walking straight at Vika with gun pointed.

The hostess fumed. How could this actress uncover her cover, get access to the papers she stole from sex-starved British intelligence officers, and now have her banged to rights and about to be shot?

'Turn,' said Louise. Vika faced the bannister and felt a gun press against her neck. 'Stocking please,' requested Louise. Vika started to remove a stocking. The gun was pushed harder now in her back. The stocking was peeled and as Louise glanced down to accept the nylon, Vika exploded. She smacked Louise's hand and the gun clattered to the floor. Vika turned and, in a frenzy tried to scratch Louise's face.

She squatted, clasped Vika's hips and lifted her using a fireman's lift. The Russian screamed as she flailed at the actress who hoisted her enemy above the bannister. A heave and the trophy wife took off.

Falling, she smashed into the giant chandelier, got caught for a few seconds writhing in fear before breaking free and plunging with bits of glass to the marble floor below. She landed face down and once in said position, said nothing. Her lunches at Harrods were cancelled.

For a moment Louise thought she was dreaming. She heard footsteps below then yelling and bolted to her room. Of course her case was packed—rule 23A in the SOE Handbook.

Down the backstairs she went, through the kitchen and out into the night. She headed for darkness. How long would it take before a search party with dogs would be let loose?

Sweeping around in a wide circle, she remembered the small lake beside the driveway and headed there. Wading through the shallows she covered about 100 yards before getting back on dry land heading for the road they used to enter the property. She was dressed for frolicking not fleeing.

Once at the front gates, her plan was to head to the public phone-box she saw in the nearest village. If she heard or saw a car, particularly at this time of the night, she would go to ground until safe to move again.

She tried to think of the Russian reaction. Would they call the police? Hardly. Not only were they highly secretive, they were breaking the laws of treason. Any dead bodies would be discreetly disposed of—nothing to see here.

Louise reached the outskirts of the village and headed towards the phone-box. Moving in the shadows reminded her of escaping in Belgium.

In the phone box she asked for a reverse charges number. Big brother Henry was sound asleep as was his entire family. He fell out of bed and croaked. 'Hello.'

The operator asked if he would accept a reverse charges call from a caller by the name of Plum.

'Yes, yes, I accept.' The operator put Louise through.

'Go ahead caller.'

'Henry?'

'What's happened?'

'I need a taxi.'

'Where are you?'

239

She told him the name of the village. 'There's a bridge over the river as you enter. I'll be under the bridge.'

'Are you in one piece?'

'I think so but Henry, please hurry.'

He did. Explaining to his wife why he was leaving at such an hour was not easy. He dressed it as a client being held hostage and the police say the hostage taker will only speak with the victim's solicitor.'

The roads were empty; Henry found the village, stopped on the bridge then nearly died when his sister tapped on his window.

She explained all as he drove her to a safe house where she gave him the mini camera. The results were an eye-opener for MI6 enabling them to capture British traitors.

After a medical check and a debriefing, she was allowed to sink in the biggest bath and then sleep. She dreamt of Farnham and her family, particularly her daughter.

It was Sunday morning, she called at Maida Vale, then caught the train home. Her shin still hurt. She thought about telephoning and having Tom collect her at the station but chose to walk. She would walk to her home, back to her family and out of her secret life of spying, lying and dying.

The sight of her daughter running full pelt towards her in the garden rammed home the "rightness" of her overnight decision. Louise Wellesley or rather Mrs Curzon was home to stay.

Her professional career, thanks to television, continued although appearances became fewer and stopped when Dickie Graves died still in harness. She took great pride in seeing several of her elocution students perform in shows with the highlight being her daughter. Like her mother, Victoria Curzon was a natural with no pushy stage mother in sight. When the daughter made her professional debut many reckoned she was as good as or even better than her mother. Louise didn't care and silently shed tears in the darkened theatre.

Chapter 33

The Cotswolds, Gloucestershire, 2002

The garden became her life, the sunhat her identity. The elderly resident was happy to live alone in her charming cottage. A dog was essential. Her daughter and granddaughter both often raised the issue of her living alone.

'But Mummy, at Farnham you can have your old room and you know there's plenty of garden for you to potter to your heart's content.'

Granddaughter Millie, mother of Elspeth the youngster who adored sleepovers at Grannie Plum's, put in her two bob's worth with less delicacy than her mother, Victoria.

'Grannie, if you have a fall or trip over Angus, who's going to help you? You could be lying there, calling out and no-one will know.'

'I have this buzzer for an emergency.' It hung around her neck.

Persuading the elderly gardener to move proved impossible. Her family worried her frailty was another red flag. She lived alone. Yes, it was a peaceful village but if a drug addict or anyone with serious mental health problems strayed into this crime-free paradise and fancied a soft touch, Grannie wouldn't stand a chance. Mind you they knew nothing of her unarmed combat skills and expertise with numerous firearms.

With Angus dozing in the shade, the gardener fancied a cup of tea. 'Angus,' she called in a sing-song voice. He knew the sound. He knew it meant a treat, his elevenses and he scampered after the mistress.

She entered the kitchen and pottered when without warning Angus went crazy. He snapped his barking and growled with intent.

'Angus,' she said. 'Whatever's the matter?'

The great-grandmother stared in the direction Angus was facing and saw a middle-aged woman, well-dressed but unremarkable although with one outstanding feature. She held a gun which pointed straight at the homeowner.

Her family's projected nightmare had come true.

'Can I help you?' seemed a logical reply.

'Lose the dog,' she said in perfect English but with a strong accent.

'Angus, here boy,' said the older woman, oddly not showing any outward signs of distress. Angus was reluctant to respond. Part of his terms of engagement at Bluebell Cottage included protection of said owner. 'Angus,' sounded more serious and the dog reluctantly obeyed. He was shown the door.

Before he could start a ruckus outside, his treat appeared and his happiness replaced his concern—for now at least.

The visitor used her gun as a pointer as she issued various orders. 'Sit down.' 'Keep still.' 'Show me your hands.'

With her quarry seated and away from any kitchen utensils, the intruder got down to business.

'I suppose you're wondering why I'm here.'

'Well I'm fairly sure you're not collecting for the WI.'

The visitor snapped. 'Don't get smart with me, bitch. You're about to suffer and we'll see how clever you are when the torture begins.'

The threats did nothing to upset the victim. 'Would you believe I survived the Gestapo? No? Well I did so I doubt you'll have anything more obscene.'

That threw the woman. She knew how Germany invaded her country and killed millions of civilians but found it hard to understand how this frail old woman could have been involved with the Gestapo.

'Are you Jewish?' she asked.

'No dear, C of E.'

The woman was being distracted and forced off script. She returned to the purpose of her visit. 'I'm here to obtain revenge for my family.'

'Right, so would this be in the "eye for an eye" category?'

'Exactly and as you killed my parents, I'm here to exact revenge.'

The gardener didn't respond and when she did the intruder copped another surprise.'

'Have you arranged your escape or will this be a murder suicide?'

'There won't be anyone coming here till next Thursday. I've been watching your place and my preparation is perfect.'

'Really?'

'Yes, really.'

'So what about the home help on their way right now because I've pressed this buzzer around my neck?'

She produced the buzzer showing it to the would-be killer. The intruder reacted with anger. 'You haven't pushed it. I've been watching your hands.' She strode towards the great-grandmother and ripped the cord with its buzzer tossing them aside.

Neck-rubbing helped. 'Temper, temper, my dear.'

'Mock as much as you like but after I've finished with you, you'll beg me to shoot you. And we can't leave the dog without its owner.'

The old woman seethed. 'Don't you dare! What has my little dog ever done to you?'

'He's given you pleasure and taking away what you hold dear is what you deserve after the pain you inflicted on me and my family.'

'You keep going on about it. When and where was all this supposed to have happened?'

'Do the names Mikhail and Vika Antonovich ring any bells?'

'Oh indeed and loud and clear. But that was fifty years ago.'

'Fifty two.'

'I remember your father trying to rape me and your mother being a promiscuous Russian spy working against the British government. Fair game I'd say.'

'Liar,' she screamed. 'My father told me the truth before he died. You seduced him, smashed his voice-box then threw my unarmed mother off a balcony. That's the truth and for which you now will die.'

She stepped closer and raised the gun.

'Wait, wait, wait; what happened to this horrendous torture you promised me? You can't have the finale without the first act.'

Enraged, the Russian would-be assassin hated being taunted. She expected her quarry to fall on the floor, snivelling, sobbing and screaming for mercy. Instead she made fun of the killer. Well, no more. About to pull the trigger, murder was about to happen in this peaceful Gloucestershire cottage.

Angus barked. It wasn't a "please let me in" bark and even the assassin sensed danger.

Then they heard a voice. 'Hello? Is anyone home?'

The script moved to the next page. Did it ever? The first visitor showed signs of panic as she wondered if the bitch did push the buzzer and the district nurse was the first responder.

'What would you like me to do, dear?' asked the gardener with ice-water in her veins.'

'Shut up.'

The new visitor called again. 'It's Megan, your family-history-buff friend from the other day.'

'Get rid of her and if you breathe a word about me, you can watch the woman and your dog die before I kill you.'

'Charming,' whispered the home-owner but thinking the latest threat ominous. She opened the top half of her Dutch-style back door.

'Oh hello, it's Megan.'

'Well done. I wish I could remember names like you.'

'I'm busy baking right now, dear.' She addressed the jumping and excited dog. 'Angus, please behave.'

'He's fine.' Megan bent and patted the Westie. 'I wanted to tell you I've had a bit of luck with my family tree and the distant relative. It's thanks to you suggesting Esmeralda at Honeysuckle Cottage.'

'Well I'm delighted for you.'

Their chat was interrupted by a sudden crashing sound coming from within. Madame Assassin wasn't checking where she was creeping and accidentally knocked a precious Jardinière—worth a pretty penny a minute ago but now no longer—as it lay in many pieces on the flagstone floor. She clearly wasn't a professional assassin.

'What was that?' asked a concerned Megan.

'Oh just me being clumsy when stacking plates. Now you run along dear and come and see me when I'm not so busy.'

Their eyes met and the gardener spoke with hers then secretly dropped a key on the grass. 'Wait Angus,' she called and closed the top half of her back door.

The woman with the gun appeared crunching crockery beneath her shoes. 'Has she gone?'

'She has,' said the victim trying to think of a way or ways to disarm the vengeful intruder. 'I don't suppose you'd care to hear another version of the events of that night?'

'No!'

'I mean I was there and can answer any questions you might have. Your father didn't witness the incident with me and your mother, and she was never able to give you the truth whereas I can.'

'The truth? What truth? Isn't it always written by the winner?'

'Well the offer's there but I think in the interest of balance, you should at least hear the other side of the story.'

The woman with the gun was being manipulated and it pushed her anger level higher. She screamed. 'No! Turn around!' The homeowner didn't move. Pointing the gun only a few inches from the old woman's face, the same order was screamed. 'Turn around!'

The victim gave in, turned and reckoned her world was about to end with a bullet in the back of her head. No whimper just a bang. She gritted her teeth and hoped Angus would find a new and happy home.

Clunk went the sound of a large dinner-gong being struck. The assassin crumpled to the floor and Megan stood there holding a large frying pan of the copper-bottom variety.

'I thought you were never coming,' said Grannie Plum.

'I couldn't get your front door key to work.'

'Yes I'm sorry; it is a bit sticky.' She picked up her phone and dialled 999.

'Police please.' She gave a brief explanation about an intruder who was armed but now disarmed and the address of her cottage.

'I'll put the kettle on if you'll take the brush and pan and please clean up the broken crockery before Angus does himself a mischief.'

The police arrived and collected statements, the weapon and the dazed intruder now handcuffed and sporting a blinding headache.

They left and Angus and Megan enjoyed a special afternoon.

'I have a confession,' said Megan.

'You're not a family historian,' said Grannie Plum.

'How did you know?' she asked shocked and genuinely intrigued.

'I can smell a journalist a mile away. There isn't a year goes by without another turns up trying to con me into giving an interview.' Megan's face collapsed. 'And I checked on your Cambridge PhD status.' Megan died. 'I still have contacts at my alma mater.'

'Mea culpa.' She paused then tried again. 'Was that woman here about something you did in the Second World War?'

'Surely you don't expect me to answer.' Megan shook her head at another failure. 'I'm afraid you've shot yourself in the foot, my dear.'

'Oh, how so?'

'Well after today, your headline will be *Journalist Captures Armed Intruder*. And when you're asked about who she was and why she was in an old lady's cottage, you won't know. But if you tell the truth you'll have rivals rushing to print to beat your deadline. It's a bit like your fictitious great-grandfather; close but no cigar.'

Megan cringed, her scheme failed. 'I've been investigating the secret life of the famous actress for ages. I know bits of it but so much is missing. What must I do to have you agree to me writing your biography? I'm happy to pay and hand over full editorial control.'

'Not necessary but I will grant you that interview.'

Megan gasped. 'What!? Are you serious?'

I believe one good turn deserves another. Of all the journalists who've come snooping around, you're the only one who has saved my life. So here's a proposal. I agree to tell you about my secret life, you pay 20% of the gross income from book sales and film money to dog charities I name, you pay me nothing with you having editorial control.'

Megan struggled being astonished. 'And you'll tell me *everything?*'

'Yes but with one inviolable condition.'

The journalist sighed. She knew. 'And here I was thinking I'd won the lottery; writing about the brilliant actress and her incredible secret life. So what's the one condition?'

'You can't publish until ...'

'... until you're dead. But that could be in another twenty years.'

The great-grandmother shrugged. 'Take it or leave it.'

'I can't say no. I'll take it and thank you, thank you so much. So what happens now?'

'I draw up a contract and once a signed copy is with my lawyer, you turn up with your recording device and I'll tell all.'

Megan was thrilled. 'Thank you for trusting me with your story.'

'Thank you for saving my life.'

'Can I ask one question before the contract is complete?'

'It depends on the question.'

'Why have you kept parts of your life secret?'

'Because from the beginning I never told the people I loved. Now my parents, siblings and husband are all gone although, as you know, my daughter and her family are still with us and if I am going to tell all, now is as good a time as any. To not speak of what I did was arguably cruel but I made the decision all those decades ago to never go public or to even tell them in private. I believed the shock may have hurt them. Yes, of course they may have been proud but I decided ignorance was bliss and the longer I remained silent, the harder it was for me to change my mind.'

Megan remained still and quiet. She was a witness to the thinking of a remarkable woman who continued remembering her life of fifty even sixty years ago.

'There were times when I thought I would tell one family member, my mother. But then she would have been under enormous pressure to tell my husband. I hated the thought I might hurt the ones I loved.

She paused and Megan did the right thing, something not all journalists do well; she remained silent.

'Being an actress I know the meaning of the word dénouement and this might be my life's dénouement, my time to reveal all.'

Angus wasn't used to his mistress being philosophical using big French words. He preferred *sit* and *walkies*.

'There have been times when alone I've wondered if other people have, as I have, kept a secret and if so, if it impacted their life. People may have committed a crime, cheated on a loved one or, on the positive side performed a life-saving deed yet told no-one.' She paused. 'How many untold secrets are out there?'

Megan dared to intervene.

'You do still have family members; your daughter, granddaughter and great-granddaughter. Won't they be hurt?'

'I hope not, I hope they'll be proud but as you'll keep to our contract, I won't be around to care.'

Megan patted Angus and looked at his owner. 'Thank you, Mrs Curzon and I'll be proud and honoured to tell the world what I believe is your truly remarkable story.'

The old woman smiled, relieved her secrets would finally, *finally* be revealed. She looked at Megan and said, 'Call me Plum.'

The Detective Joanna Best Mysteries

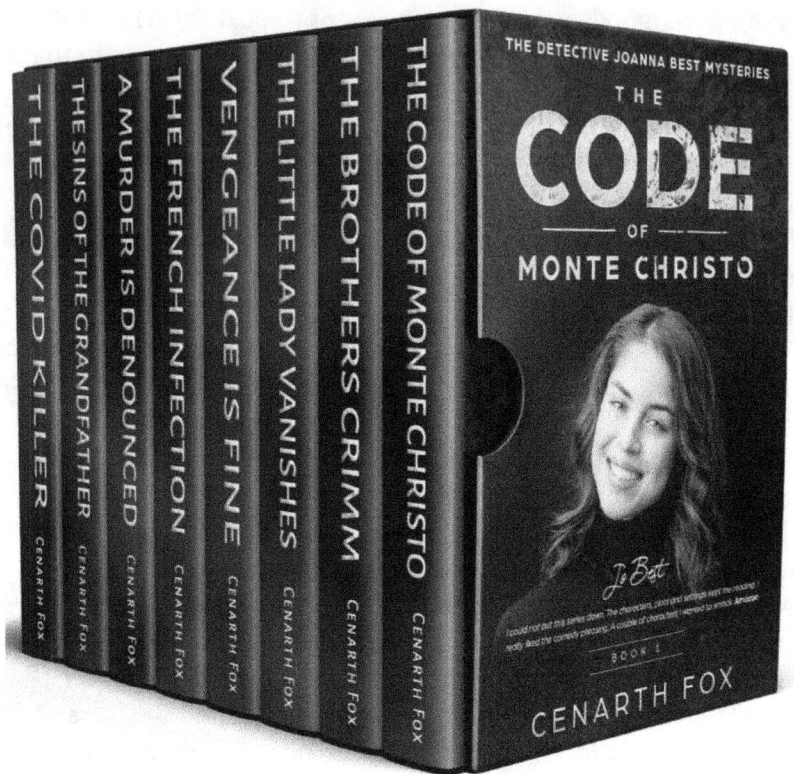

www.cenfoxbooks.com

Joanna Best is the youngest homicide detective in town. Smart, feisty and gorgeous, she's brilliant at cracking cases and rubbing people up the wrong way. Some jealous colleagues are desperate to undermine her. Certain criminals want her dead. Juggling a career with Victoria Police, having three men madly in love with her, and a strange family, Jo Best's adventures will drag you in. Her second banana is an Australian born Chinese IT guru who makes computers sing. Her best pal is a female 60ish police surgeon, a forensic genius and chocoholic.

I could not put this series down. The characters, plots, settings, kept me reading. I really liked the word comedy phrasing. A couple of characters I wanted to smack. **Amazon**

Sherlock Holmes

The great man is soon to retire. On his last night at Baker Street, the loyal landlady drops a bombshell. Holmes is staggered. Mrs Hudson has done what!? Sherlock Holmes never panics—until now. Dr Watson arrives and is stunned. It's their greatest challenge. Sir Arthur Conan Doyle is furious. A famous author turned WW1 counter-intelligence spy is on the case. *The Strand Magazine* smells a scoop. Inspector Lestrade from Scotland Yard plans revenge, and at stake is the brilliant reputation of the world's most famous consulting detective. His only hope is to 'play the game'.

www.cenfoxbooks.com

A delightfully imaginative pastiche. Recommended. **Peter Blau BSI**

An extraordinary book, one of the most enjoyable pieces of Holmesian fiction I've read in a long time ... a complex, ingenious and deliciously funny story of intersecting realities, and the conclusion is entirely satisfactory. I love it! **Roger Johnson Commissioning Editor: *The Sherlock Holmes Journal***

The George Miracle Series

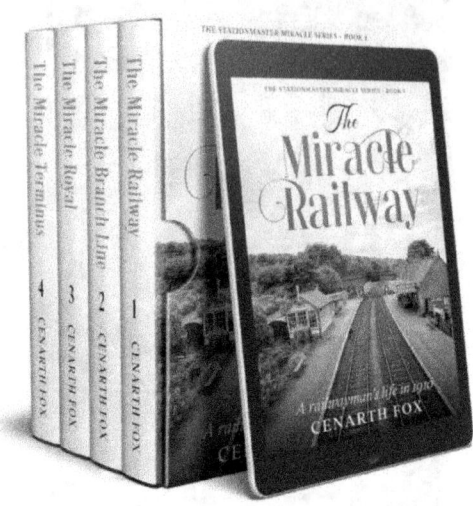

A sweeping saga with four generations of the Miracle family. In 1910, 12 year-old George Miracle started as a station lad in London. His railway career lasted 50+ years. In-between sweeping platforms, lugging parcels and helping lost passengers, he's arrested for murder, fights in a French trench in WW1, and becomes the youngest station master in England at a rural backwater where he's conned by jealous colleagues. His branch line is dying. He meets a local Capability Brown and a loveable, limerick-loving novelist. He falls madly in love and marries in amazing venues. He tackles a crazy would-be murderer and armed robbers. Book 3, *The Miracle Railway* has George the SM at the famous Royal Station, Wolferton. "Good morning, Your Majesty". As he awaits the coffin of his namesake, George V, a family tragedy occurs. Book 4 has George go underground. In WW2 he's part of the Railway Executive Committee running the entire rail network. In the Blitz, he saves a million children. He helps 300,000 Dunkirk troops and Winston get D-Day sorted before chasing an IRA terrorist though the Tube. His career ends as British Rail cops the horrific Beeching cuts. Yet even in retirement, old George finds a new life on the rail! His life is rich with comedy, crises and many steam trains. All four books available as eBooks or paperbacks.

It's like someone from the times telling their experiences; a pleasure to read. **Twitter July 2022**

World War Two Thrillers

Meet the actress turned spy. From a musty church hall in Cambridge to glitzy nightclubs in Nazi-occupied Paris, Louise Wellesley stars on stage. Even cows are impressed when she parachutes into a French field at midnight dressed as a nun. Men bombard her with proposals; most indecent. As WW2 drags on, Louise, nicknamed Plum, joins ENSA – *Every Night Something Awful* – to entertain troops. She's bored and an offer from a handsome young Belgian sees Plum do the unthinkable. She survives death beneath the Eiffel Tower, and by hitching a ride with the French Navy, stumbles upon her true love. D-Day looms with the promise of slaughter on the beaches of Normandy. Will her heart be shattered? People and pets perish. New challenges appear. New life is created and when one war ends, another begins. Can Plum survive and find happiness?

I have read 100's of books on WW2 both fiction and non-fiction. This series will go down as one of the most enjoyable. The books were riveting. I adored her. I really can't recommend these books enough. **Amazon 5 stars**

www.ingramcontent.com/pod-product-compliance
Lightning Source LLC
Chambersburg PA
CBHW070557120726
47909CB00007B/2369